HOME FOR Always

KETLEY ALLISON

Home For Always Playlist

Thinking 'Yout You - Dustin Lynch, MacKenzie Porter
Look What God Gave Her - Thomas Rhett
The Good Ones - Gabby Barrett
the lifeboat's empty! - Chelsea Cutler
Dreams - MisterWives
If I Don't Laugh, I'll Cry - Frawley
Clueless in Suburbia - Yen Strange
Flight Risk - Tommy Lefroy

Listen to the rest of the playlist:

One

NOA

"I'll take an Americano to go, please."

I tap my fingers on the refurbished counter as Maisy rings up my order.

"You look asleep on your feet, doll," she says without looking up from her tablet. Her furry gray brows scrunch together while her pink acrylic nails fly against the screen.

"Oh, it's nothing," I say, hoping my voice sounds lighter than my body feels. "Been a long week of my patients not feeling well."

"Mmm. Damn modern contraptions ... why do I need this? You think Carly would be in charge of this artificial intelligence since she's the one who demanded this nonsense. Speaking of my wayward daughter, have you seen where she's hidden my vintage cashbox? That sweet ring it made every time I lowered the handle reminds me of my gambling days." Maisy lifts her head for a good, nostalgic laugh, her smoker's voice circling the crowded cafe and drawing other patrons' attention, who immediately smile back.

Say what you want about Maisy, a bird going on seventy-five—her words—but her laughter could stop a spontaneous bar fight any time of the day.

"Here, I have cash." I shove a hand into the pocket of my green scrubs, partially aware of Past Me shoving a few dollar bills in there when I was shopping for groceries yesterday.

Maisy's cataract eyes narrow. "Tell me you have exact change."

"You bet."

"Ah, save your soul, doll." Her heavy silver bracelets clank as she gestures for it with her hand. "You just saved that gentleman behind you at least ten more minutes of wait time."

She winks at me.

Winks.

This is Maisy's not-so-subtle way of telling me there is a very available bachelor standing nearby, and here in Falcon Haven, that is no small feat. Bachelors—indeed, men under fifty—are scarce in these parts, and Maisy knows it.

I swear I am *not* turning around.

He's probably passing through on his way to New York. We're right off the highway. You can see the Empire State Building if you squint your eyes hard enough, and this man whose face I will *never* see probably wanted to stop for a pee break and caffeine hit, not a spontaneous match-up from his eclectic barista.

He'd want nothing to do with me, dressed in yesterday's scrubs with two-day hair and ... I can't remember the last time I put on makeup.

I say to Maisy, "I'll ask Carly where she hid your register next time I see her."

Maisy's lips crimp into a magenta-colored frown, disappointed I wouldn't flirt and find my future husband where she could bear witness and tell everyone for years to come that she found poor Noa-Lynne Shaw—spinster-at-large *but with such a sweet face*—a man.

Maisy shoves the bills in the tip jar, then waves me to the side. "Off you go."

I sidestep to the pickup counter, waiting for my coffee by staring at anything but the growing line in front of Maisy as the man asks whether the Mercantile does pour-over coffee.

"Do I look like I have ninja barista skills? *No.* I got milk. I got coffee. I can get you one of each if you're so inclined."

Smiling at how the man blubbers and withers under Maisy's commands, my eyes snag on the newspaper stand.

Typical papers decorate the wire spin stand, but with the Mercantile being under Maisy's ownership since the sixties, she also demands the latest tabloids and gossip rags.

As I'm idly scanning the headlines, a face cuts through my vision in the same way I picture the *Titanic* hitting the iceberg.

The headline above that devilish, dimpled face shouts, **STONE WILLIAMS IS AT IT AGAIN.**

"Noa? Your coffee's ready."

The teenager employed for the summer months inches my cup closer to my suddenly immobile limbs.

His attention darts from the newsstand to me, then back again.

"Um, I gave you an extra shot because ... you know." Chewing on his lip, he gives me one last pitying look before disappearing behind the coffee machine.

Damn, if a sixteen-year-old boy who has more of a relationship with his video games than actual people is aware of what happened ten years ago, I *truly* am a lost, pathetic spinster.

I swipe my coffee from the counter and leave enough change to cover the tabloid I grab as I walk by. Flipping the plastic lid off my drink with my thumb, I pour my fresh, super hot, extra shot coffee all over his stupid face over the trash can near the exit.

I let go, and the soggy mess lands with an audible plop.

The Merc goes silent. Even Maisy has nothing to say as she watches the sudden, if interesting, breakdown of her most reliable customer.

"She never truly got over that boy," an elderly lady mumbles behind me. "Such a shame because he's certainly over her."

"Do you think she reads about him often? I would."

"Cries into her pillow about him, probably."

"Well, he seems worth enough effort to waste a bunch of coffee on his face."

I push open the door, the bell ringing cheerily above my head.

I hate gossip. I absolutely despise when it's about me.

But just now? What I did?

So worth it.

Two

STONE

"So how do I put this?" My agent glares at me through my phone's display. He folds his arms across his desk.

Expensive fabric covers those arms like a soft, custom-tailored hug. I'm wondering how much a suit like that costs. It has to be Armani or Gucci or Tom Ford.

"I want that suit. Where'd you get it from? Our guy on Melrose?"

"Have you listened to anything I said?" Aaron Golde gives a long-suffering sigh. "Focus on the topic at hand, Stone. Specifically, your insanely accurate ability to set fire to your ten-year career in under two minutes."

I wave him off, adjusting my sunglasses as I recline against my pool chair. The sudden movement makes me wince, making me thankful for my tinted lenses. Aaron can't zoom in and lecture me about my hangover.

"I've had worse shit go viral before," I say. "It'll go away as soon as another celebrity uncouples or gets caught doing something they shouldn't be. I'm the media's breakfast today, not its dinner."

Aaron's tanned face wrinkles with concern. "Listen, I'm going to do what I can on my end, but I have to be honest. We've known each other for years, you and I."

I nod. "Sure. You're my first agent. The first guy I partied with in LA. The first man who introduced me to my ex-wife. My one and fucking only." I point at the screen. "Are you in need of a *you're pretty and I love you* pep talk today? Because I have more."

Aaron swipes a hand across his face. "Why do I tolerate you?"

"Because I make you money."

Aaron's the guy who drew me away from my bumfuck town after a few of my YouTube videos where I reenacted key Oscar-winning moments gained enough traction to catch the attention of talent agents. I was eighteen. Aaron had just graduated college and was hungry to sign an up-and-comer with true potential. It seemed a good match. Fuck, it *is* a good match. Look how far we've come.

"I may have given you too loose of a leash as my first signing," Aaron admits.

"Please. I'm a big boy. See all this?" I span the house behind me by lifting my hand and waving the phone around, though Aaron's seen my house thousands of times before. "I bought this abode with the funds from my first movie. Remember that?"

"I know, dude, but—"

"And I renovated it with my first superhero franchise."

"I'm not trying to lessen what we've gained—"

"I even moved in a wife, Aar. A *wife*. We were supposed to make a life for ourselves before we realized we shouldn't've gotten married after two days of knowing each other. See?" I perk up, lifting off my chair and forgetting my hangover for one precious second before I tilt dangerously. "There. I admitted I fucked up. Is everyone happy now?"

"You did fuck up, bro. Badly." Aaron's brows crunch together. "How can you not understand the extent of the cleanup involved? Wait—do you even *remember*?"

"Of course I do," I lie.

"Oh, fuck me."

"It's fine. So I went too hard at a club last night, and some fan caught it on video. What's the harm? I'll lay low for a bit, and as soon as *Cascade* starts, I'll—"

"You're about to lose *Cascade*."

My hand clenches around my phone. I couldn't have heard him correctly. "What?"

Aaron dips his chin sympathetically. "They called this morning. They're considering booting you from the movie."

"The *fuck*? Why?" I shoot up from my chair, pacing the pool and nearly falling in.

"I believe we're covering the reasons right now."

"No. I nailed the audition. I impressed the casting director so much she fast-tracked me through the screen test. They love me. They wouldn't just fire me because..."

"Because you threw Bradley Mitchell onto a table and broke it in half?"

I scoff and hold up a hand like Aaron's arguing right in front of me. "Wait, wait, wait. That's not what—I don't remember it that way."

"Oh yeah?" Though it's clear he doesn't want to hear it, Aaron motions for me to continue. "And how do you remember it, Stone?"

"Brad was spewing some dark shit about my work ethic

and how he couldn't believe I'd made it as far as I had on a couple of well-timed YouTube videos. He argued to anyone who'd listen he was the better fit for my *Cascade* role. He called me a talentless hack, Aar. I couldn't let that stand."

"While it's enraging being talked down to, you don't break a table with another guy's face, you know? That's not really how society expects you to win an argument."

"Then he shouldn't have made his idiot brain so appealing to squash," I point out.

"Yeah, well, he was your costar in *Cascade*, and he has pull."

"How much pull?" I laugh. "The dude is barely two movies into his career."

"He's sleeping with the casting director."

I lose my smile.

"Not only that," Aaron continues, "but he's pressing charges."

"What a pussy."

"Oh, and Ravynn contacted *The Times* and has agreed to an interview regarding the disintegration of your marriage and how your drug use played a role."

"We were married less than twenty-four hours. And *my* drug use? Ravynn had an entire medicine cabinet of Oxy and Xanax under our kitchen sink. She was so high, one time she put some in our fish tank, and you know what? I found Nemo afterward. It wasn't pretty."

My voice ratchets to a distinctly strained level. I take a few breaths to stay calm.

"I agree, I do, but the best course of action is damage control. My advice is to lie low and let me and your lawyers handle this. Get out of the spotlight, out of LA, and don't give the media any reason to film you when you're not in front of professional cameras."

My shoulders fall. The sun, so welcoming an hour before when I stepped out onto my patio and greeted the world, prickles my bare shoulders with the warning that comes before a nasty burn. "Fine. I'll stay inside for a bit."

"No, Stone. I am asking you to go. Leave."

"Go where?" I search for my favorite haunts from the past, coming up blank. "Italy? Australia? I refuse to run from that asshole."

"I couldn't give a shit about Bradley. I don't want you in a place where the press can find you. I think you should go home."

Silence.

"Stone? You frozen?"

I mutter, "I'm not going home."

"I wouldn't ask it if it wasn't necessary. It's the one place I can trust you to lie low and stay out of the public eye."

At my sullen silence, he adds, "And hey, I'll visit you, okay? Give me a few weeks, and I'll—"

"A few *weeks*?"

"Well, I was thinking you should stay there for a few months. Until Christmas."

"Dude."

"I'm serious, Stone. You're fucked. Fucked in the ass. Fucked over. I don't know how many fucks I have to say before you believe it, but we're in serious career-saving mode here. You pissed off a lot of higher-ups who swear they're putting their efforts into making you C-list. You gotta let me do my job, which means you need to take my advice."

I run a hand through my hair. "Jesus, Aar."

"I know. But it's temporary, right? And look, aren't small

towns meant to be quaint, sweet, and filled with old ladies making fresh cookies? That's exactly what you need and where I want you to be if you're ever located."

I side-eye my city-born agent. "Whatever small town you're referring to, it ain't mine."

"Well, you're not going to fucking Mallorca and renting a party yacht, that's for damn sure."

I frown at his ability to read my mind. "Hey, I'd extend Bradley an invitation, too."

Aaron doesn't laugh.

"You're serious, aren't you?" I say. "I'm in trouble."

He gives a solemn nod.

After a beat of meditative breaths, I say, "I'll give going home a try. For the few days it'll take for this to die down."

"Excellent." Aaron actually fist-pumps the air. "I'm hanging up before you change your mind. We'll be in touch."

"Coward."

But Aaron's already clicked off, leaving me alone with my artificial waterfall, gorgeous oceanfront views, and a dream career my unpredictable temper might've flushed down the toilet.

Three

NOA

1 Week Later

"Mrs. Stalinski?" I call out.

After a few moments of answering silence, I push open the front door of her small Victorian home, pocketing my keys as I step in.

She knows to call me if she becomes uncomfortable at night or needs help, but she's also stubborn, and Mrs. Stalinski would rather reach the point of piercing agony before calling for any more help than she already has.

"Hello?" I try again as I pass through the front hallway and into the kitchen at the back of the house.

The window above the sink looks over the fenceless backyard and quaint patio where Mrs. Stalinski likes to sit and enjoy a cup of coffee in the morning, hoping to glimpse the nearby family of deer.

I peer out that window, noting the untouched dishes in the drying rack that I cleaned last night.

Finding the wooden rocking chair empty, I push off the sink and walk to the base of the stairs leading to the second floor. While taking the steps two at a time, I hear a weak, "In here, dear," coming from the main bedroom.

The second floor is in a U shape with a modest guest room to the right of the staircase followed by a second bedroom turned sewing/fitness room. At the center of the U is the main bedroom.

Propriety has me knocking lightly before bursting in, worried over what I'll find.

My concern is unfounded when, at the sound of my movement, Mrs. Stalinski turns on her bedside lamp and stares at me limply from her side of the bed.

"What's going on?" I ask, coming to her side and grabbing her wrist, gauging her pulse.

"A rough night, is all," she croaks, shaking her head as if a night of excruciating pain is all in a day's work. "You know how it is."

"I do," I murmur, laying my palm on her forehead for a sense of temperature before moving to my kit and retrieving a thermometer. She feels fine, but the blanched look on her skin and her bloodshot eyes tell me otherwise.

"Did you take your pain meds?" I press the button on the thermometer, then put it into her ear until it beeps a normal 98.5 degrees Fahrenheit at me.

"Like clockwork."

I hum in thought as I pick up her bottle of opioids and double-check the dosage. "I'll call Dr. Silver today, see if we can't get you on some Fentanyl patches."

"No, dear." She's quick to alertness before her eyelids

droop once more. "You know I want to keep my faculties for as long as possible, and those things send me straight to la-la land."

"Yes, but you don't deserve to be in this much pain around the clock."

Mrs. Stalinski gives me a long look. "I believe I befriended a unicorn the last time you threw one of those patches on my back."

"Well..." I arch a brow. "Was it a nice unicorn?"

Mrs. Stalinski snorts with surprised laughter before swatting me on the arm. "Meeting one of those creatures, no matter the temperament, is always worrisome at my age."

My smile softens. "I understand. But it's more medicine or I stay the night."

"Not on my watch, dear. You're too young to be at the beck and call of a sick old woman."

"Mrs. Stalinski, it's my *job*. And one I'm happy to do. In fact, I'd much rather be here with you than anywhere else."

"Now, that's just pathetic," she says kindly.

I brush off her observation with a warm, doting smile—one I know she hates.

Mrs. Stalinski narrows her eyes at me. "You're too pretty to be holed up in this house with me all day, and you have way too much energy to be contained within these walls. And how many times have I told you to call me Judy? I'm not your high school English teacher anymore."

"It's a hard habit to break."

Mrs. Stalinski considers this. "Mmm. I was pretty frightening in my day, wasn't I?"

This time, my doting smile is genuine. "No teacher deserved more respect than you. Now, back to keeping you comfortable. I don't mind sleeping here. Really."

"Noa, dear, don't tell me you have nothing to return home to. I appreciate your help, truly I do, but the guilt that rides me every time I see you cleaning up my messes ..." Mrs. Stalinski's cheeks go pink. "There's no way this is the future you envisioned for yourself."

"No," I admit, and as soon as my mind flashes images of what could've been, I shut it off. "But it's the one I've adopted and wouldn't change for the world. Stop changing the subject." I unscrew her pill bottle and shake out her next dose. "I don't like the thought of you in agony and unable to do anything about it. So either we call Dr. Silver for an opioid upgrade, or you have me stay a few nights—to prove to me you don't need any help or even just an empathetic ear," I add when she opens her chapped lips to argue.

"There's got to be another older, world-weary-yet-content-with-her-lot-in-life nurse who could relieve you from this fate."

"There's only Berta, and she's a staunch believer in two-hour physical therapy for all her patients. Every morning."

Mrs. Stalinski mouth drops in horror. "If it's just the two of you doing home care, then I suppose a cute young stud is out of the question, too."

I laugh. "I'm all you have, unfortunately, but instead of an impressive six-pack, I do come with a chocolate and caffeine addiction, same as you." I wink at her. "Why don't you rest in bed with a good book today? I'll bring you some coffee shortly."

The brief color I brought to her face vanishes. "I've done so much reading, I'm surprised I'm not disassociating into different characters right in front of you. I was hoping to make it down the stairs with your help and enjoy the morning outside."

"Then what are we waiting for?"

With a little assistance, she lifts off the pillows stacked behind her head, accepting the palmful of pills and downing them with her bedside glass, which I note is still at the same water level I left it at last night.

A knot forms in my belly.

I'm snapped out of my concern when Mrs. Stalinski rests a hand on my arm. "I am absolutely up for it. I refuse to stay in this cream puff of a room longer than necessary."

I survey the beautifully designed space as I put her arm around my shoulders and help her stand. "I think it's beautiful. Very calming."

"Yes, calm is the word I'm thinking of as I yak up yesterday's dinner all over the cream carpet."

"You should think of that more as putting your signature of approval on it. Isn't that what cats do? Vomit in places they like?"

Mrs. Stalinski barks with dry laughter. "This is why I like you so much, Noa. Between you and me, I'd be bereft if you ever left."

"I know." I squeeze her around the waist. "Feeling's mutual."

We share a smile before hobbling forward with care. Mrs. Stalinski makes it to the top of the stairs, then has to rest. The frustration in her expression of not being able to slide out of bed and head down the stairs like she used to, before being diagnosed with breast cancer metastasizing to her bones, is clear, though she tries hard to disguise it as she shifts her weight to the banister and less on me.

"We got this." I reposition my feet so I can bear more of her. "Or I could go online this afternoon and get you one of those staircase chairs that *creeeeeeaaaak* you slowly and carefully all the way to the bottom—"

"Don't you dare." Mrs. Stalinski nails me with a withering look. "I will do this on my own two feet if it takes all morning. And you will watch me and weep."

"You're on."

She and I make it to the bottom of the stairs in under five minutes, but to Mrs. Stalinski, it feels more like an hour. I guide her down the hall and through the kitchen, cracking jokes and insulting her the way I know keeps her energy up, until I have her in her rocking chair on the back patio with a thick plaid blanket covering her legs.

"I'll be right back with a coffee," I say to her.

She acknowledges me with a nod, her eyes at half mast.

By the time I make it back outside with a steaming cup of coffee, Mrs. Stalinski is fast asleep.

Tiptoeing to her side, I leave the coffee there for her in case she wakes up wanting something for her parched throat, then creep back inside and begin the morning routine.

Some days are worse for Mrs. Stalinski than others, today being one of the bad ones. Depending on the type of day, I have a list of things to do. My job is as her nurse, but it's hard not to want to do more for her, living alone. She was my favorite teacher in high school, always there to lend an ear, even on a level outside of schoolwork, which she did with me often. It's not that I feel like I owe her. More like I want to give her at least an iota of comfort that she gave me when I needed it most.

A couple of hours later, as I'm tidying the kitchen after prepping lunch, Mrs. Stalinski stirs. I assist her into the house and onto the living room couch where she resumes sleeping. After being up all night, it's not surprising she's making up for those lost hours.

I peek in on her at odd intervals, and each time I do, I'm

resolved to stay on for more nights—pay or no pay. The woman deserves a restful sleep.

The rest of the afternoon flies by, filled with putting away a grocery delivery, talking with Dr. Silver, going to the pharmacy, and making sure Mrs. Stalinski takes her medication on time. I leave for a few hours to check in on other patients who don't require as much hands-on assistance, just washing a bathroom basin or two. By the time the evening rolls in, I'm wiping my forehead and searching Mrs. Stalinski's fridge for a pitcher of sweet tea, the one thing she demands she make herself since no one else can make it to her specifications—including me.

I'm in the middle of pouring myself a hefty, thirst-quenching glass when there's a knock on the screen door.

Tilting back, I spot my friend Carly waiting on the front porch. I pull out a second glass and pour the sweet tea into it before heading to the door with a drink in each hand.

"You're just in time," I say through the screen.

"Is there vodka in that?" Carly opens the door for me.

"Sadly, no." We head over to the two porch chairs over-looking the one-way street. "Not until I strip out of these scrubs, anyway."

Carly has come at the perfect moment, no doubt intentional. Falcon Haven's sunsets are almost famous. We're at that time of day when the pure blue becomes a watercolor painting of pinks, oranges, and reds, their brushstrokes reaching high over roofs and treetops, coating the town in a dreamy glow. One of the neighbor's kids brings out a basketball and starts dribbling and shooting for the net, the sound of rubber meeting asphalt a comforting backdrop to weekend beginnings.

"You look like death," Carly observes as she perches on the chair next to mine.

I force my attention away from the view. "Gee, thanks."

But I don't deny it. I scraped my brown hair into a bun, I'm pretty sure I put on mascara this morning but not confident it's stayed on my lashes, and I've spent more time trying to hydrate Mrs. Stalinski than quench my thirst. I'm sure my dry skin shows it.

"Man, I couldn't do what you do." Carly rests her head back, the warm September wind doing a fine job of blowing her auburn strands around her face. Unlike me, none of her healthy locks fly into her mouth.

"Doesn't it suck on your soul?" she asks.

"Not really." I shrug. "Everybody needs someone when they're at their most vulnerable. I prefer to think of it as a comfy blanket over my spirit."

Carly turns her head in my direction, smiling softly. "Sweet Noa-Lynn. You haven't changed a bit since high school."

My best friend doesn't mean it as a dig, but it smarts. Too many times, I've tried to convince those important to me that I could have claws if I *really* wanted them (case in point: melting to my ex's face with coffee last week), but ever since senior year, when I should've stood my ground with him but didn't, my arguments have fallen on deaf ears. And that was ten freaking years ago.

"Mrs. Stalinski was a fire-breathing dragon at school," Carly continues, oblivious to my critical inner monologue. "It's honestly heartbreaking to see her now. Cancer is such a fickle fucking bitch."

I nod in somber agreement, sipping on my drink as we watch the neighborhood kids hop on their bikes and skid out onto the road to catch the last rays of sun before their parents call them in for dinner.

"That's why I do what I do. To help. She doesn't deserve this. No one does."

"On that, we agree." Carly holds her drink to the side for a cheers. I meet it with a *clink*.

Carly gets a cheeky glimmer in her eyes before reaching into her small Chanel purse and pulling out a flask.

At my amused scoff, she shakes it lightly, the liquid inside sloshing. "Sure you don't want to partake?"

I look at the flask longingly. "Positive. I'm on the clock."

"When do you get off? We could go to the Tipsy Falcon tonight, see who's driving through our town on this lonely Friday night ..." Carly's brows jump suggestively. "We haven't had a girls' night where we play with a bunch of boys in much too long."

"I wish I could," I say, and I mean it. Ever since taking on Mrs. Stalinski, I haven't been up for late nights of drinking and partying, and Carly can usually be called upon to help me forget a tough day. With this patient, though, it's different. "I'm pretty sure I'm staying here tonight."

"Really? Overnight?"

"Uh-huh."

Carly leans over the arm of her chair, her focus bouncing to the front door and back to me. She whispers, "Is it ... time?"

I nearly choke on an ice cube. "No! Nothing like that. Mrs. Stalinski needs more help, that's all."

Carly raises an unconvinced brow. "Does Mrs. Stalinski know that?"

I raise my glass until it covers half my face. "Not until I magically appear next to her when she needs someone."

"Hmm." Carly rests against the chair, rocking softly. "You're terrible at duplicity."

"What's wrong with it? I think it's a good plan."

"Yes, refusing to bend to the will of a terminally ill woman. Look at you, so rebellious."

Carly winks. I smack her arm, then we both laugh.

It's dark humor to be sure, but I learned long ago that finding humor in the worst of moments is one of the best ways to cope.

"Well, well, would you look at that."

Carly's curious drawl turns my head in the same direction as hers. A dark sedan turns into our cul-de-sac, but to have grabbed my friend's attention, it's not any old car. It's sleek, fancy, black, and sticking out like a big *fuck you* to most—no, all—of Falcon Haven's residents. It would impress only one person with such a flashy show of wealth, and she's sitting beside me, her red-painted mouth open in an impressed O of want.

I put two fingers under her chin, clamping her mouth shut.

"Probably some tycoon looking to buy up more land," I say, crossing my legs and preparing to enjoy the show of whatever door this poor sod's planning to approach. I hope it's Mrs. Lu's next door. She's straight from the 1950s, using her gardening shovel to shoo away trespassers and kids who dare to trample her gardenias.

On cue, I see her scowl emerge from between the lace curtains of her front window.

"Interesting." Carly straightens. "Why's it turning our way?"

"What?" My focus goes from Mrs. Lu to the drive leading to Mrs. Stalinski's home. The car approaches us with the quiet stealth of a gorgeous black panther.

"I ... don't know," I say, straightening my back away from the chair.

Even as I say it, a large, jagged rock lands in my stomach with a *plop*.

"Is Mrs. Stalinski expecting visitors?" Carly asks with forced innocence.

My ribs are actually calcifying over my heart. "She didn't mention it."

The car slows to a stop, close enough to see the driver if someone didn't illegally tint all the windows to the point of opacity. It idles for a minute, then two, then three.

"It's a salesman," I say to fill the silence. "It's gotta be Mrs. Stalinski's insurance provider. Something."

Carly wisely stays silent.

At last, the driver's door opens. A man in dark clothing and black Aviator sunglasses steps out.

He doesn't see me at first. His back is to us as he slides his sunglasses down his nose and surveys the landscape, his broad back rippling under his tight black tee when he moves. He runs a hand through his thick chestnut hair as he rests his other muscled, tanned arm on the roof of the car, and every part of me that's held on to his memory quivers.

"Oh my God," I whisper.

"Girl," Carly says slowly, "You sure you don't want some of what's in this flask?"

He turns, and our eyes meet across the drive.

Four

STONE

"Noa? What are you doing here?"

Not the best first words to say to her after all this time, but it's all I could get out once I lock eyes with her, and the years that separated us shrink into minutes.

She's in scrubs, is my first thought.

She's still so fucking gorgeous, is my second.

Noa's thrown her waist-length, dark brown curls into a pile on top of her head. Even from a distance, her moss-green eyes are vibrant and pure. A natural red flushes her cheeks. Same with her lips, which she used to chew on constantly and probably still does. While the scrubs are boxy, her breasts round out the fabric, and if she turns around, I'm positive her ass would do the same.

Luckily, I latch onto my first observation and control my libido on the second.

She rises from the rocking chair, her hands coming together in front of her and picking at her cuticles.

"You're a nurse?" I ask.

Noa responds with a jerky nod.

"I thought you wanted to be a chef," I muse. In fact, I distinctly remember her choosing a culinary school in Paris over heading to LA with me.

Carly responds to my question with an unnecessarily phlegmy scoff. I scowl at her. "Nice to see you, too, Car."

"Oh, the pleasure's all mine, dick."

I give a tired shake of my head and open the door behind the driver's seat, grabbing my luggage. "Same ole spitfire."

I wince as I bend into the interior. Five minutes back in town and I'm falling into the accent I worked over a year to remove from my dialect.

"That's *counselor* spitfire to you," Carly says, sauntering down the porch steps and heading to a cherry-red Mercedes I assume is hers. It's definitely not Noa's taste, but the scrubs are throwing me off. Did I get it wrong? Is that why Carly's so pissed? Noa's a doctor now?

I refuse to look like an idiot, so I say to Carly, "Oh, look at that. You made it to the other side of the law instead of behind its bars."

"Gimme a minute." Carly holds up a finger and stares at her phone. "I need to call my firm and tell them under no circumstance are we to represent you on your next DUI."

"Funny *and* original. I can see why they hired you." I lift both duffels and move to get past her, but she hip-checks me on the way.

"This town hasn't missed you one bit, William Stalinski."

It's my second grimace since pulling in, and I'm almost successful at hiding it again. Noa's lashes flutter down like she knows I'm ashamed, and *she's* ashamed that I hate who I was.

"I don't go by that name anymore, as you well know."

"Oh, *apologies*." Carly flutters a hand against her total boob-job chest before rounding to her side of the car. "I'd hate for anyone to know the truth of Stone Williams."

I respond with my trademark mega-watt, fully dimpled smile. "Go fuck off now, Car."

Carly makes a face at me. "Not until Noa gives me the go-ahead." She folds her arms against her car's roof and calls, "You okay, No?"

"Fine." Noa's pained expression looks anything but. "I've gotta head home soon, anyway, to feed Moo."

"Moo's still alive?" I beam at Noa. "Awesome."

"Of course you're more concerned about a goddamned *cat*," Carly mutters, then slips into her car.

"Come again?"

She slams her door shut at my question and revs her engine.

I don't bother to flip her off when gravel spews against my pants as she reverses out, too focused on Noa fidgeting in front of me.

My strides lengthen when I think about whether she still smells the way she used to, like vanilla and oranges. I can't help but want to close the distance.

I reach the top of the porch steps, dropping my duffel bags to my feet. "Hey."

My voice comes out rougher than intended, but *damn*, it's so good to see her.

Noa does nothing I'd expect. She doesn't leap into my arms or burst into tears or scream at me for not saying a word to her all these years. Nothing a standard scorned woman from my past would do.

No, all she does is stare at me quizzically. Almost ... appalled.

I attempt to laugh it off. "I'm used to people freezing in my presence, but not in a way where they look horrified. You okay?"

Noa blinks. "I—you've just surprised me, is all."

"Okay." I span my hands. "Can't say I expected you here, either. Why are you hanging out with my mom?"

Noa's response is to further commit to her appalled expression. "Does it look like I'm visiting her?"

"Well, yeah."

Her lips curl in disgust. "No, Will—sorry, *Stone*. I'm not *visiting* her."

I jerk back at her tone. "The lip curl, okay, I deserve that from you. But what's with the venom? All I'm asking is what you're doing on my mom's porch. Did you just clock off from the hospital? Do you and that Satan's daughter of a best friend you have visit her often? Not that I mind, but ... why?" I try for a joke. "Are you making it a habit to kick it with your ex's mom on Friday nights?"

Noa stares at me. "Is this funny to you?"

"That you're hanging out with my mom? Kinda, yeah."

She ducks into my vision when I glance away. "Will, I need to know if you're kidding right now."

"Stone," I correct.

"Okay, stop with whatever character audition this is for you and be serious."

"Character audition?" I echo. It's annoyance that tightens my voice and not the effort of lifting my bags when I add, "I know I hurt you, and I'm sorry for that. I truly am."

A decade ago, I would've sworn up and down that it was impossible to snuff the light out of Noa's eyes. The older me knows better since I'm the first one who managed it.

"It's been ten years, Noa. You can't possibly hold on to

hate that long. Not you." I cock my head. "Or is it the opposite? Do you think chatting with my mother will bring you closer to me?"

"You think I'm here because I'm pining for you?" Noa holds her hands to her face, growing red with anger. "Oh my *God*, you have it so backward." She spins away, pacing her side of the small porch. "I expected Hollywood to make you cold but not obtuse."

I frown at her back. "Whatever's going on with you, I wish you the best. I'm going inside now."

She whirls with a dawning expression. "You really don't know what's going on, do you?"

Noa reaches for me, but I dodge out of her way. "Great seeing you, but if you can't be straight with me, I'm not wasting my time standing around making you feel good by looking dumb."

One of my greatest pet peeves, one I haven't been able to shake since I was a kid, is not understanding what's right in front of me when everybody else seems to. Of all people, Noa should've remembered that.

"Will—Stone—wait, please. I need to explain."

But I've already shut her down.

Shoving the door open, I call, "Ma?"

Five

NOA

I RESIST RACING THROUGH THE GAP BETWEEN Stone's body and the doorframe to get inside and block him from entering, but only just.

"Ma?" he calls again, stepping over the threshold.

I follow, wringing my hands and picturing my brain in the same jumbled mess as my fingers.

Does he really not know? How could Stone not be aware of his mom's cancer? Did Mrs. Stalinski not tell him, or is it because he's basically cut the entire town of Falcon Haven out of his life—including his mother?

I'm guessing the latter, but have trouble picturing either Stone or Mrs. Stalinski doing something so hurtful to the other.

Except, here Stone is, dumbfounded and increasingly frantic as his mind puts the pieces together.

My nursing uniform.

His mother's lack of response.

Carly's over-the-top, icy behavior toward him, even for her.

"MA!"

"She's sleeping."

Stone whirls on me, his duffel bags thumping to the floor, his eyes wider than when I last saw them. "It's seven in the evening. She should be eating dinner, not sleeping."

"Her dinner's warming in the oven." I gesture to the kitchen behind him. "She eats later these days and will probably get to it around nine."

Stone whips his head toward the kitchen, then back to me. "You made the dinner?"

"Yes."

"But Ma loves cooking."

"She does but hasn't had the energy lately."

Stone's throat bobs. His eyes stay glued to mine. "Why would that be?"

The moment of truth. I want to throw up. My gut churns like it really wants to follow through with that thought. "She..."

"Spit it out, Noa."

His voice is harsh, loud, and full of grit. Stone's hands clench against his sides, the tendons in his arms protruding and turning an alarming purple.

Against my will, my vision blurs. Time should've made this easier, but I never look forward to hurting someone. Even when it's him. "Stone, I'm so sorry."

His stare shrinks. Stone steps forward like he's prepared to shake the truth out of me. I'm certain if he steps any closer, I'll be able to hear the wild thumps of his heart.

"Honey? Do I hear your voice?"

Mrs. Stalinski's soft question at the top of the stairs makes

Stone step back. I swear cool hair brushes against my cheeks at his movement. I close my eyes and breathe in deep.

It's not that I was afraid of Stone at that moment, but he was so coiled up, so indecently thrown into a dire situation, that I wasn't sure what he'd do to release his frustration.

Not hit me—never. Stone would never resort to violence against a woman. But the wall behind me or the open door hanging on brass hinges, even the potted plant at the base of the stairs, however...

"Mom." The word whooshes out of Stone's mouth as he passes me and clings to the banister on the first step. My heart squeezes at the worry in his voice.

As soon as he sees his mother holding her robe together and her usually perfectly curled, dyed red hair flattened on one side of her head and mostly gray, I pull my lips in and bite down.

"Honey, what are you doing all the way out here?" she asks him.

He ignores the question. "Tell me what's going on, Ma. Why are you in your pajamas instead of grading papers or making dinner or hanging out with your friends at the salon or—"

"Son. Honey. Calm down."

"No fu—" he hisses as he stops himself from swearing in his mother's presence, though I'm 100 percent certain he was about to say *no fucking way am I calming the fuck down.*

"Noa?"

Mrs. Stalinski's use of my name jerks my chin up.

"How much have you told him?"

"Nothing," I say, conscious of Stone's attention prickling against the side of my face, cold with betrayal and hurt.

I don't owe him anything, I assure myself. *He lost that privi-*

lege when he left me without so much as a goodbye.

Mrs. Stalinski sighs. "All right. Help me down."

Stone immediately complies, taking the stairs three at a time. Mrs. Stalinski offers her hand, but Stone ignores it, scooping her up in his arms.

His face collapses at how lightweight she is.

My composure cracks at the sight.

Stone takes the steps with grace and care now that he's holding his mother. I scoot out of the way as he brushes past me and into the living room, where he gently places her against the stacked cushions—a favorite spot of hers.

"I'll give you two some time," I say softly, backing away.

Mrs. Stalinski catches me right before I reach the front door. "I'd love some hot tea, Noa, if you wouldn't mind."

"Of course." With one last, longing look at the front door, I turn into the kitchen, but not before going into the attached dining room and lifting expensive bourbon off the bar cart.

If Stone is the same William Rodney Stalinski from my childhood, he'll need about three fingers of this right now.

I busy myself in the kitchen, throwing on the kettle and readying two chamomile tea bags in a mug until I find myself with nothing to do but wait as the water boils.

There's no door separating the kitchen from the hallway, and Stone and his mother's voices carry like a gentle wind flowing through the space and into my ears.

Biting my lip, I lean against the wall, my head tilting back as I listen.

"How long?" Stone demands.

Mrs. Stalinski must have laid her diagnosis on him the moment I left, a move I respect. The poor man was vibrating so much with worry and confusion, it electrified the air throughout the entire house.

Or was it only the air between him and me, thick, pulsing, and heated?

We left so much between us unsaid. And so much *more* was added to our emotional baggage today.

"A few months," Mrs. Stalinski admits to her son. "It's rather aggressive."

"And you didn't tell me?" Stone's voice breaks. "Why?"

"Honey, since the moment you could speak gibberish, you were meant to take the world by storm. And by God, you have, and I am so proud of you. *So* damn proud. Why would I want my son, who's finally made a name for himself and become an independent, successful man, to return to a town that so clearly strangled him as a child and watch his mother deteriorate?"

"Oh, I don't know. Because you're my *mother*, and no fu— no way would I want you to suffer alone?"

"I'm not suffering, honey. I have my girlfriends, and my Friday night cribbage games—this evening notwithstanding— and my church on Sundays. My community. The whole town's come together to make sure I get by, and as much as I hate it, I've accepted the help. Not to mention sweet Noa, who's too young to be wasting her energy caring for elderly lost causes like me, yet here she is. I'm relying on her too much, I think."

"Don't make this about Noa."

I tense against the wall.

"Why shouldn't I? She had an entire future ahead of her, and she's choosing to clip at my heels instead, cleaning up my waste and feeding me like a toddler."

"It's the job she chose, Ma. Don't burden yourself with her decisions like it's somehow your fault she wanted to do this with her life."

There's a sudden tightness on the surface of my chest. I rub the heel of my palm against the uncomfortable spot between my breasts, but it doesn't go away. It only gets worse as Stone goes on.

"Last I checked, she was perfectly capable of escaping this town and making a name for herself, too."

"She was dealt a crappy hand just as I have, honey. Go easier on her."

A dismissive rumble escapes his throat. "I'm not concerned about Noa. I'm worried about *you*. I'm angry you didn't tell me. But I'll put that aside because you've now become my number one priority. You. I'll have Noa pack some things for you before she leaves, and then we're driving to the airport."

Mrs. Stalinski's tone hardens. "Oh no we are not."

Shoes clip against the tile as Stone no doubt prowls the room. "This isn't negotiable. I'm taking you to California to see the best doctors and get the latest treatments and get away from this Podunk fucking town where the local doctor probably still uses leeches to cure blood infections."

Leech therapy is still a valid form of medical treatment in some instances, but I'm not about to cut in despite the very real insult he's lobbed in Falcon Haven's medical community's way—which includes me.

"I am very happy with my doctor, and I'm not about to be forced into a city that I don't know, in a home I'm uncomfortable in to be poked and prodded at until my son is satisfied that I'm enough of a lab rat to be granted cutting-edge drugs that probably won't cure me."

Mrs. Stalinski's voice grows stronger as she fights. I want to fist pump the air for her going up against Stone's demands with such calm aplomb.

"I only want what's best for you, Ma, and I know for a fact it isn't here."

"Indeed, it is. This is my home. My serenity. The place I'm happy to die in."

"Don't say that—"

"Then don't run circles around me pretending that my going to California would only delay the inevitable. The cancer is in my bones, honey. You are the love of my life, and I hate hurting you this way, but my time has come, whether I see one of your famous doctors in Hollywood or remain with the comforts of Dr. Silver and her drugs, which I assure you are the same medications I'd receive anywhere."

"You can't. This isn't the end. *Mom...*"

There it is. The plea of a little boy coming out of a toughened, grown man's lips, begging for the truth to be a lie. The strangled hope for the Mom of the past to receive him into her arms and assure him this is all a bad dream.

I hold a hand to my lips.

The kettle's electric whistle pierces the air, surprising me into a heart attack and cutting off any remaining conversation. Except for my scream.

Stone bursts into the hallway, his red-rimmed eyes zeroing in and scanning me head to toe as he strides into the kitchen. "Are you all right?"

"Yes. Sorry." Cheeks burning, I rush to the stove and stop the damn kettle. Leave it to my inattention to ruin a crucial moment between mother and son so I could eavesdrop.

I feel rather than see Stone lingering in the kitchen. The back of my nape tingles under his scrutiny. It takes all the acting chops I have to go about pouring and steeping the tea as if he's not there.

"Did you hear most of that?"

His gruff question makes my shoulders stiffen.

I don't turn around. "Yes."

Seconds pass. Stone clears his throat, then exhales a long, noisy breath. "Listen, Noa..."

I whirl. "I'm happy with my choices."

He pauses with his fingers shoved in his hair. "Okay. Good."

"No, you don't understand." I point at him with the spoon I was using to stir in the honey. "The way you talked about me out there. You didn't even have to *mention* me."

Stone's brows jump.

I continue, "I'm sure it surprised you to see me like this, dressed in scrubs and tending to your mother, but I'm fine where I'm at. I didn't have to go to culinary school or pursue endless wads of cash, or gain the love of the nation. So I'd appreciate it if you didn't dissect my life choices."

Slowly, as if not to alert a wild animal, Stone removes his hand from the top of his head, then raises both in surrender. "I apologize. My social filter isn't at its best. I've just found out Ma has cancer."

"*How?*" I throw my hands up, flinging warmed, sticky honey onto his shirt. "Fuck. Shit. Sorry."

I swipe a hand towel from the oven's handle and rush to dab the mess off his chest.

Digging my teeth into my lips, I swipe at the glob but only manage to make it worse.

I'm stopped by a gentle pressure on my wrists.

His touch sends a scatter of goose bumps across my bare forearms, made more apparent as his minty exhales hit the top of my head.

This close, I can smell his cologne—probably the one he's on all those commercials for, which Carly and I cackled at every time it came on, convinced it smelled like piss water and vinegar. But because it's *him*, and he has those *eyes*, he could sell it to the most skeptical.

Including me. I've been ripping samples from magazines because his simpering, clear blue gaze keeps telling me to.

"Noa," he prompts.

I refuse to look up. I can't. Not this close. Not when he's touching me, and his skin is as warm as his tan, and his body is what I've been missing for all these years.

"What's this shirt cost?" I ask, staring at the fabric stretching across his chest. His nipples pierce through the thin material.

I'm not sure this was the better spot to focus my attention on.

"Has to be a week's salary," I add with a hitch in my voice.

"It's fine. I'll have it laundered."

He releases my wrists but takes his time moving away, his breath tingling the baby hairs across my forehead and making me wish he'd blow that sweetness over my lips before he kissed them.

I recoil. *Jesus. What's wrong with me?*

"What did you mean?" he asks. His voice is low with extra butter churned in, and I'm thankful he doesn't see me close my eyes in pained remembrance at the sound.

"Hmm?" I pretend deep focus on fixing Mrs. Stalinski's tea. It's usually done in half this time. I blame Stone's presence for mixing me up and making me stupid.

"You asked me *how*, after I told you I didn't know about Ma."

I pick up the mug and the tumbler of whiskey I'd poured for him, handing it to Stone as I turn.

He takes it with genuine surprise.

"I figured you'd need it. Because, like you said, you had no idea she was sick."

Stone opens his mouth, but I interject with, "Which I'm having trouble coming to terms with."

"Well, what would be the alternative?" With deliberate calm, Stone puts the tumbler on the countertop. "You think I've deliberately ignored my sick mother?" Stone's gaze turns colder than I expected, and the small of my back hits the counter with a distinct *thud*.

He puts his hands on either side of my hips, bracing himself against the laminate as he leans in, his expression hardened with suppressed anger. "Is that how you remember me? Being your asshole ex isn't enough, you have to add cold-hearted bastard to it, too, huh?"

"No." Hating myself for stuttering under his shadow, I inject steel into my voice to continue. "But what does a small-town nurse like me know? Hollywood keeps you busy."

Deep frown lines replace his dimples. "Just as you've asked me not to judge your lot in life, I'd ask you to extend the same courtesy to me."

He's right, but I refuse to cede to him. "She tells me you talk to her every week. Even if she didn't outright admit it, didn't you hear it in her voice? Couldn't you catch her in any lies?"

Stone bares his teeth at the same time his eyes well before he blinks it back. "I fucking *wish* I did."

I search his face, taking the time to unearth the truth, since I don't plan on being this close to him again.

It hurts too damned much.

Stone doesn't break our stare.

"I thought I'd given her the life she wanted," he says. "I bought her this house, had a designer come out and decorate it with her, made sure she didn't have to work another day in her life even though she refused to stop teaching. When we talked a few months ago and she told me she was leaving her job, I thought she was finally retiring. I was happy for her. I bought right into the lies she was selling—the ones meant to protect me, to keep me away, to prevent me from seeing her slow decay."

He slams his palms against the countertop on either side of me. I wince, but keep his gaze.

"Maybe you're right. Maybe I let my Hollywood life color what was going on with her, but I believed my mother when she told me she was doing all right. And believe me, Noa, I'll be carrying that guilt with me for the rest of mine."

My lips part. I resist the urge to run a finger down the sharp angle of his cheekbone. "You're here now. You're not too late."

"Am I?" He angles his head, his sorrow reforming into his namesake. "Is that why you think I'm here?"

I have the sudden, confusing urge to soothe him. "You must've sensed something to have come home after all these years. That's not for nothing."

Stone's hardened expression doesn't change until it splits into a too-wide, maniacal smile. Then he laughs. Long and hard, cracked and uneven, like it hurts him.

"Stone?" I ask.

He pushes off the counter, freeing me. Stone shakes his head as he tries to get his laughter under control. "You were right about me on the first count, sweetheart. I'm a cold-hearted bastard."

My brows tighten as I watch him finish his whiskey in one gulp, then pluck his mother's mug out of my hand.

"Have a good night, Noa. You're dismissed," he says, then turns into the hall.

STONE

WHEN I SEE NOA TO THE DOOR, I REALIZE MY mistake.

She'd walked out of the kitchen behind me after my not-so-subtle hysterical laughter at the piss-poor timing of my return to Falcon Haven. I could've been honest with her about why I was here and that I'd flushed my career into the California sewage system, but I'd laughed in her face instead. It almost brought tears to my eyes that my mother's terminal cancer heralded my return, not the scandal currently rocking the West Coast tabloids.

They weren't sad tears. Tears of shame, more like.

My mother's dying. She thinks I'm here because I identified the truth she was trying to hide from me.

The last thing I want to do is confess my Hollywood mistakes and make my mother sicker, or for Noa to despise me more.

I picture the way Noa braced herself as I stepped into my

mother's home like her little body wanted to tackle me and was holding herself back.

Her scent. Her *fucking* scent hits my nostrils again, and I nearly fall to my knees.

Smell is the greatest memory there is, and that mixture of vanilla and citrus recalls hiding under the bleachers after school and kissing her until both our bodies imprinted into the dirt. Taking her to the Merc and swiping strawberry milkshake on her face before licking it off. The soundtrack of her laughter in my ears.

It brings back innocence. Freedom. The weightless future a sixteen-year-old envisions for themselves.

Reaching past Noa, I open the front door a little too hard, nearly hitting her shoulder.

She leaps back in time, glaring at me through her lashes but stepping outside all the same.

I definitely did not win points with her back in the kitchen. I wasn't trying to, but now I wish I didn't dim that sparkle in her eyes.

"I assume you still want me here at six tomorrow morning? Or am I fired?" Noa waits for my response before descending the porch steps.

She asks it nonchalantly, but I notice how she works her jaw while I stare at her, one hand on the open door.

"You're not fired."

Noa's face tightens. She must sense pity in my voice.

"You don't have to keep me because you feel bad. I have other patients." But her face darts to the window into the living room. Where Ma's sitting.

Noa's had months to reconcile her favorite English teacher with a devastating diagnosis. She's been there for Ma in ways I haven't. It isn't fair, but I resent her for it. We have our history, but if she didn't see me around and wondered about it, she could've called me. Hell, if the tables were turned, I'd be on the phone in a hot minute to let her know her only family, her best friend, was dying.

An unnatural cold envelops my body at the thought. Numbing and therapeutic as I stand across from a woman who haunts me, hates me, and has me all at the same time.

"You have a routine with Ma." I swing the door shut. "See you at six."

I break our stare-off before I can register any wounded look on her face.

"That went well."

Ma's wry tone comes through the hallway as I walk back to her.

"How'd you expect it to go?" I snap, before remembering what we're doing here.

Ma reclines on the couch, her thin body almost boneless with exhaustion and purple bags under her eyes. Fuck, she's lost so much weight.

"Don't be doing that." Her snippiness matches mine.

"Doing what?" I round to the bar cart in the dining room, needing a refill. Or three.

"Look at me all pitiful, like I'm a wounded deer you spotted on the road."

The decanter's lid clinks as I lift it off.

"I don't think that." I glance over my shoulder. "'Cause then I'd have to shoot you in a ditch to end your misery."

My lips uptick at Ma's snort. Good that I can still make her laugh with our shared love of dark humor.

"Still, I don't need my grown son to stare at me like I'm already dead." Ma grunts as she shifts to get more comfortable. "This is a bad spell, is all. I have good days, too. I've

43

found the clinical trial to be so much easier on my body than chemo."

"What clinical trial?" I return to the living room with a full glass and take a seat on the sofa chair next to her.

Her eyes slit at the suspicion in my tone. "Before you get on your high Hollywood horse, it's being done by a well-respected oncologist and has Dr. Silver's full approval. Even better, all it requires is a few pills a day."

"Except you could be on the placebo and not the actual drug."

Ma shrugs. "The mind is a great healer, too, and so long as I believe I'm taking a cure, it's been better for me."

"Ma, that's not realistic."

"Does it look like I appreciate reality at the moment?" Her arched brow mimics mine. "You didn't see me on chemo—"

"Because you didn't allow me to."

Ma levels me with a weighted look, the type with the full knowledge of what she did and has no regrets. "The trial is for a few months. Then if it doesn't work, I go back on chemo."

"And during those months, the cancer will have time to grow."

Ma's lashes lower as she sighs. "Hon, it's *been* growing. It's in my lower spine, my hips, and parts of my skull."

With each body part she lists, I wince. But her *skull* … "Jesus, Ma."

She opens her arms. "C'mere, baby."

I refuse to break down. I'm too big and too grown of a man to curl up on a mamma's lap, but I sure can sit next to her and hold on tight.

I do just that, cradling her head under my chin and marveling at our switch in roles. She used to do this for me during my nightmares as a kid.

"Were you ever going to tell me?" I ask over the top of her head.

She squeezes my arm. "I was. I promise you. I didn't know when, or how, but maybe you coming home right this moment is a gift. I'm glad you're here. I want you to know that."

I bury the lower half of my face in what's left of her hair, closing my eyes. "I am, too."

She wraps her arms around my waist, pulling me in as tight as she can. "And now that my surprising news is out of the way, let's talk about you and your penchant for whipping around furniture in public like you've regressed into toddler form."

I play dumb. "I don't know what you're talking about."

"You think your own mamma isn't aware of what's going on with you?"

To clear the guilty phlegm out of my throat, I answer, "I thought you didn't read the tabloids."

"I don't, but my cribbage group sure does. Maisy Hitchins being at the forefront."

"That fucking family," I grunt.

Ma smacks my arm. "I allowed you a few f-words when you were upset, but you watch your language."

"Sorry, Ma."

"Besides, she's just the messenger. You're the problem, and returning to town with your tail between your legs, no less. You must've really done it this time, huh?"

I pull away to grant space between us, though the last thing I want is to be scolded by my mother. She may be reduced in size, but her glare sure isn't. "I may have crossed the line slightly."

Ma clucks with disapproval. "Then we have some work to do."

"You don't have to do anything. This is my mess. You rest."

"Oh, please." Ma waves me off. "I'd love to be a part of your redemption tour. You can start by getting in some work around here."

I scan the room. Her floral fabric sofa furniture is spotless, as is the glass coffee table in front of us. No finger smears on the windows, and the fan above is devoid of any dust bunnies on its blades.

"It looks like your monthly cleaners do a fine job."

"I wouldn't expect any less from Jean and Nelson. They do wonderful work outside with my lawn and garden, too."

I pull my head back so I can study her better. "Okay, so what's the problem?"

"I'm not talking about my home, hon."

"Then I need more information."

"You remember that Carter boy, the one who was always beating up the neighborhood kids?" she hedges.

"Yeah." I draw out the word as my mind works to recall past events. "He should be about eighteen now, I'd think. Took over my detention record at Falcon Haven high."

"That's right."

"And he has to do with this because..."

"He quit his job at Talon Ranch to pursue a wrestling scholarship at Duke."

"No way." My surprise is honest. I figured that kid would be doing jail time by now.

"Turned his life right around. We're all proud of him."

"Well. Good for him."

"But Rome's having a heck of a time filling in his role, what with all the kids back in school."

I scrunch up one eye, not entirely enjoying where this conversation is going. "Ma, I'm not a stablehand."

"I know that." She pats me lightly on the arm, then rubs it.

Her go-to manipulation tactic. "It wouldn't be permanent and you could do with some honest work now that you're aiming to get away from all that bad behavior." She adds sweetly, "That's what you're doing here, aren't you? Re-writing your reputation?"

"I was thinking I'd spend more time with my mother, actually."

"You can do that, too, honey." She frickin' pats me again. "This would only be part-time. A few hours in the morning."

"Not that I'm entertaining this idea *at all*, but how early are we talking about?"

"About four, so you can help haul in the feed to the Merc store."

I pause. "The only four o'clock I know is the one where the bars close and I stumble home."

"Mm-hmm. And how has that been going for you?"

"Nope." I stand, pointing at her before pacing away. "You're not psychoanalyzing me. Not now, when I've only recently been told about your health and kicked off my movie and given a stupid amount of ammo to Ravynn."

"That girl." Ma curls her lip. I smile at her immediate response. "Not that I'm about to use her as a valid defense to your current behavior."

My smile falls.

"You'd be doing Rome—and Maisy—a great service, and she's been a wonderful friend to me during this horrible time."

Ma folds her hands into her lap, allowing the meaning of her words to sink in.

I squint at her. "Ma! You're using your cancer to get me to do this."

"I sure as heck am."

"That is not cool."

"Hush, now." She pats my hand, then uses my thigh to push to her feet. "Noa made an excellent lasagna for this evening and I'm hankering for a meal after sleeping for most of the day."

I let my head fall back to the sofa before sighing and getting up. "Lead the way."

The cushions don't shift as Ma rises. It takes a second to collect my heart from the bottom of the well my stomach has become. But I do.

I offer Ma my elbow. "Her lasagna as good as I remember?"

"Better." Ma leans her head on my upper arm as we head to the kitchen. "She adds this thing she calls a *rue* now."

"Excellent."

I don't know what the hell that is.

All I know is, Noa's meals used to fix anything rough going on in my life.

I kiss the top of Ma's head, praying that fact still holds.

Seven

NOA

News of Stone Williams's return surges through Falcon Haven like an uncontrolled STD.

I hear about him on the local radio as I drive. He's mentioned as I walk into the Merc, first from the elders of our community clustered around a round table, whispering in disapproval about the antics landing him back here, but doing it with a saucy glint in their eye, like if only they were younger, they'd really give him hell.

Then I hear it while waiting in line for my coffee, the young baristas behind the counter discussing whether he's hotter in person or as his superhero persona, Blue Flood, with his silver armor outlining his pecs.

Worse, I dreamed about him last night.

I prefer to call it a dream and not remembrance, even though the image was freakishly close to the times I woke up to him in bed with nothing but a crumpled white sheet separating me from him. Or how parallel the moment his eye cracked open and caught me staring was to what really happened, when he sprang from his side of the bed and landed on me, pulling the sheet over our heads and shielding us from the world as he slipped inside me. So easily, because I was always wet for him.

He smelled the same, too. Smoke and cinder with a small wave of soap. How his back felt so warm, but the skin over his heart so much hotter. How his mouth played with my lips the same way he enjoyed sucking on my nipples. Tender, with a little *nip* of dominance now and then.

As our lips met, as his tongue stroked mine, he stops his pumping, pulling his mouth away and asking roughly, "You're not still mad at me, are you?"

My eyes shot open, and I almost fell out of bed. In a cold, dark, lonely room.

Another cold splash of reality hits me when I hear the ladies waiting behind me chime in to the morning gossip, pondering which came first—his defined torso or the molded superhero outfit.

The brunette directly behind me murmurs to her neighbor, "Do you think that question could be applied to his nether—"

"Thank you!" I practically yell when I grab my coffee from the counter and sprint away from the whirlwind that is Stone's return.

The ruminating turns into curious wonderment as I breeze by, feeling the eyes on me like butterfly wings brushing relentlessly against my back.

"I wonder why she..."

"Do you think the poor girl's still heartbroken?"

"Does she want him back, or...?"

"How hard it must be to see that handsome face again and not be able to mess it up for real this time."

My head whips around at the last comment and I catch Carly sitting there at a table with her younger sister, Mae, where they have their usual early Saturday breakfast before Carly drives back into the city. She winks at me.

My lips pull up, and I shoulder open the door and step outside.

September hits hard today, bringing an abnormal chill compared to how it was even yesterday. The weather hasn't scared off the regulars wandering Falcon Haven's narrow sidewalk in search of breakfast, exercise in the nearby public park, or catching up with acquaintances on the wooden benches carefully placed near the decorative tree wells lining the sidewalk.

Falcon Haven is the type of town that looks good on the Fourth of July, Halloween, or Christmas—with banners hanging from the streetlights for each season, of course. At the moment, green leaves fight for survival against their inevitable submission to fall.

The nip in the air adds a pleasant cold to my cheeks as I slip into my car with the laughter of children collecting on the park's playground and tired parents holding the Merc's coffee cups, leaning on strollers to watch their kids.

I fall back into my seat, straightening my arms against the wheel. It would be the perfect start to Saturday, if it weren't for yesterday.

Stone's back.

And I'm about to drive straight to him.

Feeling a lot like those errant green leaves, I turn on the engine and drive down the hill of Falcon Haven's main strip and into the larger plots of land with perfectly landscaped houses.

Stone moved her into the richer, north part of town soon after scoring his first big paycheck in LA. I shouldn't have been being attention, but I can never seem to stop with him. Besides, the town kept tabs on Stone Williams, too. Even during my most desperate times when I tried not to give in to Google, my neighbors were perfectly happy to do it for me.

Seen as a good thing, I guess. It helped make me impervious to the mention of his name—the real or the fake one. It was certainly necessary, since the one way I could truly escape Stone Williams was impossible—by leaving Falcon Haven.

I thought I had my feelings for him, if not completely gone, then under control. Then he had to show his face in this town again.

Mrs. Stalinski's driveway comes into view all too soon and I creep into it as if my car's on the fritz. I lean over the wheel, my chin practically bumping against the leather as I search the darkened windows for his presence, my thoughts about as slow and heavy as I'm driving my Civic.

As if it wasn't enough to arrive unannounced on a literal doorstep I was sitting on, he had to get that look on him, that adorable, heart-rendering, shook expression where I could practically breathe in his pain as he learned the truth about his mother.

Stone wasn't acting. Of that much I know. Before yesterday evening, I was certain Stone was avoiding his mother because he didn't want to deal with her diagnosis and the fate that would follow. I figured his selfish ways had bled into his future, including dealing with his mother's shortened one, which is why he never came around when Mrs. Stalinski first got the news.

I hate being wrong. But I give myself full permission to keep hating him.

When my bumper's about an inch away from the garage door, I accept defeat and turn the engine off.

The wind bites my cheeks during my trudge to Mrs. Stalinski's front door. I squint up at the sky. Gray, dreary, and threatening to storm.

My keys jangle as I dig them out of my pocket, but I pause with the key inches from the lock.

Normally, I'd walk right in and begin setting up while Mrs. Stalinski sleeps. Doling out her medications, pouring her juice, tidying the kitchen if she came down late at night for a nocturnal snack, as many cancer patients do since that's about the time the nausea from their meds wears off. That sort of thing.

Mrs. Stalinski encouraged I enter without ringing the doorbell so I don't disturb her, but now...

There's another occupant.

I take a sip of my coffee, contemplating the closed door and whether I should knock. It would be the polite thing to do. The nice thing.

Poor, sweet, Noa-Lynn...

Screw it. Mrs. Stalinski would tell me to come on in, regardless of who's staying with her.

Even if that person were her hot, wayward, famous, heartbreaker son...

Taking a deep breath, I unlock and swing the door open.

That's the extent of my rebelliousness.

"Hello?" I ask in a quiet voice.

The foyer lights are off, no different from any other time. It isn't even seven yet. The house is silent, no footsteps or muffled voices.

I step farther inside, setting my purse and keys on the sidetable. Above it sits a mirror and I can't help but smooth down the fly-aways the wind kicked up and tighten my low ponytail. My make-up is minimal, as always, but I might've applied more concealer and blush than usual and glossed my lips. I wasn't about to be caught unawares by Stone Williams a second time. Not that he deserves an increased beauty routine, but I also don't want to look worse than he does.

His absence as I continue to move deeper into the house comes as a relief. Maybe Stone stayed at a bed and breakfast last night or found the Tipsy Falcon, had a bit too much to drink, and was sleeping in.

Either way, I could get Mrs. Stalinski's morning routine done without having to see—

"Morning."

The soles of my sneakers squeak against the hardwood flooring as I grind to a halt.

Stone stands at the stove in low-riding gray sweatpants and nothing else.

His back muscles bunch as he uses a spatula to flip what resembles a pancake.

"Hi," I respond with a tight voice, shifting in place which will hopefully summon the confidence to appear unaffected and casual. "I didn't think anyone was awake."

Stone glances over his shoulder at me. "I've been up since before dawn. Went for a run."

His statement brings up an image of him running in those very sweats and nothing else, beads of sweat forming on his muscles and running a straight line down his spine.

I tread into the kitchen, eyeing the cabinet over the fridge with worry.

Stone catches my stiffened approach, asking, "Something wrong?"

"No. It's just, I need to get into that cupboard."

I don't want to tell him I'm staring at the cabinet like it's a venomous snake because I have to scoot past him to get to it.

And possibly touch him.

Probably grazing his butt with my stomach while I'm doing it. Or, if I turn the other way, pressing the small of my back and part of my butt to his.

Physical contact isn't supposed to be part of the equation. Hating him means keeping my distance, speaking only when spoken to, and redirecting any conversation back to his mother. Nothing else. No reminiscing, no wishing.

Stone swings his gaze in my direction, narrows his eyes, then eats up the space in one step and reaches for the upper cabinet. "What do you need out of it?"

"Your mom's medicine," I say, pointing. "In that front container."

Stone glances up and grabs the clear container with about a dozen pill bottles in it. Any pensive thoughts about him and I disappear from his expression as he lowers the container and studies it. "She takes all this?"

"Not at the moment, no." I gently take it from him and place it on the counter, pulling out the mini spiral notebook tucked in the middle. Attending to professional business loosens my tongue. "She's on a clinical trial and gets two of these." I lift the plastic bottle and shake it lightly. "Then for pain, every four hours she gets this. And on particularly bad days, these fentanyl patches or lollipops if she has dry mouth, too."

I don't watch him while I explain, instead crossing out yesterday's dosages and moving onto today's column.

Satisfied with my final check, I look up.

I shouldn't have.

Stone stands on the other side of the counter, unmoving. His eyes shine with anger.

My stomach turns to slime. I gave myself full permission to be cold to him, but not when it comes to his mother. Too late, I realize how clinical and uncaring I sound.

I open my mouth to truly apologize, but the scent of burned butter hits our nostrils at the same time.

Stone whirls. "Shit—the pancakes."

He grabs the frying pan and angles it over the sink. The blackened chunk formally known as a pancake doesn't shift.

Stone turns his head this way and that, holding the pan over the sink. "Where the hell is my fucking spatula?"

His expression twisting and face reddening, he uses his fingers to pry the blackened pancake off.

"*Ah—fuck!*"

"I got it." I rush to his side as he shakes off the pain. I don't know where he put the fucking spatula either, but my finger pads have years of burn experience behind them and I easily un-stick the pancake-coal. It falls into the garbage disposal with a crunchy plop.

Taking the pan from him, I run it under the tap; the steam coming up with a *hiss* of smoke.

"Are you okay?" I ask as I grab his injured hand, inspecting the scarlet skin.

"I'm good," he grits out.

I prod the tips of his fingers gently, happy to see his frustration merely caused impatient man burns and nothing serious. "You don't need salve. Run it under cold water for a few minutes and you'll be fine."

I pull his hand into the running water, holding on as I angle his hand.

I'm watching the water cascade over his calloused palm when it occurs to me I can feel the soft hairs of his forearm under my grip. And smell the soap from his shower. And inch closer to the heat of his body.

Then I lift my chin and meet his eyes, blue as the spring sky on our faces when we skipped school to go to the football field.

I drop his arm. Not expecting the move, his hand falls against the still-hot pan in the sink.

"Ah—*Jesus H.*!" He recoils, his back slamming into the fridge as I stand there, not sorry at all that I let him go.

"I should get these to your mom." I use the gap he created between us and get back to pill counting.

Stone doesn't move, his bewildered stare following me as he holds his injured hand. "Oh, no worries, Noa. I don't need both hands working to resume my roll for *Blue Flood 2*. It's not like I need to hold on to anything ever again."

I send him a droll look over the pills, wondering if he's making it easy to dislike him after what happened between us on purpose. "You'll heal in less than a day."

"Well. Good." He holds his hand up, turning it to make sure I'm not lying.

I pick up the small bowl where I'd dispensed her morning medication. "I'll take this up to her now."

"Wait."

Not much could get me to stop from doing my job, but his soft plea does.

He blinks. Swallows. Holds my stare. "Last night was rough on her."

My shoulders slope. "I'm not surprised. I was hoping she

wasn't holding something back when she told me she was okay at night, but I should've listened to my instincts."

Stone nods. "I wanted to call you, but Ma demanded I leave you alone, so we called her doc instead."

"Dr. Silver? What did she say?"

"We have three options. One is to put Ma in a home of some sort for round-the-clock care."

He and I shake our heads at the same time.

"That's a no-go," he agrees.

"What about the second?"

"Take her out of the clinical trial."

I stare over his shoulder, thinking. "She won't want that either."

"No." He sighs. "She seems to want anything other than chemo."

I've had enough patients on chemo to sympathize with Mrs. Stalinski's decision. "So we're left with the third."

"Well..." Stone combs his fingers through his hair. "You mentioned something to her about staying over nights?"

"Oh." I jerk back despite there being nothing to recoil from. "Yes. I remember."

Stone looks at me through his thick chestnut lashes. I can't stand that look. I despise it because it's like the one where his lashes shine auburn in the sun.

"Would you still be able to do that?" he asks.

"I—well, you're here." My voice comes out screechier than I want, but the meaning is the same. "And there's only one bed aside from your mother's."

"I'm staying two weeks." He raises his hands. "And I can take the couch in the den. Or stay at a bed and breakfast in town."

"I wouldn't ask you to do that." In no way did I want to

separate a mother and her only son during the time she needs him most. Even if that son came by on happenstance. Stone wants to stay, and that's all that matters.

"I'm not qualified to care for her the way you do," he continues. "I can't stand the thought of sending to her to a home or making her reliant on another nurse she doesn't know, or the—I don't know, this is all so much and so sudden and I don't know if I *can* stay longer than two weeks but now Ma takes precedence and I have calls to make—"

"Okay." I raise a hand to stop him from jumping off the ledge. Stone's forehead crinkles with foregone agony and it makes me want to hug him, long and hard.

I step back, creating more space. "To be honest, I was about to stay over last night, but then yesterday kind of ... threw me for a loop."

"Yeah." Stone gives an understanding, lopsided smile. "For you and me both."

I resume walking to the stairs, trying not to fall into his smile. "I'll see to my other patients after this, go home and pack some things, then I'll be back."

"I appreciate you rearranging your schedule. Even if it's temporary and Ma fights you on it, it's absolutely the best solution. Especially if you have someone waiting for you at home..."

I pause at the balustrade. "There's no one but Moo."

"Bring him." Stone perks up. I'm thankful he's not like the rest of the town and doesn't question why I'm single or why there's no one but an elderly, grumpy cat at home. "I'd love to see that old fucker again."

A smile pulls at my lips until I yank them back. "I'll see if it's okay with your mom first, but it would make it easier to have him here."

I start up the stairs as Stone says, "I could always rely on you, Noa. I'm glad some things haven't changed."

There's a hitch to my step I hope he doesn't see and my grip tightens on the bowl to the point it might crack if I don't loosen my emotions.

Other than that, I have no reaction to his words.

None at all.

Eight

NOA

Mrs. Stalinski takes the news of her new roommates with grudging acceptance. I have the sense that with her son here, she's more amenable to changes she'd otherwise resolutely deny. Stone softens her the way she redirects him, and it's amusing to watch them try to out-manipulate the other into doing what they want.

I catch myself smiling as Stone tries to hand Mrs. Stalinski a coffee without sugar after she rustles awake midmorning.

She's suspicious the instant she cups the warm drink, wrinkling her nose and sniffing it before shoving it in my direction, stating, "I don't know what Hollywood's done to you, son, but Noa understands how I like it."

"Almond milk and collagen peptides have great benefits, Ma." Stone leans his elbows on the kitchen countertop, watching the cup exchange hands like he's witnessing his mother giving away his new puppy.

"I've taken my coffee with cream and sugar since before

61

you were a seed in my belly," Mrs. Stalinski says before gesturing to me with a *hurry up and fix it* motion.

With a subtle laugh, I shut my patient log book and slide off the countertop's barstool. "If it's the last thing I do before I leave, it'll be to get you a perfect cup of coffee."

"I like that sound." Stone angles his head as he watches me round the kitchen island. "Haven't heard your laugh since coming here."

My grin wilts, its petals lying dry against my tongue. "You've been here half a day and one night."

The idea of him thinking I'm depressed or unhappy while stuck in Falcon Haven while he lives it up in Los Angeles grates me the wrong way.

"Wasn't meant as an insult," he says, straightening and heading for the hallway. "You okay without me for a few hours?"

I open my mouth to retort, *I've lived ten years without you just fine,* when my brain catches up and shuts it before I make the gaping wound he left behind that obvious.

"I'll be fine," Mrs. Stalinski says, rolling her eyes in my direction. "Most I get up to these days is reading and sitting in the garden, and I'm fairly certain I can be successful at both activities without you hovering."

"It's all to get you back for that helicopter parenting you did to me in high school." Stone swivels around and winks at his mother. I wonder if it's just me who catches the painful shard of glass in his eye before he does it. "Do you remember the harvest dance, Noa?"

Against my better judgment, I respond, "How could I forget?"

Mrs. Stalinski *tsks* at the two of us. "I couldn't get you two off each other without resorting to chemical glue remover. Sue me for thinking that showing embarrassing baby pictures of you both while you were being crowned harvest king and queen would humiliate you enough to un-stick yourselves and scramble to take them down."

"A mortifying acceptance speech by my mother would've been better than that," Stone says.

Mrs. Stalinski's lips spread into the widest smile I've seen in months. "The one of you pooping in the bathtub and holding it up with pride was my favorite."

"All right, Ma."

"It was during your potty training days. I couldn't get you to relieve yourself on the toilet, but squatting on the floor and in the bath? Good to go."

"*Ma.*"

Mrs. Stalinski catches my attempt to swallow my laughter.

"Don't think your days of running butt-crack naked through the backwoods were any better, Noa," she says to me. "Thank goodness your mother was just as eager to publicly humiliate her child as I was."

Stone's baritone laughter fills the air, familiar and contagious. "Damn, I totally forgot about that. You wore mud pie hats for a while there, didn't you, Noa? How's your mom doing, by the way? Still making that prize-winning cherry cobbler?"

I straighten, my hands sliding off the counter and going for my bag on autopilot. "I'd better go. I'm going to be late for Mr. Childs."

The lines around Mrs. Stalinski's lips soften. "Off you go, dear. I'll be here when you get back."

Nodding, I squeeze her shoulder as I pass and take a wide berth around Stone.

"I'll see you later, too," Stone calls behind me, likely to get under my skin. "The guest room will be ready by the time you get back."

His statement forces me to turn around and acknowledge his sacrifice. "Thank you."

I focus in his direction long enough to see Mrs. Stalinski lift her coffee to her lips while her eyes ping between us both, sharp and assessing.

"Fate better be on my side," I mutter to myself as I open the front door, "because I refuse to allow two weeks of living with that man to be my second ruin."

MY REGULAR PATIENTS are easy and unproblematic, giving me plenty of time to head home for lunch and pack for my stay at the Stalinskis'. If I were a superstitious woman, I'd think the town was hatching a plan to return me to Stone as seamlessly as possible.

The town is split on the benefits of Stone's presence. He's been here less than a day and strange cars have popped up, likely hiding a camera behind their reflections. Falcon Haven welcomes strangers, except for those who unjustifiably pry into town residents' business. The key word there is *unjustified*. The town can pry into the town's own at will.

It's impossible not to overhear tidbits of conversation as I'm running errands. A cluster of girls at the bus stop fawn over one of their phones after she took a picture with Stone. It's clear the younger generation will forgive any transgression after Stone beams a dimpled smile their way and poses for selfies, whereas the elders of the community grumble over their chess games and coffee about his poor choices in life and debate whether fame has poisoned his soul.

I'm debating where I fall. Emotionally, I'm in the elder camp. Physically, my body betrays me whenever he's in my proximity, and I become a hormonal millennial.

Moo is in the third camp. After bribing, pleading, forcibly prying off my couch, then giving in and drugging Moo to get him into his carrier, I stop at the Merc for a couple of sandwiches to take to Mrs. Stalinski in case she's feeling peckish. Getting Moo to transfer away from his favorite spot and into the type of confines he only gets when he goes to the vet made me burn enough calories to eat Mrs. Stalinski's share if she doesn't want it.

Maisy rings up my order of two turkey sandwiches with the smooth movements and a watchful eye consistent with being fully aware of my temporary housing situation.

"Got everything you need, doll?" she asks, dripping with sweetness.

I sigh, envisioning the conversation I'd have to endure if I don't give in now. "You better add another sandwich."

"Already in the bag."

Shaking my head and fighting off a smile at her not-so-subtle inclusion of Stone, I lift the paper bag off the counter.

"Threw in a couple of cups of coleslaw, too, in the off chance you're hungrier than normal."

The bag freezes in mid-air. My vision slits. "Why would I be hungrier than normal?"

Maisy tries to cover her sly expression with an offhand shrug. "I hear he's a handful, is all."

"Maisy." I plop the bag back by the register. "I'm not there to rekindle anything with Stone. I'm staying over to take care of Mrs. Stalinski, and I hope you're telling anyone who asks exactly that."

Maisy flutters a hand near her heart in mock horror. "I

know that. I'm not contesting your wonderful care of Judy. You're the best nurse she could've ever hoped for." Maisy lowers her arm and rubs my hand. "But I understand how it can get frustrating and lonely. All I'm saying is, if you need to unload some of that baggage, there's now a handsome young man, one you're vastly familiar with, who could help you loosen an overworked muscle or two."

I press my lips together, then puff them out with a long exhale. "That I'm receiving this kind of advice from my best friend's mother should give you some pause, Maisy."

"Why should it?" Maisy raises a brow. "It's not my daughter we're talking about, now is it?"

I lift the sandwich bag one last time in farewell. "Caretaker, Maisy. That's the only label on me you'll find."

"Mm-hmm."

I feel her eyes on me as I walk out, no doubt coupled with a crafty grin.

Moo meows his displeasure for the entire drive to Mrs. Stalinski. I cajole him while watching through the rearview mirror, but he's having none of it and continues his horrifying wail all the way into Mrs. Stalinski's house.

"Jesus Christ." Stone covers his ears as he comes down the stairs. "Is he dying in there?"

I place the carrier on the floor and bend down alongside it. "He doesn't like small spaces and voices his opinions. Loudly."

"Who needs a dog? Just have that sound echoing throughout your house and you'll scare all the criminal assholes away."

I glance up at him, debating a retort. Too easy. Instead, I unlatch the carrier door and say, "Get ready."

A flash of white and caramel fur bursts out, followed by the panicked scrape of nails against hardwood as Moo tries to find the closest dark space. He flies through the V of Stone's legs, stopping long enough to swipe at Stone's bare ankle before moving on.

"What the—that's not the fluffy fritter I know!" Stone hops one foot and looks down, horrified at the long, red scratch on the side of his leg.

"He's fully embraced his crotchety old man status." I press my palms to my knees and rise. "I tried to warn you."

"Forget what I said." Stone lowers his leg. "*He's* the asshole."

I snort and turn back for the door. "Moo's never been one for change."

"I'll get him to come around," Stone says as he follows me down the patio steps. "Is Moo still willing to sacrifice virgins for an anchovy?"

My lips lift into a smile. "Every time."

"Good. I bought some this morning with that thought."

He thought of Moo this morning? As much as I hate to admit it, Stone's remembrance of Moo's favorite snack warms me.

"You didn't have to get anything for him." I round to the trunk of my car, pulling it up. Stone comes up beside me, the heat of his—bare chest, which I've just realized is happening right now—pulsing off him with invisible waves.

"I got that." He cuts in front of me and lifts my two suitcases.

"You don't have to—"

Stone twists toward me before straightening. "Let me. I didn't just follow you out here to admire your ass."

Heat blooms on my cheeks.

"Which looks considerably good in scrubs."

I lick my lips, then step back and away from the fragrant

warmth of his body. He's showered again. "Just like Moo doesn't need your platitudes, I don't need your compliments."

His disarming grin wavers. "I didn't mean anything by it."

"I think you did." I straighten my shoulders. "If I'm living here with you, we need to set some ground rules."

Stone lowers my suitcases on either side of his body, his biceps rippling with the weight. "Fine with me."

"You've gotten by with flirtation and flattery in Hollywood, but not with me. I'm your mom's nurse, and if I absolutely have to choose another label, your ex. That's it. That's all I want to be. Nothing more."

Stone cocks a brow. "Was I misleading you into thinking I wanted sex from you?"

I jolt at his casual use of what was once so special between us. So right. If our sex hadn't been so imprinted in my memories, I wouldn't believe this man had been my first, and I his. I wouldn't think about the women who came after—the *wife*—and how I cried for a month straight when I thought of Stone making vows to someone who wasn't me. I definitely wouldn't remember the low-key champagne celebration Carly and I had when his divorce was announced.

What tortures me the most is that, while every sweetness that passed between us runs through my mind when he says *sex*, none of that shows on his face. His expression is remote. I can't even say it's a blank one, because it's controlled. Stiff. Carefully affected.

Exactly how a talented actor would approach the situation.

To combat the wrenching of my heart, I mutter, "Wow, Hollywood really did a number on you," before lifting the bags myself and doing a lopsided walk to the house.

"What's that supposed to mean?" The gravel crunches as Stone catches up.

"Nothing."

"That's exactly what a woman says when it's a goddamned truckload more than nothing." With a flick of his wrist, Stone takes one of my bags.

"Hey!" I make a grab to get it back. "I was doing just fine."

Stone lifts the bag out of reach and I catch air. The uneven balance catches up to me and I trip into his chest. "*Dammit*, Stone!"

Stone glances down at my face pressed into his chest. "You were doing just fine. Sure."

I push off, smoothing my hair, hopefully soothing my pounding heart as well. And ignoring the bittersweet feeling that the beat of his into my ear brought. "That wasn't fair."

"Take some help from a gentleman, Noa."

"No. Not from *you*."

The sudden vitriol sobers his cocky attitude. He squints, studying me as I pull my lips in and gather what little control I have left.

"I don't want anything from you," I say before he can utter more cavalier and charming sentences meant to sway me. "Except maybe some respect. I'm here for your mother. You don't need to be the movie star with me or the most popular guy in the club or any other man you feel you have to be with other people. All you need to be with me is Mrs. Stalinski's son. Not my ex, not a celebrity, not a gentleman."

At his sudden silence, I prompt, "Okay?"

"Yeah." He blinks. "Fine, okay."

Stone drops my other bag, stepping over it to get into the house. I don't see his expression, but I notice the stiffness in his shoulders and the hard line of his back as he takes the steps two at a time and disappears inside.

I refuse to mull over whether I hurt him and lift one bag, dragging it up the stairs, then going back for the other. Why I felt I had to bring so much stuff...

Why I suddenly needed to unload on Stone...

Why I ripped my chest open and showed him the raised scars of our relationship when he's so clearly moved on...

All of that is better left for another day, so I swallow it all down, straighten, and walk into my new lodgings with my head held high.

Nine

STONE

Noa moves in with the stealth of a mouse. Ma's asleep, which I'm sure is why Noa's being so quiet setting up the guest room rather than doing anything to inconvenience her. Noa works fast, buzzing past me more than once and pretending I'm not there.

Noa made it perfectly clear on the front lawn that I was just below cleaning up Moo's cat shit on her list of priorities, so that's just fine.

At least I know where we stand.

Being in her company again punched me right through the chest, both in longing and, it surprised me to figure out, remaining connection. All these years should've lessened the strike, yet I'm still hit by lightning every time I see her.

Apparently, that's only true for one of us.

I push away from the desk in Ma's sewing room, closing the script I'm supposed to be going over and pulling off my headphones. They drop with a *clunk* beside the monolithic screenplay that's allegedly about to change my career into the more critically acclaimed side of acting. I've made it a quarter of the way through, and my vision's blurred and thoughts distant.

Without the soundproofing of my headphones, I hear the low murmurings of conversation coming from the kitchen. Ma must finally be awake. I haven't seen her since early this morning and start toward the hallway when my phone rings.

I check the caller ID and answer. "Aaron. Hey."

"How's life in the sticks?"

The beat of thumping bass comes through with his voice and I check the time. LA is three hours behind. He can't be at a club at this hour, so gym it is. "Slow and steady. How are the gym bunnies doing this morning?"

"None as fluffed as I'd like." Aaron chuckles at his own joke.

"There's still time if you spend less of it on the phone and more of it showing off your hot bod while lifting those weights you constantly avoid."

"I told you. I like the sauna and the cooling green tea infused towels offered."

"All complimentary, I'm sure."

"For me? Always."

I keep one ear trained on the sounds in the kitchen, Noa's light melody and Ma's tired, sleep-roughened voice. "What can I do for you, Aar? I'm kind of in the middle of something."

"Busy reading through *Cascade*, I hope."

I glance at the script, shut and barely creased. "Are you calling me to tell me I still have the role?"

"I'm working on it," Aaron hedges. "And you going twenty-four hours without being in the tabloids is helping. Are you lying low like you promised?"

I stare through the open door and into the hall, where Noa's voice seems to swirl. "As low as I can go, truthfully."

"Good. I have a meeting set up today with the studio exec to preempt the damage Ravynn's impending article threatens to do, and we'll go from there."

I reluctantly ask, "Do I need to be there? Or Zoom in?"

"Nah, you stay where you are and be a good boy. So long as you don't add to this shitstorm, we can come out of this."

"Uh, about that."

The thumping bass fades and a door slams. "Fuck. Why did I feel like I had to go somewhere private to hear this? What have you done? Can you even get coke in a haystack?"

"No, no, nothing like that." I swivel on my feet, staring out the window, scraping a hand through my hair, then leaving it there to pull on the strands. The jolt of pain should ground me, but I still feel like I'm floating outside my body. "I got some news when I got here. News I wasn't expecting."

"Oh yeah?"

"My mom. Ma has..." I clear my throat. "She has cancer."

Aaron is silent for a few seconds. "Shit, buddy. I'm so sorry."

"She's not gonna be all right," I say, even though Aaron didn't ask if she was. Maybe I'm mentioning it because I have yet to believe its truth. "It's spread, and she may only have a few months."

"That's fucking terrible. How are you holding up?"

"As good as expected, I guess. In an ironic twist of fate, my high school sweetheart is her nurse."

"Is that right?" Too late, I sense Aaron's wheels spinning, and I regret the confession.

"Aar, I'm telling you this as my friend, not my agent."

"Yes, obviously, but..."

"No."

"Hear me out."

"Not a chance." I pull the phone away from my ear.

"This is your redemption story!" Aaron shouts through the speaker before I can hang up. "You've gone home to take care of your ailing mother with your high school sweetheart, forsaking Hollywood in the name of family. This could look *so* good for you. And before you attempt to strangle me through the phone for being so crass—which admittedly, I am—I'm your agent. I can't ignore this in good conscience. This could absolve you of your shitty behavior for the last ten *years*, never mind last week."

"Dude, I get that you're acting as my agent, which is why I won't hire someone to punch you out since I can't do it personally right now, but I refuse to use my mother as a news piece. End of story."

"All right, all right, I understand." Yet I can still hear him thinking. "How about the ex angle? I can check her out, make sure she's as sweet as a small-town girl should be. That could absolutely compete with anything Ravynn says about you."

"I'm not using Noa as an angle against my bad decisions, either. Ravynn is my mistake, not hers."

"You're upset. I don't blame you. How about I give you some time to really think about this and what it could do for you? Be with your mother and take all the time you need. But sometimes the truth is better than fiction, and with how close you are to imploding what you've worked so hard for, you have to be smart about this. Please."

I gnaw on my lower lip while staring out the circlet window in the hall. Evergreens behind the street tower over the smaller, color changing oaks, but those sunset leaves draw the eye even under a larger shadow. "I don't think so. I've never spoken publicly about my past or my family and I don't intend to now."

Aaron releases a disappointed sigh. "Let me help you. Your rough patch just got a lot bumpier. I'd like to see some good come out of it. As your friend, I'd like the public to see you for who you really are."

"Right now, I'm a brokenhearted son and the public has no right to see that. I'm sorry, Aaron, but no."

Pause. "Fine. But you do not make my job easy."

"And another thing. I'm probably not coming back for a while."

Another pause. "How long's a while?"

"I don't know. Ma needs me. Noa's been handling this herself and I don't feel comfortable with that, either. Things are ... complicated, and I'd like to stay until I figure some things out."

"Take all the time you need." Aaron's tone brightens. "I can work the getting back to your roots, small-town reminiscing angle. I'll keep in touch regarding any news and truly, Stone, I wish you all the best with your family. I'm so sorry about your mom."

Aaron's genuine sentiment cleans away some of the dirt left on me after his career proposal. "I'll call you."

Noa's faraway tone becomes frantic. I tear my gaze away from the fall foliage and frown.

"Talk soon," I finish saying to Aaron, then hang up and stride into the kitchen.

I'm not sure what I thought I'd find, maybe a grease fire or a spill or a pissed-off cat ripping into a can of sardines, but I wasn't expecting Noa facing off with my mother, hands on her hips and an expression somehow being both stern and horrified.

I look between the two of them, Ma sitting primly on a barstool and Noa's body practically vibrating with the need to unleash beside her.

"What's going on?" I ask.

My voice draws Ma's attention. "Oh, hi, honey. How's your script reading coming along?"

"Fine." I drawl, my gaze sliding from her to Noa. "How's it coming along in here?"

"Noa and I are simply going over my schedule for the next month," Ma says.

Noa slits her eyes at Ma, then whirls and says brightly, "I'll start dinner."

"You don't have to cook," I say at the same time Ma pipes in, "Do you remember Noa's dream to go to culinary school?"

"Sure I do." I walk deeper into the kitchen, conscious of Noa banging pots onto the counter. "I was often the happy recipient of her food experiments."

"What's everyone feeling like tonight?" Noa asks loudly while facing the stove. "Pasta? Chicken milanese?"

"Either sounds lovely, dear." Ma folds her arms on the counter. "Great!"

Noa's exclamation comes out high-pitched and frantic. Conscious of the plot thickening between these two, I lower myself onto the stool next to Ma, readying for the show.

Ma continues as if Noa hasn't spoken. "Now I, for one, think it's high time for Noa to expand her skills, or at the very least exercise the ones she's gained."

She leaves a gap of silence, of which I have a son's obligatory urge to fill with a supportive, "Yep. Definitely."

"Excellent!" Ma claps her hands together with a burst of energy I haven't seen since arriving home. "Then you won't mind accompanying her to the *C'est Trois* cooking classes I bought her."

I straighten. "Wait, what?"

Noa spins, her oil-coated wooden spoon coming with her and splattering across my shirt. Again. "Mrs. Stalinski, I've told you, I don't need—"

"Judy, dear."

"—to go to these classes. Not if you can't go."

Ma looks to me, choosing to ignore how I have to reach around her to get a napkin and dab at my shirt. "The classes were my gift to her, meant to be for the two of us to enjoy together. A small token of gratitude for all she's done."

Noa audibly sighs. "I'm a *nurse*. Your insurance pays me to do this and I'm happy to do it. Please, you don't have to give me anything to help you."

"You are *not* a nurse." Ma sticks her nose up. "You are a cook. A chef. Saucier. Chef de *partie.*"

"Now you're just showing off your fancy words," I say wryly.

"Mrs. Stalinski, I've chosen to be a nurse."

"If by *chosen*, you mean you were pushed into the role."

"I truly wasn't!" Noa throws her hands up, splattering more oil. *Hot* oil, I might add. "I enjoy what I do.."

I jerk back, but not in time to receive a second coating. Neither of them hears me curse under my breath. Or acknowledge another reach-around for a paper towel.

"You do not belong at my bedside, dear, or in the bathroom with me, or seeing to my needs all night."

"That's for me to decide." Noa huffs, folding her arms and thankfully tucking the spoon behind her.

During their spat, Noa's come closer, her arm a scant inch

77

from mine. If I leaned sideways enough, I could kindly return the favor and stain her shirt, too.

"We can put a pin in it for now," Ma allows.

Noa visibly relaxes, the tension around her eyes disappearing. "Thank you."

She goes back to the stove.

I stare at Ma.

I know my mother and have full confidence she's not finished. Crossing my arms, I wait for her to drop the mike.

"Because either way, you're still attending these cooking classes."

There it is.

"Mrs. Stalinski." Noa presses her hands on either side of the stove and drops her head.

"What?" Ma widens her eyes innocently. "I dislike the airing of financial discussions, but I must insist that these classes are non-refundable and booked months in advance."

Noa lights up. "Then we can sell them. I can get you the money back."

"That just won't do." Ma clucks, shaking her head. "There are distinct rules, one being that the tickets are non-distributable or shareable."

I squint one eye at her as she continues to bat her eyelashes.

But are they really?

Noa is so distraught that I decide to be helpful, even though I'm mostly insulted that her distress is largely due to my going with her to these supposed classes. "Ma, I'm sure we can inform them about your circumstances and they can make an exception."

"Yes!" Noa points that damned spoon in my direction again. "That!"

"I swear to God, woman," I mutter before swiping the spoon from her and making my way to the pot she's filled with some sort of onion and garlic mixture.

Noa's hand goes slack, startled, but, since her argument with Ma is more important, she allows me the space to take over the stirring.

"I'm afraid not," Ma says. "I've tried, and Chef Bernard insists the tickets must remain with us."

I look up from the pan. "Then how can I take your place?"

Ma's lips flatline and I re-center my attention on the mixture rather than face her laser-eyed glare in my direction. "I explained my situation and he's willing to allow a substitute for myself."

"Any substitute?" Noa asks behind me with way too much hope.

"Like who?" Ma counters. "We both know Carly sets fire to butter and scares wild animals away with her leftover cooking, and anyone else you're attempting to think up doesn't have the space in their schedule the way my son does."

For a moment, the only sound is the spitting coming from the pan.

Ma prompts, "His schedule's opened all the way up, hasn't it, Stone?"

"Not really," I say. "There's the screenplay I have to get through, and my free manual labor that you've offered Rome, as well as all the rearranging I want to do now that I'm staying here for a while. I have to get my affairs in order in LA, get someone to watch my fish..."

"Just as I said." Ma flaps her hand. "He's got time."

"I can't," Noa bites out. "*We* can't. If taking these classes mean this much to you, I'll go alone, but I don't think Stone joining me would be to anyone's benefit. You don't like cooking, do you?" Noa asks me, although it sounds more like a threat.

"I don't hate it." I shrug.

A sliver of white shows through her lips, almost like her teeth blocked a venemous hiss, before she pastes on a sweet smile for my mother's benefit. "You're right. I'd love to take cooking seriously again, but I doubt having the town's movie star next to me while we cook in Falcon Haven's latest restaurant would do me any favors. He'd be a distraction."

"Maybe not," Ma says. "The class sold out immediately. We get so few trendy places moving into the area. It's not like anyone who hears he's there will sneak in, and one couple that signed up for the class is from my cribbage club, and they know my boy well enough."

Too well, I think with a wince. I was a little shit growing up and Ma's friends were often the victim of my frustration outlets.

"Does *he* have a say in this?" I cut in, pointing to myself.

The smell of burned garlic slips under my nostrils as I say it. Noa catches it as well, muttering as she shoves me out of the way like a football defenseman and yanks the wooden spoon from my grip.

"No," she says. "You don't. Not if you can't cook garlic."

"Hey, now," I say. "I refuse to let that pan be your answer to my kitchen skills. You two have been enough of a distraction for me to have burnt boiled water by now."

Noa lifts her head, meeting my eyes for the first time since I wandered—naively—into the kitchen. "Do you even want to do this? This is a *couple's* class, and we are so far away from that it's almost laughable."

Though her matter-of-fact assessment of our relationship status digs. "I didn't know I had an opinion on the subject."

Ma scoffs. "Don't be such a martyr. You have nothing better to do except tuck tail out of Hollywood for a while."

"Ma!" I say, a little offended.

"Don't think I don't know what you've been up to." Now it's Ma's turn to use a slitty-eyed glare. "You have not been acting like the boy I raised. I'd like to think it was California influence that did this to you, but we both know it's not. This is a time for you to rediscover your roots and get the town back in your blood, a town you've rightly disgraced."

Noa discreetly turns down the stove and backs away.

"Noa," I say after a beat of silence. "Would you mind?"

"No problem." Noa doesn't put forth any argument, sticking to edges as she leaves the room to give us privacy.

Hot flame licks at my cheeks. I check to see if Noa really turned down the gas burners, but I know it's not that. This is coming from an internal place, an area of puberty and hard lessons and making stupid mistakes while growing up. It's a part of me only my mother could locate, grab, and yank through my throat.

"I love you, I always will," she says. "You have my whole heart. If you truly want to prove to the public, and most of all yourself, that you are a man to be admired, you will do this for me."

"It's a cooking class," I say between my teeth. It's a low tone, non-threatening, but pissed.

"I'm well aware of what it is," Ma retorts. "And I had every intention of attending it with Noa until recent weeks have proven to me I simply don't have the energy for it anymore. She deserves this, son, regardless of what she says. An opportunity like this never comes into this town. If Noa refuses to leave Falcon Haven, then this is it for her. And it's mostly for her, let me tell you, not you. You reap the benefit of being in the middle of Falcon Haven so people can see you're still the boy I raised, helping a girl he scandalized get on her feet."

Putting *Noa* and *scandal* in the same sentence turns the shame in my throat into a curdle. I talk through it, mostly because I can't stand ruminating on our past for too long. "Ma, I'm not here to make waves, and it's fairly obvious Noa doesn't want me near her any more than she has to endure me."

"She's earned that right." Ma straightens in her stool, lacing her fingers together.

"Who's side are you on, exactly?" I ask.

"No one's. My own. I don't know, possibly I'm in the mood to fix as much as I can before I go."

My heart lurches. "Don't talk like that."

"While it's tempting to play cancer card against you at this moment, I will not. I want this to be your choice. I can bring Noa around easy enough—she has a genuine passion and you should've seen the way she lit up when I told her about the classes the new French restaurant was offering to promote its opening. I even weaseled my way in as a patient and her nurse rather than a traditional couple in love. She'll do it. The only question remaining is, will you?"

"I'm not sure." I glance through the open doorway Noa just vacated. "But I am sure I'll be wearing a bunch of hot oil stains by the time we're finished."

Ten

NOA

I DID EVERYTHING I COULD NOT TO EAVESDROP, including using this time to search for Moo's latest hiding place. As it is, the house is silent save for the noises in the kitchen and there are only so many crevices before I have to give up and circle back again.

I catch snippets of *earned this* and *scandal* and *genuine passion*, but it's not enough to sway my determination *not* to attend the class with Stone.

I'll go on a dating app if I have to, though Falcon Haven's phone tree system has gone through all eligible bachelors and back when it comes to Noa-Lynn Shaw. Most of the good men are married, gay, or moved out of town. The ones that remain are the leftovers. Like me. Pitied by those who've found happiness and grew old here.

With a dating app out of the question, I decide to beg Carly on my knees to join me, or pay her sister to do it for her. Mrs. Stalinski will not let these reserved seats go to waste and I hate to see her disappointed when she has such tough days to begin with. Or maybe I can go by myself and *say* Carly's going with me, then swear everyone involved to secrecy...

"Noa? Hun? You out there?"

Mrs. Stalinski's voice reaches my ears in the den, where I think I've found Moo under the armchair by the fireplace.

I pull up the embroidered dust flaps, finding the two yellow beams of his reflective eyes, then make kissy faces at him. "See you soon, pal. Glad you found a safe space."

He pissily swipes at the flap as I drop it back in place.

Instead of answering Mrs. Stalinski, I return to the kitchen, using an extreme amount of effort to keep my expression calm and blasé as I study Stone, his mother, and the after-effects of their conversation.

Did Stone convince her it was a dumb idea? He must have. A guy like him has a million better things to do than go to a small-town date night cooking class once a week for two months while the restaurant readies for its grand opening right after Christmas. He has agents to talk to, famous friends to hang out with, gorgeous actresses to swipe right on, and a sick mother to care for. No way would he want to spend his precious spare time learning the specialties of fine French dining.

"Here's how it's going to go."

My brows jump at Stone's official tone, but I don't argue, angling my head with interest instead.

"It's obvious you don't think I'd enrich your experience at ... what's this place called, Ma?"

"*C'est Trois.*" Mrs. Stalinski answers with a thick French accent.

"Yes, that. You believe I'd make these cooking lessons worse for you somehow," Stone says to me.

I don't answer. My silence is enough of one.

Stone doesn't react to my acknowledgment with hurt, or despair, or ego-wounded anger. No, he rounds to the side of the fridge, swipes the apron off the hook, and throws it over his head.

Stone fists his hands on his hips and puffs out his chest. *Get Your Fat Pants Ready* splays across the front of the cream fabric in cursive font.

"Let me prove it to you," he says.

I look at Mrs. Stalinski for further clarification. Her perfect posture shows me nothing. I go back to Stone. "What do you mean by that?"

"Let me cook dinner tonight. If it's terrible, I won't be your weekly date. No argument, not from me or Ma. Right, Ma?"

Mrs. Stalinski pushes out her lower lip. "I suppose."

"But if I *do* cook something delicious, you let me do this with you."

I rub at my cuticles, suddenly desperate to pick at them. "Why would you want to do this for me, Stone?"

Stone's confident expression falters. "Consider it a two-way street. You get fabulous lessons from a Parisian chef, and I get some redemption in the way of improving my reputation."

Here is the moment it all makes sense. Stone would never do something purely for someone else. There has to be a benefit in it for him. Good to know he hasn't changed and his selfish ways remains his most prominent quality. The reminder shouldn't be surprising, or cause a hollow *ping* in my chest, yet it does.

It always has, no matter how many times he reminds me.

No matter how many times I'm disappointed, Stone is the only man who keeps me wishing for more.

All such *stupid* wishes. Wasn't I just going through the ways I could avoid him? Why is it suddenly so important that he acknowledges my importance to his life?

"I see," I respond tightly.

"Is that a yes?" Stone's brow arches in tandem with one side of his mouth.

I'm about to say no, that my dream shouldn't be reduced to an impulsive bet, but then I catch Mrs. Stalinski's face as she watches her son.

There's color to her cheeks, a flush of excitement.

"I hope you make it difficult for him, Noa," she says. Then she laughs, a full-on, pre-cancer laugh. "But I still want him to win."

The vision of Mrs. Stalinski's pure joy stays at the backs of my eyes as I turn to Stone. "You're on."

Stone takes a spatula and smacks it on his open palm. "What were you making before the thought of having me as a partner made you run from the room?"

Choosing to ignore his statement, I almost lie instead. It's tempting to give him a complicated recipe guaranteeing failure, like the chicken milanese I mentioned. The Stone I remember couldn't toast bread without burning the center, then smearing butter all over it to cover up his mistakes. That analogy also applies to his personality, charming in all the right ways when he does the worst to a person.

But tossing such a difficult recipe his way wouldn't be fair or enjoyable to watch. As much as he grates on me, I want a fair win with no openings for him to complain that I cheated or stacked the odds against him. I'm still not sure why joining me at the restaurant is so important to him, but that's probably not the point anymore.

Stone likes to win. Always has.

But so do I.

"Spaghetti bolognese," I say to him, joining Mrs. Stalinski on the stool beside her.

Stone purses his lips. "Easy enough."

I add, "With homemade meat sauce. Nothing from the jar."

Mrs. Stalinski smacks the countertop. "Now we're talking."

"All right." Stone nods. "No problem. I can do this." He stares down at the sizzling pan of onions and garlic. "Look at that, you've already started my *mis en place.*"

I roll my eyes.

To my surprise, he turns down the heat under the pan, then goes to the pantry to bang around. After reappearing with an arm full of canned and fresh tomatoes, some dried herbs, and brown sugar, I fear I misjudged him.

He finishes his foraging by going into the fridge and pulling out the ground beef.

"Funny thing," Stone says as he goes to the sink to wash the tomatoes, then to the cutting board to chop them.

Shit, he's actually prepping.

"Living on my own in LA and becoming so busy," he continues, "I was really homesick. Desperate for a home-cooked meal. So I called Ma and she told me how to make a delicious meat sauce to put over pasta or stuff in peppers or put in a hoagie. You get the idea, right?" he asks me with a glint in his eye.

I fight against a glower. "How great for you."

"Isn't it?" Stone flashes his teeth at me before spinning and sliding the ground beef into the pan. "Don't get me wrong, it took eight or twenty tries to get it right. But once I did..." He picks up the wooden spoon and stirs, sending me a dimpled grin over his shoulder. "Magic."

I turn to Mrs. Stalinski. "You were perfectly aware of this, weren't you?"

With the most innocent expression I've ever seen, she blinks at me and shrugs.

"Traitor," I mutter, then jolt as something clanks on the counter in front of me.

Stone bends to my level after setting down a healthy glass of red wine.

"Here. You're going to need this," he says.

My tongue feels stuck to the roof of my mouth. I reach for it and take a nice, long glug.

STONE'S SPAGHETTI bolognese ends up somewhat dry, over-salted, and stupidly delicious.

It takes all self-control not to lick the plate clean as the three of us sit at the breakfast bar and finish our meal.

To Mrs. Stalinski's credit, she keeps her cat-got-the-canary expression to a minimum as she picks at her food and converses with Stone.

Stone is another story, asking after every bite, "Is it good, Noa? It's delicious, isn't it?"

I'm ready to toss my licked-clean spoon at him to shut him up when Mrs. Stalinski lets out a small moan.

It was tiny, not meant for our ears, but being with her all these months has made me attuned to every wince and whimper.

"Mrs. Stalinski?" I ask.

Stone pushes away from his third helping. He stands and puts a hand on her lower back. "Ma? You good?"

Mrs. Stalinski waves us both off. "Don't fuss, you two. I need some rest is all. Your little pissing contest took the last of my energy."

"Rigged pissing contest," I add, but I also slide off my stool with concern.

"I'm fine, I'm fine," Mrs. Stalinski insists.

She moves to set her feet on the floor, then buckles. If it weren't for Stone, she would have fallen. He catches her under the arms.

"Guess I had too much to drink," she jokes. Mrs. Stalinski maybe had two sips of wine.

"You're not making it up the stairs," Stone says at the same time I jump into action and say, "It's time for your nighttime medication. That should help."

"I told you both—I'm *fine*."

Mrs. Stalinski doesn't protest as Stone leans her into his strong body. I'm fully aware of the weight she's lost and how frail she's become, but next to her tall, powerful, and incredibly fit son, she turns into a broken bird.

A rock lodges in my throat. Swallowing it down, I open the cabinet above the fridge and pick out her necessary meds. I get her a glass of water and hand everything to her, which she takes without protest.

"There," she says. "Once these babies hit, I'll be snoozing and snoring and you two can bicker long into the night."

A note of pain laces her tone and I immediately wish there was a bedroom on the first floor so she wouldn't have to navigate the stairs. I assumed it would have to happen eventually, but with the way this clinical trial is progressing, it might be sooner than anybody imagined.

Stone solves the problem for me when he lifts his mother into his arms.

"William!" she protests. "You do not need to carry me like a darned baby. Put me down this instant."

"Not a chance, Ma," Stone says, his face grim. The muscles in his jaw pop and undulate, holding a frustrated roar prisoner.

Without glancing in my direction, he strides out of the kitchen and to the stairs, Mrs. Stalinski batting him on the shoulder and demanding to be released the entire way.

I should leave them to it. Mrs. Stalinski is in good hands with Stone, but there is a pull to follow them I can't ignore.

Maybe she'll need me, I rationalize as I pad behind them in my socked feet. *Or needs assistance to the bathroom. She won't want Stone for that.*

All things Mrs. Stalinski could probably do for herself, but I'm staying overnight as her nurse. Not as her friend or Stone's ex-girlfriend. The dinner allowed the three of us to dismiss my role for a time, but cancer never likes to be overlooked. It'll push itself back into the spotlight at every turn.

When I reach Mrs. Stalinski's bedroom door, Stone is laying his mother gently on the bed and pulling the duvet over her. His arms tremble as he does it, the blue veins down his forearms bulging.

It's been so long since I've seen him in person, yet I can spot his battle to keep himself under control a mile away.

I come up behind him. "Let me. It's why I'm here."

Stone glances at me with his expression a mixture of guilt and relief. Relief that there is someone in the vicinity who knows exactly what to do, and guilt that he doesn't want to, or can't, do it.

"Thanks." His throat bobs and he moves away.

"Allow us ladies get prepared for bed," Mrs. Stalinski says, her eyelids drooping. The fentanyl patch works fast. "Go clean the kitchen since you made such a mess of it."

"I thought the rule was the chef cooks, the gluttons clean." Stone tries for a smile, though it falters around the edges.

"In this instance, the winner humbly accepts their win and tidies up after themselves," Mrs. Stalinski slurs.

Her head lolls to one side. A wrenching keen comes from my left, and I realize it's Stone. It kills him to see his mother's slide into a helpless drug stupor. His lips are glued shut, his eyes a sheen of blue. His pulse beats so hard, I can see it fluttering like a dying butterfly in his neck.

"Go," I whisper, squeezing his arm. It's warm, firm, and with a familiar, downy softness. "I'll make sure she's as comfortable as sleeping on a marshmallow."

Stone's jaw works. He won't tear his gaze from his mother.

"Thank you," he grits out, and then he's gone.

With the image of Stone's agony battling with my nurse's to-do list, I help Mrs. Stalinski take off her clothes and have her use the bedpan before putting on her pajamas, since she's in no condition to walk. She slurs her thanks and at some points smacks at my arms feebly, demanding that she can do this all herself until the pain killers take over and she falls asleep.

Mrs. Stalinski is snoring softly by the time I ensure the baby monitor I brought with me is working on her side table so she can call for me at night if she needs.

Even though it would take a zombie Apocalypse to wake her, I tiptoe down the stairs and follow the sounds of clattering dishes and a running faucet at full power.

"Need any help?" I ask, entering the kitchen.

Stone's so busy slamming dishes into the sink and spraying the hell out of them that he doesn't hear.

"Hey. Stone," I try again.

The muscles under his T-shirt flit under his skin like rapidly blinking eyes.

I walk up behind him, laying a hand on his shoulder.

He whirls with such speed that I yelp, and I'm met with fire.

Heated cheeks, rippling skin, molten eyes.

"Hey." I cup both his arms. "Take a breath. It's okay."

"It's *not* fucking okay!" he roars. Spit flies into my face, his voice shatters my soul, but I don't flinch.

"You're right. That's a stupid thing people say when they can't think of anything else to make you feel better. I'm sorry."

I seem to surprise him with those words. His arms go slack in my hands. I still haven't let him go. I don't think I could if I tried.

Stone's softening should've come as a warning, but I'm just as keyed up as he is, just as heartbroken. It's why I'm not prepared when he cups my face and yanks me to his lips with a desperate, blazing desperation.

It's such a familiar pain that I submit to his lips without thinking to fight. His full mouth sucks on mine, his tongue as silky and skilled as I remember, tasting like a home-cooked meal. My hands slide around his neck. My body softens against the hard lines of his chest, and with arms that could crush my bones as seamlessly as he shattered my heart, he lifts me until my legs wrap around his waist and we topple against the fridge, kissing each other like we're both dying.

His hands travel to my ass, squeezing through the thin material of my scrubs and dipping into my crease, prodding and spreading my wetness into my clothes.

The cooling slickness of my need is enough to wake me out of this pointless dream. Pulling my mouth from his, I fight to get down, pushing against his chest and saying, "No, we need to stop, we can't do this."

Stone complies, likely as taken aback by our actions as I am, dropping my legs and retreating while wiping his palm against his mouth.

He smells me on his hands. Stone's pupils dilate the moment his pointer finger slides under his nostrils and I internally command myself not to react. Not to fall to my knees, pull out his dick, and smell him, too. And lick him, taste him, *have* him like I used to.

"I apologize." Stone's tone is hoarse. "That was totally unacceptable."

"Understandable, more like." I cross my arms and press my back into the stove. "You're dealing with unimaginable pain and it's only been twenty-four hours."

"You're too compassionate sometimes." Stone laughs tonelessly. "My grief is no excuse to try to fuck you on my mother's kitchen counter."

The words send another gush of need between my legs. Having rough sex with Stone would be a healing ointment that I'd love to rub all over me, until it stops working. And something like that always requires repeat uses. Stone is the most addictive drug I've ever come across.

I press my thighs together. "I'll give you one hall pass. That's it."

Stone offers up a half smile. "Deal. It won't happen again."

We should go back to tidying the kitchen, but both of us continue standing in the middle of the room, staring at each other.

"I had no idea it was like that for her." Stone's voice cracks. "Ma puts up such a front that I..."

His agony brings me closer to him. I can't help but touch

him and soothe during times like these, so I reach up, pressing my hands on his shoulders and squeezing. "She's the strongest woman I know and likes to think that making herself seem okay puts other people at ease."

Stone lowers his head, his eyes searing into mine. "I can't thank you enough for what you've done. The way you've been there for her. I'm angry you didn't tell me and frustrated with her for keeping something like this a secret for so long, but ... Fuck, you got this handled. And for that, I'm forever thankful."

My hands slide down his arms, but he catches them in his before I let him go.

"No thanks needed," I say, but it's on autopilot. So many people thank me for what seems to me to be the right thing to do, but maybe that's because I'm just too close to see that not everybody would want to do this.

"No. You're going to listen to me say it, repeatedly. She needs you. I need you. You're here because neither of us can live without you right now, and I—"

"Stone, stop."

"—want to say how sorry I am for everything that happened between us. I didn't leave this town in the best of ways back then and—"

"I said stop." I try to pull my hands from his, but he holds them strong. "Don't go there. Please."

"But I have to. For too long, I've let you go without an explanation, made you hate me, and despite all that, you've dropped everything to take care of my mother."

"I said *don't*." Seething, I yank out of his grip.

Now I own the fire.

Stone blinks at me, startled.

"You don't get to thank me for taking care of your mother after what happened between us like it shouldn't be the case that your *scorned* ex-girlfriend wants to help her. Despite what you think, I have not gone through life as your ex, telling everyone that I dated a famous actor who dumped me—though God knows, the whole town knows that, anyway. I'm doing this because I love your mother. I love her, she was there for me during the years I needed someone, and I would do anything for her. It has *nothing* to do with you. And it's selfish, so *selfish* of you to think that I've overcome bitterness toward you in order to be there for her."

"I ... Jesus, Noa." Stone lifts his hands in surrender. "I was just trying to say thank you."

"Yeah, well." I blink back frustrated tears. "It should be pretty damned obvious that I want nothing from you. Gratitude being the least of it."

Stone shakes his head then looks to the side, as if he can find answers through the window. "You know, for someone who insists I mean nothing to her, you're sure fucking passionate about it."

"*I was pregnant!*" I shriek.

The vehemence surprises even me. I jerk all the way to my toes. My heart's on fire and the flames char my throat and singe my eyes.

Stone takes a deep breath, his hands still out like he could ever soothe the ache in my chest. "I know, Noa. I was a dumb kid and if I could go back, I would."

"You left me," I somehow garble out through my rapidly closing throat. "You left me to deal with it, all without a goodbye."

"What? No. I had a plan, but then it—"

I slam up my hand. "Not another word. If you say one

more thing about this, I swear to God I *will* smack you and I won't be able to stop."

My fingers tremble in the air. They blur through my tears along with his stricken, confused, handsome face.

The world washes into watercolor until I lower my arm and sprint from the room, leaving him no further space to smear his butter over the burn.

Eleven

NOA

I manage to avoid Stone for the rest of the night and morning. By the time I wake up in the guest room, Moo angrily wriggling aside when his human pillow gets up, Stone isn't in the house and when I glance outside the front window, his car is gone.

Curious, I check my watch. 5:30. Stone must be starting work at the ranch this morning. I take these quiet hours without Stone and where Mrs. Stalinski is still sleeping and go for a run, my cardio in tandem with the sunrise until I return and take a shower.

"You can face him," I tell my reflection in the bathroom mirror. My hair is damp from a shower and my face freshly exfoliated and frowning. "You don't care how he reacts anymore. He is who he is."

My reflection nods along with me, expression highly unconvinced.

"Shit." I rest my palms on the edge of the sink and lower my head.

What was I thinking, freaking out like that last night? I was like a popped balloon, fragments flying into his face as I screamed our past at him like he wasn't a part of it.

Like he didn't leave me, regardless.

It was ten years ago and I confronted him like it was yesterday. I rub my forehead, then massage my temples to prevent a headache. How *mortifying*. Now Stone'll believe I've never moved on and clung to our high school relationship like Rose from *Titanic*. Moving forward, but not.

"He is *not* my Leonardo," I say firmly to the mirror, then spin away and get dressed.

"Noa?"

Mrs. Stalinski's tenuous voice comes through the monitor at my bedside. I finish pulling on my shirt and answer by pressing the *TALK* button. "Be right there."

I throw my wet hair into a high, messy bun as I head down the short hallway and into her room, knocking on the door.

"Morning," I say softly, approaching her bed.

"Hi, dear. Mind opening the curtains?"

"Sure."

I study the color on her cheeks before I round to the window and pull the curtains open. She looks better, more pink than white to her skin, and she's greeted me with a smile.

"Can I get you some coffee?" I ask, returning to her side.

"I'd love some. Make yourself a cup, too, and sit with me. I'd like to talk to you about last night."

Mrs. Stalinski must notice something in my answering expression, as much as I try to stifle the unease. She adds, "Nothing bad, child, but I'd like to explain my reasons for substituting my son in our restaurant plans without consulting you."

"You don't have to explain."

"Noa." Mrs. Stalinski lowers her chin. "I'm cancerous, not senile. You'd be a saint not to despise me just a little for my surprise switcheroo."

"You had your reasons."

Mrs. Stalinski levels me with a look.

"Okay, fine. I dislike you a *little* for not discussing it with me first."

"As I figured. Now, go make that coffee and we'll talk more."

She rests her arms on top of her covers, waiting expectantly.

I do as she asks, but I'm not looking forward to dissecting the subject of Stone any more than my over-anxious brain already has. I also don't enjoy begrudging Mrs. Stalinski anything, so I stir creamer in both cups and resign myself to more Stone talk.

Jeez, even when he's not here, he takes over my life.

I make myself comfortable in a sofa chair near Mrs. Stalinski's bed, glad that she lifts her coffee to her lips first. It means I get a shot at nullifying the conversation before we dig any deeper.

"I'm sure you hope he and I will make amends. You also want to keep Stone out of trouble, and placing in ranch duties and cooking classes will ideally force him to stay busy while he's here."

Mrs. Stalinski's cheeks lift over the rim. "You always were a smart girl. I'd like to add to your foregone conclusions about my motives, if I may."

I lean back, sipping my coffee, certain I covered everything that needed covering.

"I won't insult your intelligence by denying that my boy has always tried to behave himself around you despite his innate nature to make trouble. And I'm hoping you'll continue to rub off on him, as he's about to face the most difficult hurdle in his life. Losing his mother."

I lower my mug to my lap.

"Thank you for not denying that," she says, cupping her drink. "We both know Stone likes to react when matters don't go his way and I'm afraid as I decline, he'll be moved to make a mess of his life and do something worse than he already has." Mrs. Stalinski moves her head in a sad arc. "My boy's imploding in so many ways, and while I'm positive returning home will help him heal, I need you to control the rest. It's a lot to ask of you, I know," she says as I open my mouth, "but he has no one else."

I chew on my lip. "I'm not sure I can be that kind of light for him."

"I wouldn't ask if I wasn't certain you are the right person for the role. What went on between you two, I will never try to disrespect. But it's been ten years, and if it's possible, I would be forever grateful. And eventually, so will he."

"I don't need his thanks," I automatically say, then shut my mouth.

Mrs. Stalinski responds with an empathetic curve to her lips. "I will defer to your initial point that forcing you two into proximity might fix all those holes in both your hearts. But to be safe, I'll refrain from making that my dying wish."

Mrs. Stalinski chuckles and I go along with her dark humor, since that's the only choice we have sometimes.

"And I really cannot do those classes with you, even though a month ago I was ready, energetic, and willing."

"I believe you." Rising, I take the mug from her hands and tuck the sheets around her. "And we would've been hard to beat."

"You have that right." She accepts the palm-full of pills I give her. "I'd argue my son shares my DNA, but sadly, the cooking gene swooped right over him and went into the family dog instead, rest his soul."

I laugh. "Stone proved himself last night."

"To both of our surprise. Maybe California isn't so bad for him after all, or more likely, he learned one dish to impress the ladies, and that was it."

"Well, he can chop onions. I suppose I can always delegate veggie duty to him."

"Does that mean you'll do it?" Mrs. Stalinski's question rises with hope.

I offer a confused smile. "I thought we resolved that last night when he won the bet to cook dinner."

"True, but I would never force you to agree to terms that make you uncomfortable, ridiculous wager or not. You realize you always had a choice to say no, right, dear?"

"Of course. Yes." I try for a dismissive laugh, like I hadn't just lectured my reflection on how to cope with my new sous chef for the next two months. "It means a lot to you, so I'll do it. Try, I mean. I'll give it a try. If Stone's game, then I am, too."

If anything, it'll give me a chance to redeem myself after my outburst and show Stone how cool and collected I can be—*will* be—around him. He doesn't affect me anymore, and if I have to cook with him to prove it, then I will.

After ensuring Mrs. Stalinski is comfortable, I take my leave and get ready for my other patient stops today.

If moving into the same house as Stone, taking care of his mother, and attending weekly classes with him as my partner weighs heavy on my heart and confusing in my mind, I don't allow the weight to settle onto my shoulders as I push through the door and into a bright and cheery fall day.

Twelve

STONE

I haven't stacked hay since I was a sixteen-year-old quarterback. I'm ashamed to admit that these days, it's triggering my sciatica.

The nerve screams like a banshee but I paste a smile on my face as I grab another bale from the truck and "toss" i.e. roll it, to the waiting teenager who should then load it onto the waiting truck.

The bale comes to a stop near the backs of his legs.

"Hey," I say to get his attention. "I got another one here for you."

He doesn't hear me over the blaring music coming from his earphones. Contrary to popular belief, I do *not* cause everybody to fall to their feet and gush over my celebrity status. This one, Devon, gave me one cursory look underneath his cowboy hat when I introduced myself before the crack of dawn and hasn't said a word to me as we drove into the field to the *very* tall stacks of hay, climbed out of the vehicle, grabbed a bale, and swung it at my chest.

Death by hay squash. That is what this knee-jerk of a sperm sample almost did to me.

"Dude!" I try again. "Another's incoming and we're running out of room."

Devon turns enough for me to see his lips moving, but I'm confident he's mouthing the lyrics to a song and not responding to me.

"Have it your way," I mutter, then round to swing another bale in his direction.

Devon moves just enough for me to clock him in the chest with one and he goes down.

"Shit!" I lean in to move it off him as his muffled screams come from under. "I told you I was incoming!"

Thundering hooves draw my head up as I'm mid-lean, angling the hay bale enough for Devon to roll out from under.

"Heard I had a new hire," a lazy, graveled voice says from atop a gray gelding. "As I suspected, he's a pretty boy who tries to kill all the other pretty boys in his vicinity so he can stay king of the pretty boy castle."

"Rome," I greet while wiping sweat off my brow. Except I think I smear more dirt on it. "Good to see you."

"Wish I could say the same." Rome swings his leg over his horse then drops down beside it with a cocky grin and pulls me into a one-armed hug. "How long's it been?"

"Not long enough." I stagger away from the truck, the stacked hay bales, the stumbling kid who's found enough of his voice to curse at me while pulling twigs from his mouth. "I forgot how shit this job is."

"Good thing I ain't paying you then." Rome's gray eyes

shine bright under his cowboy hat. "Remind me to send your mama a stack of pies as thanks for the free labor."

"Don't be surprised if you find a pile of these hay bales in your bedroom tonight," I retort.

"That would mean you'd have to carry them there and we both know that ain't happening." Rome looks me up and down. "I thought you were meant to be a big flood man now."

"Shut up," I say. Spotting a kerchief looped through his belt, I swipe at it and use it to wipe my face. "And don't you use your fucking cowboy stance on me."

Rome Miles, my nemesis and best friend from high school, stands with his feet apart and hands on his hips like he's still on his goddamned horse. He's dressed in a Canadian tuxedo and rounds out his fashion choice with beat-up cowboy boots I would consider murdering Devon over, now that my ruined Jordans cover blistered feet.

"How long you been out here?" Rome asks.

"Dunno. Before the sun came out and after everyone sane went to bed."

"Devon welcome you properly?"

I glance at the boy, who's recovered enough to step into the driver's side of the truck and slam the door. "Sure. Real friendly."

"He's efficient. You can ride with him to the Merc, drop off the bales, then come back and uncap a beer with me." He studies me again, his expression unreadable but his eyes saying enough: *look at how much you've changed and how different we now are.*

I pull at my dark-green tee, realize the uselessness, then just peel it off and use it as a sweat collector, too.

Rome whistles. "I see what has all the ladies hollering!" He tosses a pitchfork at me, which I manage to catch before I'm stabbed. "Prove those muscles are more than just for looks and tidy up the stray blades. Devon'll wait till you're done."

"You are too kind." I blow out a breath, tie my shirt through the belt loop of my jeans, and get to collecting. I can't bring myself to banter with my old friend or complain about my current farmhand circumstances. All I can think about is Ma, then Noa, then more Ma, then a ton of Noa.

Obviously, I've drawn more of a silver lining around our past than she has. I remember her as shy and obedient until I got my hands on her. I convinced her to break into the fair-grounds after hours, climbing up the darkened Ferris wheel as high as we could go without falling to our deaths. It's where we shared our first kiss. Her tongue tasted like the cotton candy I stole for her after leaping over the snack counter and picking the storage door's lock. It's also where we found a stranded, half-starved kitten that I jokingly said looked like a rabid mouse and a mad cow had a baby and Noa insisted we take him with us and name him Moo. I introduced her to pot. I dragged her onto the rocky lake shore and dared her to swim with me under the moon. Naked. I watched her bloom from a quiet, unnoticed sixteen-year-old into a confident, clever woman who would then challenge me to a swim race, naked.

Then I broke her.

The years helped heal me, or so I thought. Keeping busy was crucial. Becoming famous is an insanely useful tool. I didn't have time to think of the girl I left behind or the pain I left her in.

It's safe to assume she had all the time in the world to hate me. To wish me dead for the callous way I brushed her off when she told me she was pregnant, or for my utter silence when I learned she'd miscarried while shooting for my first role in a Netflix series that ended up a huge success and changed my career.

I shove that feeling aside with the strength of slamming a pitchfork into the dirt, leaning on it, and cursing.

"You almost done, man?" Devon asks.

His head pokes out from the orange pickup truck, hair flopping over his forehead and eyes as he watches my cleanup with the amusement of a teen boy who'd rather be looking at his phone.

I wipe my hair off my sweaty brow, suggesting, "You could always assist."

"Nah." His head pops into the interior, and I hear an added, "You're good."

"Little fucker," I say, but get back to work.

"Put your back into it." Rome comes up behind me, and I jolt.

"Shit. I thought you'd left."

"The stealth I used to steal us beers from my pop's cooler never left." He tosses another pitchfork he pulled from somewhere between his hands.

"Funny. I was just thinking about our youth." I toss more loose hay into a pile that a handy machine will collect later. I could use this moment to ask why we aren't using machines to pile hay bales onto the truck, but I assume Rome has me doing manual labor as passive-aggressive punishment for not coming around more often.

It's a legit grudge, so I keep my mouth shut and let him watch me suffer.

Better than facing the agony etching across Noa's face when she confirmed she'll never forgive me.

"We had some good times," Rome says as he arcs a tangle of dried grass onto the growing mound. He glances over his shoulder. "Not like these soft jellyfish men who think online comments hold more power than good, honest work."

I bark out a laugh. "You sound like your pops."

"Shit," he drawls, then sticks his pitchfork in the dirt. "I do, don't I?"

"He harped on us all the damn time for being boneless fuckheads who'd rather chase girls than muck horse stalls."

"And look where it got me." Rome spreads his arms. "A farmland all to myself and my best buddy mucking stalls for me."

"You better be joking."

Rome chuckles. "Today, I am. Go on with Devon. You should learn the ropes at unloading at the Merc since I heard you'll be here for a while." The laugh lines around his eyes and mouth, deepened by his constant presence under the sun despite his relatively young twenty-seven years on this earth, soften. "I'm real sorry about your ma."

"Yeah." My chest deflates. "So am I."

"I had no idea. Otherwise, I would've found some way to let you know."

I nod, believing him.

"Though you're a hard man to contact these days with all those suits surrounding you."

"Those suits are a lot, I know, but they allow me to keep my private moments private."

Rome's easygoing stare narrows. "From what I've read, you're making your team work overtime. What happened over there? Did it become too much for you? Are you as neck-deep in drugs as they say?"

Deflecting, I say, "I didn't know you kept up with the gossip rags."

"Nice try. I may be a lowly farmhand, but I can read you as easily as I could a decade ago. What'd you do?"

"Got a bit too public with my irritation." I shrug it off, handing him the pitchfork. He takes it willingly enough but keeps his stare pointed.

"I admit, I worried about you when you got into the bad stuff. The coke and shit."

"Coke is like water over there. Don't worry about it."

"Oh yeah? Because here it's a real problem." Rome slides his gaze to Devon and back, then steps closer. "I took Devon under my wing after he got too into that stuff. His momma—Serena Lanson, remember her? That's his mother. She couldn't find him one night after one of these kids' stupid ragers at an abandoned barn in the outskirts of town. Dogs from a search party found him sleeping by the creek with a nice purple egg on the side of his head from falling and hitting it on a rock. I offered to take him in, teach him the ways of old, and get him away from temptation. Kinda like what I have to do with you now."

"Hey. I'm not a dumb kid. I can handle myself just fine."

"It's not my responsibility to keep you on the up-and-up." Rome's gray eyes harden into metal. "I'm doing your lovely ma a favor, a lot like I'm doing for his. You'll forgive me if I add that if you fuck around enough to bring Devon back into temptation, I will be forced to fuck you up."

"You're serious?" I guffaw, then set my jaw when Rome doesn't laugh back. "You really think I'll give coke, if I even *want* to find any in this hick town, to a kid? Who do you think I've become, Rome? What the fuck? I'm here for Ma, and I'm not leaving her until she all but tells me to get lost, and even then, I'll be damned if I leave. I'm not some addict trolling the streets for crack, and I'm sure as hell not some heartless asshole willing to hand lines over to a country teen. Or *any* teen, might I add."

"Oh yeah? Prove it."

I am truly thrown by the way my old friend stares at me. Like I'm horse shit he stepped on with his boots. I say slowly, "What I choose to do and how I do it is none of your goddamned business. I shouldn't have to explain my past actions. You of all people should understand."

"Not anymore." Rome backs away. "I've grown up. And I wish to hell you did, too."

"Don't talk to me like you're my father," I snap. "All high and mighty with your farm and good morals and *boring fucking life.* I've made mine exciting, and I sure as fuck can't wait to get back to it." I wish I still had the pitchfork so I could toss it at him instead of handing it over like we had some kind of friendship after all these years.

I stomp to the passenger side of the truck, throwing the door open.

"I really am sorry about your ma," I hear him say as I slide in.

"Me, too." The door latches with a hard click, and I jerk my chin at Devon. "Drive."

"Uh..."

"Your boss isn't mad at you, he's pissed at me. You'll be fine."

Devon's pacified enough to turn the engine. He's stopped from pressing the gas when Rome steps up and folds his arms on the open passenger window.

"Damned old trucks with manual window rollers," I mutter.

"Despite your shit, I'm glad you're back," Rome says.

I palm his face and push him out of the window. His rough laughter almost overpowers the rusty cough of the engine.

Jesus, and *I'm* the one who's fucked up.

Still, the tightness in my chest eases as the last thing I see through the blinder is my old friend's quick and easy smile.

After a few minutes of driving down the gravel road, I say to Devon, "So. You were into coke?"

Devon's chin juts out, but keeping his eyes on the road, he gives a single tight nod.

"Why?" he finally asks. "You got some on you?"

I smack him upside the head. Devon turns to me in what I will now always refer to as gobsmacked horror.

"That's right," I snap. "The Blue Flood just hit you. Eyes on the road."

Devon blinks rapidly, but does as I say.

I add, "And don't be a fucking idiot. Because I'll hear about it, and if you think you're afraid of Rome, wait until I tell all the girls in school that you're chalk full of gonorrhea."

Devon's jaw hardens and he stares through the car's window like he wants to shatter it.

I smile to myself while leaning back in the seat. "And they say I don't set a good example for kids."

Thirteen

NOA

THE NEXT TIME I RUN INTO STONE, I DIDN'T EXPECT
him to be sweaty, shirtless, and intent on a rampage.

The interior of the Merc is in its familiar frenzied state
when I arrive for lunch. I choose to forego a pre-made sandwich and do a light shop for groceries instead. I have enough
time off to get back to Mrs. Stalinski and make us a warm meal
and give Moo the rare treat of my presence. He'll be thrilled.

The Mercantile is a one-stop-shop for almost anything one
might need while searching for items in Falcon Haven's down-
town district. It has all the necessary groceries, a sandwich and
ice cream shop, and a gourmet cafe. If one also feels like a quick
beautifying, Maisy also rents out the attached space to Jenny
Ridge, a certified esthetician. Maisy also allows local items to be
featured in her store, like handmade jewelry and artwork.

I'm distracted from my groceries and holding up a beautiful silver, hand-hewn upside-down crescent moon necklace
made by a local metal worker when the shouting begins.

"Dude, all she asked for was a selfie, and I gave it to her."

I inch closer when I register Stone's voice.

I round the grocery aisles and into the small gap between the back of the store and the loading and storage area.

Stone stands amid overstock boxes and a tower of hay, small pieces sticking to his heaving bare chest. One's even sticking out of his wind-tousled hair. It doesn't make him look goofy, or boyish, or any of the things a stalk of hay sticking out from a man's head should.

He makes it look rough-hewn, like the grass belongs on him because he's been working the fields all day and gained all that muscle through stubborn hard work. The stubble along his jaw and the chestnut hair curling around his ears and forehead add to his homegrown, working-man air, as well as his low-slung jeans and his favorite brown leather belt, beaten up and used since he was a slimmer, ganglier version of himself.

If you didn't know him, if he wasn't famous and recognized by the world twice over, no one would guess he'd gained those muscles in a California gym with a professional trainer and a celebrity nutritionist. None would think those jeans were designer or that belt something he grabbed out of his teenaged drawer, his personal preference for it long forgotten.

Another man stalks into my eyesight, bringing me back to the present. I hold my grocery basket against my middle with both arms, my eyes wide.

"You touch my girl, you get a punch to the fucking face, I don't care how famous you are, you pansy-assed bitch."

Wow. Even I, ever the pacifist and against all forms of aggression, can call those fighting words.

Movement and shuffling sound out on either side of me, the exchange between the two men drawing a crowd.

Stone throws up his hand, his manicured nails dirt

encrusted and the palm blistered and bleeding. Rome must not have given him gloves. Deliberately.

"Talk to your girl. I was doing my job, man," Stone says.

"With your fucking shirt off in a grocery store?" the other man asks.

"Baby." The woman of the hour creeps out of the aisle she was hiding in (with her phone held up and in video mode). Long, raven hair falls in waves to her elbows, her white tee tight and braless and in cutoffs. "I had to. It's Stone freaking Williams! Do you know what this will do to my follower count?"

The big man spears a finger at his girlfriend. "Don't you fucking post that. He's not wearing a shirt, and your nipples are showing. You post something like that, I'll be the laughing-stock of my club, and I ain't no punchline. Defy me, and I'll make sure you regret it."

I parse through his toxic masculinity enough to latch onto the word *club*.

Shit. He's part of the White Tigers, a motorcycle gang living on the outskirts of Falcon Haven. They come into town occasionally to grab food, cigarettes, and meet up with those willing to assist them in their underground trafficking. In a small town like this, it's more people than you'd think.

They're enough of a presence that those not in their pockets know not to fuck with them. Stone knows it, too, though by the current look in his eye, he's decided to ignore their violent warnings.

"You usually talk to your girl like that?" Stone asks casually. I sense a threatening undercurrent, both in his stiffened lips and curled fingers.

More phones go up. I step forward. "Stone."

Stone's attention snaps to mine as if I'd whistled loud and

hard. He catches my eyes with ease, locking in place and registering my presence, softening slightly in apology before hardening again.

"Stone," I say again with harder whiplash. "Don't. It's not worth it. Let's go."

"Isn't it?" Stone cocks his head, answering me but looking at the gang member. "He disrespected me, he disrespected his girl, and now he wants to throw a punch at me in front of you. All of which are shitty actions deserving of consequences."

"What are you gonna do, Hollywood?" The man laughs. "Those muscles of yours are all for show. You have makeup people who do better work than you ever will. I bury people while you're in your trailer running lines on how to be a pretend superhero. The most you do is jack off while real men do the work for you."

"Mostly true." Stone nods sagely. "That playing the good guy shit? It's all fake."

Stone swings before anybody predicts, causing gasps and cries at the same time a skin-to-skin *smack* rings out.

"And I'm so goddamned tired of assuming the role," he grunts when the man collects himself and swings back, clipping Stone's chin.

"Stone!" I yell.

Stone bends low and runs at the man's middle, toppling them both to the ground. The girlfriend screams, then centers her phone. The people who gathered scatter like a flock of geese. Lunchtime on a school day at the Merc is mostly filled with retirees or farmers finishing their day's work before the sun gets too hot. There aren't too many willing to stay and film the action, which I'm thankful for, since Stone just rolled them into a pyramid of glass spaghetti jars on sale.

Glass shatters, and sauce flies everywhere, including my

face. The sudden, dramatic fracturing of one hundred pasta jars brings Maisy running full on into the fray with a broomstick and a battle cry.

"Goddamned hooligans!" She smacks the gang member on the head, but he just shakes it off and continues boxing-style punches into Stone's chest. Stone has the wherewithal to block him, but with glass shards flying, he's bound to bleed.

"Noa!" Maisy shouts. "Help me!"

The grocery basket I was holding drops to my feet. I fly into the fray, too worried about Maisy breaking them up on her own to think straight and maybe call the police first before I kick at a motorcycle club member.

On my way, I pick up a pasta jar that somehow survived and swing it at the side of the motorcycle guy's head as he rolls on top of Stone to land more punches.

"You *bitch!*" I hear before someone yanks me back by the hair, and I'm slammed into the mess of pasta and glass, sliding a few feet on my back like an overturned beetle. "*Nobody* touches my man but me!"

The girlfriend shrieks and lands on top of me, using her acrylic nails to her advantage and scraping them along my cheek.

Crying out, I swipe back and buck like a wild stallion to get her off me. I've taken enough self-defense classes to use my legs to wrap around her and drag her down, then crawl on top of her and hold her by the wrists, yelling into her face, "I'm not your enemy!"

She won't hear any of it. This girl has turned feral, snarling at me and promising threats against me and all those I love.

There's no reasoning with her, so I let her stumble into a stand, heading toward Stone. She, of course, tries to drag me back into it, but I catch enough to see their fight is more brutal than ours, grunts, curses, and bone-breaking *thwacks* ringing out. Maisy is still there, adding cleaning spray to her arsenal and aiming for their eyes.

Until a shot rings out.

The shock is so stunning, no one screams. Everyone freezes. I lose all hearing, and the girlfriend goes slack with surprise.

Then my heart drops.

"Oh my God," I whisper, sounds of the Merc tunneling back into my ears. "*Stone?*"

I fumble through the mess, my sneakers squeaking, then slip and land on my stomach, my chin ricocheting off the linoleum with a fiery sting in its wake. I rolll onto my back, moaning.

Stone lies still on the floor as the club member stands, brushing at the wet stains on his pants like the nuisance they are.

"That should fucking teach you," he mumbles, then limps to his girlfriend. "Come on, Veronica. Look what the hell you've done. Let's get out of here before the cops arrive."

Then with the help of Veronica, he pockets his gun and they both disappear.

"Noa. *Noa!* Are you hurt? Jesus, say something!"

Stone flies into my vision, the worried lines of his handsome face rippling overhead like an avenging angel I've summoned from thin air. His firm hands pat me down, decorum forgotten as he does a full-body search, pressing against my breasts and inner thighs searching for a bullet wound.

This isn't the time for that kind of molten fire, yet it comes scorching between my legs and sparking into my nipples as soon as his frantic touch leaves my skin.

His frenzied search returns to my face, his hot, wet palms cupping my face. "You're bleeding."

The switch from hot to soft is so unexpected that I relax in his hold, keeping eye contact and giving his wrists a reassuring squeeze. "I'm okay. I'm not shot."

Adrenaline that had been leaking from my body halts with a clog of fear. "What about you? Did you get hit?"

I do a quick scan of his body, unable to tell blood from spaghetti sauce. Red covers his chest, his lip bleeding, and one eye's starting to swell.

"I'm not hit," he says.

I sag with relief as he digs his fingers into my hair, tipping my head up.

Stone's eyes grow hooded, but it doesn't contain the spreading wildfire. His fingers stroke the side of my face and the sharp pain that follows tells me he's found a cut. "They hurt you."

Stone says it so flatly and with such certainty that I stiffen even as he helps pull me into a sit.

"Stone, don't go anywhere near him again." When Stone doesn't acknowledge me and stares down the aisle where the motorcycle couple took their exit, I repeat, "That man just fired a gun in a crowded store to win a fistfight with you. He's reckless and dangerous. Stay away from him, okay? *William?*"

My use of his birth name causes him to blink and come back to me, the depths of his eyes, like black oil on blue fire, ebbing into smoldering embers.

"There you are." I breathe out in relief.

Stone smiles at me, confused. "What are you talking about? I didn't go anywhere."

Yes you did. You transformed into a cold-hearted assassin right in front of me.

119

Sometimes I forget that when he's acting, Stone doesn't always have to reach too far inside himself to find the personality he's looking for. It's all there, a tempest of emotions he keeps at bay until he's called upon to use them for someone else's entertainment.

Without voicing my fear, I take his hand and come to a stand. His eyes won't leave my face.

"You sure you're all right? You didn't hit your head or anything, did you?"

"No. Just slipped." I take a moment to scan the detritus around us and I'm about to voice my dismay when Maisy comes storming around the corner.

"Police and ambulance are on their way. Anybody hurt? Everybody okay?" she asks.

Her voice draws the ones that hid behind display items and fled into the storage room back into the light. The ones I spot seem stunned but fine.

"Good." Maisy puts her hands on her ample hips before her stare beelines to us. "And you two. What in the *hell* was that?"

"That man was part of the White Tigers," I say before Stone can open his mouth. "He was looking for trouble."

Maisy squints at my explanation, weighing the truth of my statement. My reputation precedes me, because she says, "Fair enough, though they try to keep their antics out of my business most days. Seeing him must've set them off." She jerks her head at Stone. "You should know better than to engage with them."

Stone gives her an *aw shucks* smile. "Lost my head for a moment, ma'am."

"Literally," she retorts, having none of his charm. The sound of sirens redirects her attention. "I'll let them in.

Nobody goes anywhere until you give your statements. Those fuckers damaged my property and nearly killed someone."

It's not like Maisy to swear. She worked her tail off to buy this building from the previous owner and be granted a business loan. She converted it from an old bread factory to what it is today, and nothing like this has ever happened on her watch. I bet she feels as violated as I do after being attacked by a woman who started this whole thing, then walked away scott-free.

The sheriff approaches us, his mouth grim under his hat.

"Sheriff Miles," I greet, just barely resisting the urge to lower my head and shuffle my feet like a chastened kid.

His square face and broad frame screamed authority back when he was a rookie police officer dropping off his kid at elementary school. As sheriff of Falcon Haven, he essentially holds the keys to the town and often meets any malfeasance under his supervision with the highest punishment.

"Mr. Stalinski," his tobacco-laced voice grinds as he considers Stone. "Been a while since I had you under my thumb."

"Sheriff." Stone tips his head. "I apologize for all of this."

"Don't be sayin' sorry to me, son. You owe Maisy that and then some. From what I've gathered so far, this all began with a selfie request."

Stone rubs his chin. "I try to be gracious to all my fans."

"Uh-huh." Sheriff Miles's flat gaze shows just how much he appreciates Stone's humor. "I liked you better on the other side of the country. How long are you here for?"

"Originally? A couple of weeks. Since finding out about my mom, as long as it takes."

The corners of the sheriff's lips soften ever so slightly. "Yes. Rome told me what's been going on. With that in mind, I'll let you off with a warning and your promise of a sworn statement over what occurred here today. I'll do everything in my power to track down the man responsible, but we all know how OMGs work."

Outlaw motorcycle gangs. The White Tigers had a nice agreement with the former sheriff, but, once Sheriff Miles took over, that contract was severed. As a result, the gang has become more trouble within town and less agreeable to cleaning up their messes.

"We'll stay behind and help clean up," I say, picking up Maisy's discarded broom. "We won't leave until it's done. Right, Stone?"

"Yeah." Stone picks up the spray bottle of cleaning solution. "Least I can do."

"Uh-huh," Sheriff Miles repeats. "You'll have to do a bit more convincing than that. Mr. Branson over there told me you threw the first punch. Don't think I'm so small town I'm not aware of what kind of mess you've gotten yourself into in Hollywood. I won't be having the same shenanigans in my town, do you understand? If you have beef with the White Tigers, piss them off on their turf and stay out of ours."

"Yes, sir," Stone says under his breath. His muscles tense with contained frustration, but he says nothing more, instead unleashing his irritation on cleaning up the broken jars and overturned display cases.

Sheriff talks to both of us separately along with the other witnesses, but I don't hold out a lot of hope that anyone will meet swift punishment. My worry centers on Stone as I watch his jerky movements and locked jaw throughout the cleanup process. Soon, Maisy joins in as well as other regulars and within a few hours, we have the Merc back to how it should be.

Maisy dismisses us with a wave of her hand, her expression more annoyed than forgiving as she watches Stone leave the store.

It's not lost on me that Stone has taken shit from almost everybody he knows since coming home. I'm half convinced he'll declare a *fuck this* moment and hightail it back to Hollywood, but he takes each insult with a clip to the chin and forges on.

If I wasn't battling my own bitterness against him, I'd almost respect it.

I'm torn from my thoughts when he comes to a halt in the middle of the sidewalk. "Shit."

"What's wrong?" I ask.

"I came here with Devon. I sure as hell don't know where he fucked off to when all this went down, and it looks like he escaped with the truck."

I dig my keys out of my purse. "I'll give you a ride."

Stone regards me suspiciously. "You sure?"

"Don't make me regret it," I snap, but one look at his red-stained chest and I'm back to when I thought he was covered in his own blood. I say in a gentler tone, "We're going the same way now, remember?"

"Yeah." His gaze softens for a moment, too, as if he's recalling the same terrifying seconds after the gun went off. "But you have clients—or patients—to still see, right?"

I shake my head. "I called my supervisor and explained the situation. I've got another nurse covering my afternoon appointments for me."

"Shit. Right." Stone's eyes widen. "I gotta call my agent and tell him what went down. No doubt something's going to hit social media if it hasn't already."

The chasm between us is wide, but his statement makes it so much deeper. I have a boss to contend with. He has fame.

"I'm supposed to be here on the down-low," he explains as we walk to my car. "Aaron won't be happy I'm involved in a minor felony."

I snort. "Forget what your agent wants to do," I say as I press my key fob and the car beeps. "Mrs. Stalinski's going to kill us."

Fourteen

NOA

NOT MANY PEOPLE CAN MAKE ME FEEL LIKE A teenager who just disappointed her parents for the final time, but Mrs. Stalinski can.

Standing in her foyer as she lectures us on public decency and getting red sauce on her carpets, I'm transported to the times the adults in our lives caught Stone and me. It wasn't often—Stone is as wily as I am afraid of authority—but when we *were* nabbed by someone paying attention, it was serious, and we became the discussion of many weekly cribbage games.

This is one of those times.

"Thank God you two weren't injured," she says as she faces us down. Mrs. Stalinski is a head shorter than me, her spine bowed with fatigue and illness, but today is a good day, since she has the energy to stand before us and lecture us as efficiently as she did when we were kids. She turns to Stone. "But you should know better than to approach those boys. They're more trouble than they're worth."

"I'm sorry, Ma," Stone says, head down.

He means it, but by being around him so often, I've noticed just how much he's apologized to everyone who demands or even deserves it. The words probably have no meaning to him anymore. I'm not sure how I feel about the battering he's receiving from the town. My heart is in constant argument with my brain over what should be more important —Stone's pain or his repentance.

Mrs. Stalinski puts a hand to her forehead. "I raised you better than this."

"You're tired." I come between them, ending the war in my body by going with my heart this time. "I'll help you to your room."

"No." Stone's large form steps in front of mine. "I'll take her. C'mere, Ma."

She folds into his arms and they take the stairs together. I remain a respectful distance behind, separating from them when I reach the top of the stairs and heading to the guest bedroom to shower and change.

The stale smell of garlic and tomatoes has dulled my senses and I'm tempted never to make another pasta dish again. I eagerly twist the shower faucet and strip out of my ruined scrubs, noting the stains leaked through onto my white bra and underwear. Moo appears through the open bathroom door, sniffs at the discarded clothing, kneads it with a loud purr, then does one circle and curls up on it.

"Not you, too," I moan. "If you don't get off that pile of store-bought sauce I'll take you in the shower with me to wash the smell off."

Moo blinks his green eyes at me.

"I swear I will," I threaten.

Moo licks his chops and stares blandly.

Aware that I'm lecturing my cat while naked, I give up and step into the shower. The cleanse feels good, the water hot and my familiar soap sudsy and comforting. I take longer than necessary before finishing and wrapping a towel around myself.

I'd left the door ajar for Moo to go in and out of and I'm not surprised to find him gone when I pull back the shower curtain.

My relaxing spa moment ends when I push the bathroom door the rest of the way open and find Stone sitting at the foot of the bed petting Moo who is curled up on his lap.

I greet him with a choked scream and clutch my towel.

Stone raises his head, his hair damp. He's dressed in a new pair of jeans and T-shirt.

I expect a sarcastic comment about my grasp for chastity when he's seen all there is to see of me and it's nothing new to him. I brace myself for it.

Stone's gaze runs down my body, snagging on my most sensitive parts, his ice-blue eyes melting at the sight before re-hardening when he comes back to my face. He says nothing.

"Can I help you?" I prompt. "We used to be familiar with each other, but not anymore. If you don't want to knock first, at least respect my privacy and let me get dressed."

"I knew what I was doing when I agreed to take a picture with her."

I pause, then pad closer to him. "What?"

"In the store today. That woman. It was obvious who she was and who was with her, and I did it anyway."

I ask tentatively, "Why?"

"Because I'm angry." Stone chuckles darkly, pausing his stroking of Moo to cast his gaze to the ceiling. "I woke up at three this morning to get to Rome's ranch by four, because Ma wanted me to. I submitted to a tutorial from a teenaged ex-druggie on how to stack hay bales, then listened to my former best friend explain what a screwup he thinks I've become. This, of course, is after I realized how you truly feel about me and having to face the reality of my mother dying. I exploded. I wanted the fight. I fucking *relished* it."

I clear my throat and pull my towel tighter around me. "So you've come in here because you want me to feel sorry for you."

Stone's eyes lock on mine, growing small with surprise. Moo, sensing the tension, leaps off Stone's lap and finds a spot on the rug.

"Did you expect me to console you?" I boldly continue. "Because what I saw in that store was a complete disregard for everyone, including yourself. You're from here, Stone. This is *your* town, and you're fully aware how dangerous and vindictive the White Tigers are. If you think your fame makes you untouchable—"

"That's not what I'm saying at all." Stone rises from the foot of the bed, his hands clenched at his sides. "I'm trying to explain to you the thoughts behind my actions, because I can't stand the way you've been looking at me all afternoon."

"How have I been looking at you?"

Stone releases a disbelieving scoff at my honest confusion. "Like I'm someone you don't know anymore. Like I'm a stranger."

"You are."

"No. I'm *not*. I'm still me and I'm sick of this entire town assuming fame has poisoned me or that I'm a spoiled rich brat who's forgotten his roots. I'm doing everything I can to be what everybody here wants me to be, and it's still not enough."

"But you did. You left this town behind and completely ignored us."

I'm using plurals, but with the way my voice cracks and the sudden hoarseness coming on, my subconscious wants me to use the singular. To talk about *me*. My hurt. My years of loneliness when he wasn't with me. When I didn't come up in any of his junket interviews, like I had no effect on him.

"I was trying to protect you!" he shouts, then snaps his mouth shut like he didn't mean for his outburst to be so vehement. "I don't talk about this town, or my mother, or you, in the press or anywhere else, because I don't want anyone but me to fucking know about it, okay? No stranger deserves personal knowledge of my past or how I became the man that I am. That's not what they want, anyway. They want the superhero, the nice guy who's hot and sexy and buff, the guy who smiles off his screwups and fucks models and kisses babies and gives autographs on any body part they want. They want the jokester, the hero, the confident swagger. You think they love the small-town boy with a deadbeat father and a single mom who worked double shifts just so she could have the bail money ready for when I inevitably landed in an overnight stay in the sheriff's cell? You think they want to know about the kid who ran with the White Tigers for a minute to see if he liked the idea of that kind of family more than his own? You think they fucking want that?"

Each of Stone's points brings him closer to where I've glued my feet. My hands ache from clenching the top of my towel. My jaw muscles tremble from how my teeth lock together. His argument hits me like the bullet that missed us this afternoon, zinging by my ear with too-close accuracy.

"That is who you *are*, Stone," I say. "I was never ashamed of you. I loved you exactly as that boy. If you can't handle the choices you've made, then you need to look deep inside and ask yourself why." I muster up the courage to say what I do next, not because I mean it, but because he needs to hear it. "But I'm not your girlfriend anymore and I'm certainly not your therapist. Unload your anger on someone else."

Stone stares at me, shell-shocked. "You're serious?"

I stare over his shoulder though my heart beats a million times harder than normal. "Maybe I'm not the person I used to be, either."

"Since when did you become so cold?"

Stone meant to aim his shot and fire, and it works. Pain blooms in my chest.

I meet his eye. "Since the day you left."

Stone blinks rapidly, his shoulders sloping and his hands slackening. He nods. "Fine. Message received."

He exits the room, shutting the bedroom door firmly behind him.

I collapse onto the side of the bed, allowing the towel to fall in a damp tangle around my form. Facing off with Stone took the remaining courage I had after the day we endured. I hate that I share another traumatic moment involving him, another memory to belatedly delete from my Stone archives. The disastrous ripple effect he causes comes back with a vengeance, and I cover my mouth, trying not to sob.

Moo jumps up beside me, brushing against my arm as he rubs up against me.

"Thanks Moo-boo," I murmur, picking him up and burying my face in his side.

He endures it, sensing my distress.

Tears build in my eyes when I smell Stone's cologne in his soft fur.

Fifteen

STONE

I GET THROUGH THE NEXT SEVERAL WEEKS WITH MY head down and mouth shut. Oh, and staying out of trouble.

Not my strong suit, but possible.

My agent kept busy sending cease and desist letters and taking down all mentions of my scuffle at the Merc online, and I pulled extra hours on Rome's ranch to prove to the town, and maybe to myself, that I could go weeks straight without ending up front page news. Fully apprised of the situation with my mother, the production company agreed to delay filming *Flood Surge 2* until after Christmas. *Cascade* is another matter, the director remaining stubborn and threatening to replace me if I don't show up in Madrid in three weeks time.

Work isn't overtaking my thoughts, however. Noa's cool dismissal during a weak moment where I let my heart bleed in front of her affected me more than I let on as I politely greeted her in the mornings and waved good night in the evenings before bunking on the living room couch.

I knew I was a fuck-up—there' no beating around the bush when one's dirty laundry airs over TikTok, but there's an overtly raw feeling in Noa's disapproval of my choices. Almost like I harbor the need to impress her and prove my success has made me a good man, despite all the evidence otherwise. That I'm so much better than the immature kid who flew to Hollywood on a hell-bent dream.

That I'm sorry.

I finish drying the breakfast dishes, staring out through the window above the sink and into the forest beyond. A fawn pokes her head out, sniffing cautiously, then darts back into the protective brush after she senses danger.

"Good plan," I say to her.

"Hi, honey." Ma's voice comes from behind me and I turn.

She strides into the kitchen with a healthy glow to her cheeks. "Hey, Ma. You're looking well."

"It's those pancakes Noa left for us. They've given me the kind of sugar rush that needs an outlet. Come with me?"

I set the last dish on the drying rack and hold out my elbow. "Where may I escort you, madam?"

Ma smiles. "So cheeky and handsome. It's such a lovely fall day. Let's bike around the neighborhood and see what kind of Halloween decorations the neighbors are trying to pass for Thanksgiving so they don't have to take them down."

Concern lifts my brow. "Are you sure you're up for—?"

"If you finish that sentence with *are you feeling up to it*, you will force me to explain to everyone that my son's body is the new scarecrow in my backyard."

"Dark, but point made. Let's go for a bike ride."

In the way mothers do, Ma has forgiven me for the Merc incident, especially now that I've kept my nose clean and plan to keep it that way. The last thing I want is to cause her stress, so I happily guide her through the foyer and out of the house, grabbing our scarves and her puffy down jacket along the way.

The tires of our old bikes in the garage need air and I use the hand pump to get them ready while Ma zips up her coat and ties a kerchief around her thinning hair. Her expression is more alive than I've noticed lately, and I realize, with a pang in my heart, that I'd do anything to keep it that way, including taking her for a ride without the permission of her doc or nurse.

Bikes ready, I swing onto the seat, wincing slightly when my groin rubs up against my tight designer jeans. I make a mental note that my life is more Wrangler than Tom Ford these days.

Ma gets on her baby blue Cruiser like she never left it, gripping the handles and zipping down the drive with her plastic flower basket leading the way. With a happy scoff, I follow her on my old, well-loved, fire engine red Schwinn.

The fall bike tour is a welcome distraction, considering Ma's clinical trial ended the week before and results are due any day. She doesn't want to talk about it and neither do I. We keep to mundane topics while meandering through our street, commenting on the pumpkins, scarecrows, shrunken zombie heads, and (shudder) hay bales.

"The neighbors are going more harvest chic this year," Ma muses while we cruise past the corner house with an impressive gourd display.

I make a noncommital sound in my throat to let her know I'm listening. Noa made breakfast for the house then rushed out to take care of her other patients with an odd pep in her step. Did she have a date tonight? She had to be looking forward to something, what with the reinvigorated brightness to her jaded eyes, a cascade of sunlight I was all too responsible for taking away. She was different this morning than all others preceding it. I'd taken to studying her and predicting her thoughts rather than asking directly. She wanted me to leave her alone, so I did, but that didn't mean I had to stop watching her. Noa is an irresistible force, a reckoning of my soul I hadn't considered I'd have to face when moving back here. I figured she'd be happily married with kids or living in Paris as an in-demand private chef. Last thing I expected was to find her taking care of my mother.

And now she's moved in. We avoid each other in that mature way adults do when they don't want to talk about their problems, but we're still forced to see each other every day. She's a constant, like a cut inside my cheek I keep tonguing to prevent from healing because I'm addicted to the textured ache.

"I, for one, prefer to scare the children and make them work for the turkey feast they'll no doubt inhale in minutes while I worked for hours on it," Ma says.

"Huh?" I look across the road at my mother.

"You heard me," she says primly, her eyes ahead but with a sly slant to them. "Back in the day, we had the scariest house on the block. You remember?"

"I mostly recall turning our home into the Boo Radley house because I lived in it."

"That too. But those kids loved it when you handed out candy to them. It meant they got to meet the rebel of Falcon Haven."

"C'mon, Ma." I gently rib her. The wide-eyed kids I begrudgingly handed candy to are the same adults who poo-poo me when they see me in town today. "Maybe that'd be funny if those kids hadn't grown into the assholes they are now."

"This town isn't full of assholes, dear. You only think that way because you still have the vision of how it was when you were a boy and thought the entire world was against you. This place is healing, if you let it be. Quiet, peaceful, friendly and involved. Close-knit and loyal."

"That's for damned sure," I mutter as we turn into the neighboring street.

Ma rides closer until we're side-by-side. The wind paints red circles on her cheeks and her blue eyes are clear, the colored leaves crackling under our tires. I spent a long morning corralling Rome's cattle before the even the sun woke up. I'm exhausted and should nap, but I can't think of anywhere I'd rather be than accompanying my mother through the quiet streets of her neighborhood.

Maybe Ma's right. This town could heal if I let it. And it's not wrong to hope it heals her.

"I bet we can come up with a nice, traumatizing front lawn display for the kids," she says and I laugh.

"You missed your chance on Halloween." Ma wasn't up to any Halloween celebrations, so Noa and I kept it quiet with the lights dimmed. "But I could call in a few favors, get some props that have been retired."

"Sounds fabulous." Ma beams. "You and Noa put your heads together, come up with something grand."

My brows lower and my speed slows. "Ma."

"Yes, dear?"

"I know what you're doing."

"You know nothing of the sort. She lives with us now. She deserves to be involved in the holidays."

"What about her family?"

"She has no one besides that Carly, and we all know that girl is more flighty than a bird changing seasons."

135

"That can't be true. What about her mother? I remember them being tight. Did they have a falling out or something?"

Noa's father died when she was a baby in a car accident, but I always remembered Lynn Shaw to more than make up for his absence.

Ma reaches over and pats my arm. "That's a story for her to tell if she wants to. For now, I'm glad she's with us and I want to make her as comfortable as possible in our house. She needs to feel like she belongs."

I ask wryly, "Are you saying I'm making her feel less than belonged?"

"You do have a talent for that."

"I'm making up for it." I sigh, leaning forward on the handlebars. "I'm staying out of her way, letting her live her life and giving her the space to take care of you."

"If you think that's doing the right thing," Ma says, "you are so far from reading women, you're in outer space."

I frown. "She told me in no uncertain terms to let her be."

"Yes, and did she also tell you she didn't want you as a partner anymore?"

"A partner in what?"

Ma smacks me. "In the cooking class! Don't tell me you've forgotten. Noa's been bouncing around the house for days looking forward to the first session tonight, as much as she's trying to contain it."

I'd completely put the deal we'd made at the back of my head, what with so much else to unpack.

"Shit. I mean, shoot," I amend at Ma's sideways glare. "It slipped my mind, but before you smack me upside the head, I have no plans for tonight and can still do it."

Ma nods with more confirmation than required. "Exactly as I thought."

We reach the end of the street. Ma's breath comes out shorter and I casually turn us around, heading back to the house as if it were my idea. She'd never admit the need to go home. "What exactly are you thinking, Ma?"

"Noa didn't fire you from the sous chef position. That's a sign if I ever saw one."

I roll my eyes. "I'm hardly a sous chef. More like I'm her only option, and if she wants the small chance at pursing her passion in this town, she has to tolerate my presence."

"She could very well tell you to bugger off, but she didn't." She glances at me sideways before adding, "if you can't read the room, then there is no hope for you, son."

I give a befuddled shake of my head. "If she wants me to go, then I will."

Though, I can't disregard the swell of relief at the answer to why Noa's so excited these days. It's not another guy. It's cooking. I'm shocked she'd want me around, but I'm not about to bring up our sore spot and re-hash the pain that was the night of the Merc incident.

It'd be a nice change from the wake up before sunrise, clean manure, go home and eat breakfast, nap, talk to Ma, repeat. If she wants to put aside our emotions like mature adults, then I'll be her vegetable cutter or oven opener or whatever she needs.

How hard could it be?

"That's all I'll say on the subject," Ma says. "Oh look, a hill."

"Ma—"

She turns left before I can stop her, flying down the same dip of roadway I flew over when I was a kid, both on a bike, on a winter sled, and on the rubber of my soles when fleeing cranky Mr. Jenkins after throwing manure on his lawn.

Ma takes similar flight, releasing her handlebars and holding her arms out wide. I come to the top of the hill and throw one foot on the ground and letting it scrape along with my back wheel until I'm at a standstill.

Ma's kerchief comes off, billowing in the wind that carries her laughter into my ears.

I don't chastise her when she has trouble pedaling back up the hill. When I meet her at the bottom, I give her a high-five.

Sixteen

NOA

FORMER CATTLE WORKER SAM BARNES HAS SOME trouble today and I work overtime to get him comfortable and as pain-free as he can be before giving instructions to his wife and a tight hug. She pats my cheek and wishes me good luck in my class tonight.

Word has gotten round that the new French restaurant, *C'est Trois*, offered professional cooking classes to couples as a friendly introduction into a close-knit town. Because I've grown up with the residents, it's a given to them I'd be attending, but what's become most curious is who I'm taking it with. My last boyfriend was two years ago, and he was from Sutton Falls, the next town over. At the moment, everyone assumes Mrs. Stalinski will accompany me, and when I show up with Stone tonight, I'm basically confirming myself as the talk of the town tomorrow.

It's worth it, I think as I turn the ignition and pull out of the Barnes' driveway. This is an impossible dream come true, a decorated chef deciding to put down roots in a town like ours. A chance like this shouldn't be possible, yet it's staring me right in the face and I'd be an idiot to let pride impede me from learning from someone so accomplished.

I'll deal with Stone by considering him my assistant, or an intern, or any other number of labels besides an ex-boyfriend who cratered my heart. He may be famous to the world, but to me, him crying over the chopping of onions can be the topic of the hour, nothing more.

With a curt nod of confirmation to myself, I pull into Mrs. Stalinski's property and hop out with the car still running. I changed at the Barnes', opting for worked-in jeans and a loose black T-shirt. My hair's twisted up into a bun, held together with a claw-clip.

The screen door creaks as I pull it open, but the wooden door opens silently, telling me Stone's oiled the hinges. I'm noticing small improvements around the home while he's been living here, things Mrs. Stalinski misses but become noticeable when Stone walks away from them. Like the hinges around the house, doors, and windows, and the dripping faucet in the powder room no longer *plinking* throughout the day. Not to mention Moo's litter changed before I get to it. Those little improvements and Stone's presence has brightened Mrs. Stalinski's demeanor in ways nothing else could. While Stone's return to Falcon Haven was under less-than-ideal circumstances, I'm so glad he came when he did.

The very man I'm thinking about tiptoes down the stairs with a finger to his lips, dressed in loose, stained jeans and a charcoal Henley shirt. His hair curls damply above his brow and I get a whiff of his woodsy, clean scent before he reaches the bottom.

"Is she okay?" I whisper, still holding the door open.

He nods. "She's sleeping. I knocked her out with a bike ride."

My eyes widen. "Was it too much for her? Did she get hurt? Her bones..."

"The opposite." Stone grabs his black wool coat off the hook and quickly steps outside like I'm about to lecture him for spending time with his mother.

It gives me pause. Does he think I'm a stick-in-the-mud nurse? That I don't know how to have fun and don't want my patients to find any joy? And why should I care what he thinks?

"I'm glad you two had a good time," I say.

Stone glances at me like I'm being sarcastic.

Jeez. I give up. Heading to the driver's side of my car, I ask, "You ready for this?"

"Yeah, why not." Stone shrugs, then stop shorts in front of my headlights.

I look at him. "What?"

"Why are you getting in your car?"

"...Because I'm going to drive it."

Stone stares at my blue hatchback, aghast. "Like I'll fit in that thing."

"Oh, come on. You had no problems with it ten years ago."

"I was a scrawny trash compactor back then. Now I pump weights and eat the amount of protein an MMA fighter does. If I get in there, my knees will hit me in the face."

My mouth drops in a fake *O*. "Oh no, not your pretty face."

"Hey, this mug makes a lot of money." He points at his cheekbone, a smile crinkling it along the edges. "And if I remember correctly, the last time I could squish in there was when we rolled the passenger seat all the way down and you straddled—"

"Your car it is!" I cut in a little too loudly. Opening the door, I shut off my engine and follow Stone to his space-age technological advancement of a vehicle.

He smirks. "Nice jeans, by the way. Don't think I've seen you outside of scrubs since coming here."

I brush off his compliment—and the warmth in my cheeks —by retorting, "I work a lot."

"I've noticed." His black beast unlocks with a beep and flash of angry-looking headlights and he opens the passenger door for me. "And what I've figured is, everybody loves you and wants you as their nurse, and you don't have the heart to say no."

"Are you saying I work too much?" I ask suspiciously.

Stone's lips purse into an innocent frown. "Just observing that you're young, intelligent, and beautiful, with a long life to lead."

"What am I supposed to do with a statement like that?"

Stone shuts my door, and it latches almost silently. I stare at the buttons on the handle in wonder as he gets in his side and flicks the car on—literally *flicks*—on his phone's screen.

"Good lord, are you about to time travel me?"

Stone's perfect white teeth flash through the stubble he's grown out. "She's almost as gorgeous and lovely as you. Wait till you hear her purr."

"Enough with the compliments. Please."

The strangled tone to my voice shuts down the conversation. Just like I wanted, but I feel hollowed out because of it.

"I was just trying to be nice," he says while pulling up the rear-facing camera and reversing out of the drive.

"I don't want you to be nice. I don't want to like you again."

The truth spills out before I can bite it back, and I press against the cool leather seat as stiff as a piece of torn cardboard.

"Fair enough." He spins the wheel and as he promised, the car turns soundlessly. "You've been looking forward to this night for months. I won't ruin it for you."

I stare at his profile with cautious gratitude. "Thank you."

He gives a single nod. "Contrary to popular belief, I'm trying not to be dick. Especially to you."

My cheeks grow hotter and I squirm in my seat. I thought I wanted a pliable, respectful Stone, but all he's doing is casually swinging a pickax at the bricks I've built around myself since he left. It makes me wonder who is worse—nice guy Stone or selfish, careless Stone Williams. Either can smile their way out of anything.

Thankfully, the drive into Main Street isn't long. The sun hasn't set and a warm, golden glow casts its rays across the red-brick lined tree wells and black, old-style lanterns with banners showcasing a happy turkey hanging from them. The trees lining the strip have changed from lush green to burned orange, translucent yellows and scarlet reds, casting a painting across the two-lane road.

Stone parallel parks with one-armed ease. I refuse to be taken by that surprisingly sexy ability and step out onto the sidewalk before he can round the car and charmingly pull my door open again.

We are not on a date.

With the dumb luck of a famous celebrity, Stone found a spot two cars down from the restaurant and we talk to the front door without speaking.

It's not in Stone's nature to hold in smart-ass quips, and I glance over at him. He's busy studying the restaurant's facade with a pointed squint, as if he's assessing its worth, but I know him better than that.

His shoulders are practically to his ears and he folds his arms like he's the bouncer *C'est Trois* never knew it wanted.

Stone is *nervous.*

It's not often Stone wanders into areas where he's unknown or for purposes other than being told to show up, smile, and charm the pants off everyone in the room. This is a cooking class, a place he has no reason to be at, no desire to learn, and no freaking idea how to act.

For the first time in a long while, Stone is baffled.

I bite back a smile as I open the door and gesture him inside. "It'll be fine. I promise."

"I'm not worried." Stone snorts, then grabs the edge of the door above my head, ushering me in first. "I got this."

"Uh-huh." And then I actually *wink* at him in jest before going inside, my heart feeling light as air.

What is *wrong* with me? I'm supposed to despise this man. A man who atones for the town by doing grunt ranch work, then spends all day with his sick mom, then attends cooking classes he'll all but fall asleep in so I can stay enrolled in the class...

Shaking myself out of it, I use stronger strides to get to the hostess stand, where a gorgeous natural blonde dressed in a tight black cocktail dress waits with a pen and headset.

"Can I help you?" she asks after her gaze arcs from my head down to my toes. Then it moves sideways and snags—nay, *glues* —onto Stone.

"Omigod, you're Stone Williams. *Hi,*" she says. "I'm Amy."

"Hey there, Amy." Stone angles his head and perfects his relaxed, yet gracious energy with a lopsided smile.

I watch him, bewitched and just as enchanted by his ability to what I can honestly call a shapeshift.

"I can't believe it's you!" she squeals, then holds her hands to her heart and collects herself. "I mean, I knew you were here, but I didn't think I'd get the chance to meet you, and here you are, saying hello to me!" She risks peeling her eyes away from him by looking over her shoulder, then leaning forward on the podium and showing off her ample, flawless cleavage. I look down at my A-cups, thinking my neck wrinkles are currently bigger than my girls.

"I could get fired for this but seriously I don't think I'll get another chance ... can I take a selfie with you?"

My head snaps up, automatically searching for a motor-cycle boyfriend nearby.

Stone has no such worries. "Not a problem at all. We'll do a quickie so you don't get caught. I don't want you to lose your job over me." He winks, and it's *so* much sexier coming from him.

I'm shot back into reality when he smoothly adds, "Noa, do you mind?"

The hostess blinks at me. Not hostile, not interested, not concerned that I could be a threat. I paste a smile onto my face. "Sure."

Taking her phone, I wait for the hostess to mold herself to Stone's body, pressing her breasts against his side and palming one of his pecs until I'm sure his hard nipple is directly in the center of her hand. God knows what her hand at the back is doing, but I brush the thought away as I center the camera and click a bunch of times so she can choose which photo best represents her first touching of Stone.

Stone's eyes twinkle on the screen, his laugh lines stark and amused as he focuses not on the lens, but on me. Like he's enjoying me squirm.

Why am I uncomfortable, anyway? And why is he amused by my reaction to a fangirl moment? I shouldn't care. Neither should he. This whole thing has me confused and more than a little regretful that he's my cooking partner. Will I endure this from everyone we come across tonight? And for the next two months?

What if there are more gorgeous youthful girls who want to climb him?

Ugh—*I shouldn't care!*

I pass the phone to the hostess more aggressively than normal, but she barely registers my presence nevermind my movements as she gushes to Stone about his last movie and that she's totally on his side in the Stone vs. Bradley debate on social media.

Stone suddenly grows uncomfortable. "Right, well, I wish Bradley the best, regardless of how we feel about each other."

"Seriously?" The hostess guffaws. "I totally thought after you *broke his head* that you were mortal enemies—"

"Nice meeting you, sweetheart." Stone grabs my elbow and steers me to the back.

I dig in my heels, both confused and disturbed by what the girl said. "Wait—Stone, we don't know where to go."

"Pretty sure a cooking class is gonna happen in the kitchen. Let's go."

"But there might be instructions or a pamphlet we have to grab."

Stone pushes against me firmly, stumbling me back into a walk. "Put your rule-following instinct aside and let spontaneity guide you to the pots and pans for once. I know you have it in you. I drew it out of you any chance I could."

Slightly hurt, I say, "It's not that I need someone to tell me what to do all the time. I just like to know what I'm walking into without looking stupid."

Stone slows his steps, his clasp on my upper arm loosening. "You're right. I'll go back and ask her if she has anything for us."

I glance back at the same time as Stone, both of us noticing the hostess tapping on her phone with the fury of someone explaining to a chat group what just went down.

I lay my hand on his flexed, tense bicep. "Don't worry about it. If we go in unprepared, I have you to use your Stone magic and smooth it over."

Stone smiles at that, but it's a sad one. "Yep, I'm reliable like that."

As we approach the back of the restaurant, I venture, "So ... you used your fists to end an argument?"

The way I phrase it makes Stone's chest shake with laughter. "Don't tell me you didn't know about that. It's the whole reason I'm in Falcon Haven."

I think back fondly to the time I pulled Stone's glossy, still face from the magazine stand and tore it up to dump in the trash—back when my feelings were black and white. "I tend to avoid anything written about you."

Stone sobers. "Right. Well, my agent sent me home for a time-out to think about my actions."

"And have you? Thought about it?"

Stone halts between the tables. "Who are you, my mother?"

His harsh tone brushes over me with the sharpness of a

blade. "I'm not asking if you've learned your lesson, I'm wondering what caused you to hate a man so much you wanted to humiliate him."

Stone stares at me, his lips thin and his eyes shrinking with confusion. Silence passes between us, the type where I've either cemented my status in his head or caused irreparable damage to whatever our relationship could now be called. His eyes leave mine, tracing my face instead, leaving a trail of stardust in their wake. Sparkling, ethereal, invisible. I shouldn't be able to feel the weight of his study so deeply.

"No one's ever phrased it that way," he says quietly.

I'm truly taken aback. "Why not?"

"Because my team wants me to keep paying them. They're afraid of making me moody and unable to work. Aaron, my agent, is the only one who tells it to me straight and even he didn't have the cajones to be that direct."

"Well..." I move back, creating needed space between us. "I'm not trying to start anything. I was genuinely curious."

"I get away with a lot of shit back home—back in LA, I mean. And for the first time, standing here in front of you, I'm thinking it might've been too much, because I honestly don't know how to answer your question, other than to say because I could."

I raise my head, meeting his eye and sharing in the perplexity of this strange, sudden moment of revelation. The type of unraveling that creates an unwanted bond.

Until we're interrupted by a smooth, velvet baritone asking, "Are you the last of them? Class has started."

I break my stare from Stone's, but not before I notice his jaw cutting forward to make room for his massive frown.

Turning in the same direction, I face the man who just

beckoned us forward. The name *Toussaint* is embroidered in black on his chef's coat. His frown mirrors Stone's.

Chef Toussaint is nothing like what I imagined a French chef opening his doors in Falcon Haven instead of a big city would be.

My new teacher is young, tattooed, and gorgeous.

Seventeen

STONE

SHAME IS LIKE AN EXOTIC PET I HAVE NO BUSINESS owning. It rubs up against me all wrong, with a spiked tail and scaled skin. I don't appreciate the way it's staring me in the face, either, but somehow Noa brought it out.

Why did you hate a man so much you wanted to humiliate him?

She asked it with an unblinking stare. Like she saw right through me and pulled out the teen idiot who would do anything short of setting himself on fire to get her attention and impress her. All kinds of excuses bubble up, such as *he started it* and *Bradley Mitchell was a complete dickwad to me the minute we met.* And especially, *that fucker slept with my ex-wife and couldn't wait to tell me about it.*

All but that last one is something a toddler would say to defend their actions. And the most credible excuse, the one most likely to be accepted by Noa and shut down our conversation with an audible *pop* of a celebratory balloon, is a confession I don't want to say out loud to her. Not because I'm ashamed, but because I don't want Ravynn and Noa to ever come across one another, whether it be through words or a physical meeting. Somehow, saying Ravynn's name out loud would give her a power she doesn't deserve to have. Ravynn was a one-minute mistake ending in an annulment. Noa was never a regret of mine, and to confess to her I unleashed on Bradley because he slept with Ravynn would somehow belittle my feelings for Noa.

And that just can't happen. Even though Noa's made it obvious there is no second chance for us, I can't bring up Ravynn. I can't hate Noa so much that I want to humiliate her.

Standing before Noa at this moment, at least two heads taller and definitely two lengths bigger than her toned form, and be stared down by her, is in a word, humbling.

Luckily, I don't have to roll around in the muck too long once we're distracted by a taller, darker, inkier version of ... *me.*

I almost choke on the instant territorial growl that comes forth as soon as I see him seeing Noa.

Chef dude folds his arms over his chest and lowers his chin like he's guarding the kitchen doors and hasn't yet decided if we can enter.

I'm not sure what I expected a cooking teacher to look like. Maybe like that chef in *Ratatouille*, with a tall French hat, curly black mustache, and portly belly. Someone jovial and heavily accented.

The last person I expected was a guy around my age, with wavy, thick black hair, cheekbones that rival mine, *dimples* where mine are, and one fucking additional dent in the middle of his chin. Muscles are obvious even through his apron jacket thing.

Well, he has one thing over me. Tattoos. Black tendrils stick out from the cuffs of his jacket and indecipherable symbols decorate his fingers between the joints.

My vision shrivels, with him at the center.

"I'm sorry we're late," Noa immediately apologizes.

Of course she does.

"You don't exactly leave clear instructions at the front on where to go, not that you advertised very well before that," I pipe in.

Noa frowns up at me and elbows my side. I ignore her.

Chef dude narrows his gaze to where it mirrors mine. "We've kept enrollment exclusive to those couples interested in using advanced techniques in the kitchen, not every Joe and Mary who watches the Cooking Channel and wants to try the latest food trend."

"You've basically named all of Falcon Haven."

He ignores me. "And, using a standard restaurant layout, we assumed those amateur chefs would understand that said lessons would occur in our open kitchen. But I guess you're the exception."

My snarl doesn't reach across the room, but Noa hears it and sends her heel down on my toes. I bite back a howl, fisting my hands instead.

Chef dude cocks his lips, amused.

"Again, so sorry." Noa steps in front of me. "It won't happen again."

"Good, because you only get one mistake. You want to cook at a professional level? Start with being on time. Any chef above you would fire you on the spot."

Noa nods eagerly, like this shithead has any power over her. Or *anyone,* considering where he's decided to set up shop.

"Yes, chef," she says.

Gag me.

The guy gives a curt nod, satisfied with his little show of authority.

"I'm Chef Bernard Toussaint, but friends call me Saint. You're not my friends. Get inside to your prep stations where everyone else has set up and wastes their money while waiting on you."

Noa scurries forward, eager for this shithead's approval. I amble behind her, giving him the once-over in tandem to his.

Don't mind us, just two panthers figuring out where best to leave their piss-mark.

Bully for him, because I'm known for pissing first.

I smirk.

Saint curls his lip at my expression before reaching behind him and revealing two navy blue aprons.

"A welcome gift," he says.

Yeah, I feel real welcome.

Noa accepts it with a genuine smile. It's followed by a sharp pang in my gut. I've worked my tail off trying to get her to use her lips on me like that, and I can barely get a twitch from her. But this guy? With his chef coat and tattoos and title, gets it in less than a minute.

Noa has the apron straps over her head and is tying it at the back when Saint hands me mine.

I stare down at it hanging limply in his hand. "I'm not wearing that."

"Oh yes you are." Noa yanks the apron out of Saint's hands and tosses the strap over my head with a little jump.

"Hey—I didn't give you permission to touch me," I grouse. All Noa does is shove me around until she's in the back and strapping me in.

"You were happy enough wearing your mother's apron a few weeks ago with *Get Your Fat Pants On* written in bold at the front," she says while tying what I can only assume is a double-knot so I can't slip out of the thing.

"Would you like me to bring you that one instead?" she continues.

A huff of sound comes from my left. I don't care that I dressed up in Ma's apron, but that Noa said it in front of this guy makes me want to deck him.

"I promise there will be no cameras inside," Saint says. I detect an undercurrent of sarcasm. "Your fame will remain as precious as you normally care for it."

A muscle tics in my jaw.

"So you know who I am," I say with my usual cocky grin. Anything to remove this oily slime from my mouth. "I wasn't sure, what with you trying to drum up business in the sticks, if you wanted the worldwide attention I normally bring."

Noa's gaze flicks to me and she shakes her head in a disappointed arc with a disgusted twist to her lips. That's enough to shut me up and move me forward. I almost let my alpha-need to best this guy become more important than her time here and it takes effort to remember what I'm here for.

For her.

"Do you see our table?" I ask her.

Attention successfully redirected, Noa leads the way into the back of the restaurant, which is actually a larger space with more tables and an open kitchen. I've seen a lot of these types of restaurants in LA, featuring tables where patrons can watch the chefs cook and see their food being made fresh. Those who prefer an average restaurant experience can sit in the front.

I think it's an excellent idea to feature both options in Falcon Haven, attending to traditional and evolutionary needs, but hell if I'm telling Chef dude that.

The restaurant isn't open for business yet and they pushed

aside dining tables in favor of four metal prep tables lined up in a row directly in front of the food run station.

Couples surrounded by bowls, vegetables, knives, and other kitchen stuff occupy three tables. Our table is super shiny in comparison, probably because there's nothing on it.

I take position behind it while Noa greets each table individually. I recognize some, namely the elderly Mr. and Dr. Stanton, the latter being my pediatrician as a kid and Ma's cribbage partner. Noa says hello to another pair and I catch their names as Danny and Rad. I don't recognize them, but they do me. The older one, Rad, has a jaw-drop moment as I pass and feigns fainting into his partner, who backhands his arm and demands more decorum in the presence of a superhero. The last couple is young, like right out of college young, and they peel themselves off one another to politely introduce themselves to Noa. The woman, Claire, gives me shy smile while her guy glances sideways at me a lot like I did to the chef.

The man of the hour takes his place at the center of our tables and behind the food run station, the red mosaic tiles behind him adding somewhat of a blood-thirsty charm.

"I thank all of you for enrolling in *C'est Trois's* exclusive French master class," he says, drawing upon a handy French accent when deciding to sound like an authority on the subject. "While I vastly appreciate your support, I must warn you, there will be no coddling during these lessons. I'm here to nurture talent as much as you've arrived to prove yourselves, and I will meet any lack of effort with immediate dismissal." Saint scans the tables, silent throughout his speech. "My father's the nice guy. I'm not. You will not receive accolades, a degree, a chef's hat, or any kind of reward for completing my classes. You're here out of passion, a desire to learn in a subject that perhaps passed you by when you had the chance or circumstances have prevented you from pursuing a professional chef's career."

Noa's body goes limp next to mine. I glance down at her, noting how fiercely she's staring at Saint while her body betrays her sadness. Somehow, she missed her chance, and the why of it eats away at me. I make a mental note to ask her about it the next chance I get. A girl like her with such dashed dreams shouldn't have to lay herself at the feet of a shitstain like this, who acts like an overlord in his little slice of Falcon Haven.

You deserve better, I want to say to her.

As if sensing my intensity, she looks up, notices my attention and jerks her head toward Saint, silently demanding me to listen.

"With that in mind," Saint continues, "We'll start today with blank slates. I'll reserve judgment until a moment of indignity reveals itself." He stares pointedly at me while stating that.

I meet his gaze. *Game on, buddy.*

"Before you are the ingredients for traditional French cassoulet. Mr. and Mrs. Williams, you'll have to grab the ingredients yourselves since you arrived late."

"Oh—we're not married," Noa says. Too loudly, in my opinion. "Or together, actually."

Saint raises his brows. "Oh?"

"I thought this was couples only," Claire whispers to her boy-toy.

Noa, realizing her faux pas, shuffles beside me.

"I believe my mother called *C'est Trois*," I say, putting beautiful French emphasis on the name (I'm a talented motherfucker with accents), just for his benefit, "and explained our circumstances, which I'd prefer to keep private if you don't mind."

I grin handsomely at Claire and send her a wink. She flutters against her guy, confused feathers smoothed.

"That must've been my father, the owner," Saint admits. "I'll talk to him to confirm, but for now, let's move on. We've lost enough time as it is."

Noa jumps to attention and I'm forced to admit how much I enjoy observing her in her natural environment, collecting utensils and ingredients and instructing me on how to do the same without batting an eye.

I never noticed how cute it is when her brow scrunches with concentration as she chops, or how she bites her lip when she slices. What floors me the most is how the tip of her tongue pokes out when she works the saucepan on the hot plate. They adorn each table with in substitution of a stove. Her tongue shines a rosey pink, pointed in my direction, and when a piece of dark hair falls in front of her face, I want to tuck it behind her ear and suck her tongue into my mouth while doing it.

The part of me that's not supposed to be present twitches at the thought and I readjust my pants and show an intense focus on preventing the beans from burning. I'm hot, I'm sweating, and the apron tie is wildly uncomfortable against my neck, but to my surprise, time passes quickly, especially when I put all my energy into observing her.

Chef Saint wanders our way. I move in front of Noa protectively.

If he notices, he gives me no sign as he clasps his hands behind his back and hums deep in his throat as he assesses our progress.

"The fat on your duck breast could have better knife scores," he says while prodding the meat Noa just finished searing. "And you could have rendered it better."

Saint pulls a knife and fork from the cup of tasting utensils on our table. Without asking permission, he cuts into the middle of one of Noa's painstakingly prepared duck breasts and clucks his tongue. "How disappointing. It's raw in the center."

"*Raw?*" I can't help it despite Noa's warning expression to shut the hell up. "That's a perfect medium-rare in my books and I've been to a lot of ritzy places where snotty chefs like you take charge, and every single upper-crust asshole that dines in places like that would accept this breast as a fucking beautiful one."

The room goes silent. Heating saucepans continue to sizzle, the pop and spit of fat seemingly louder than normal.

"Stone," Noa hisses. "Don't talk to him like that. I'm here to learn from him and if he says it's undercooked, then it's undercooked."

Saint crooks an eyebrow at me. "Anything more to add, Mr. Williams?"

"The name is Stone, dick."

There's an audible gasp from Rad.

"Right." Saint rubs his lips together. "I forget I'm in the presence of *the* Stone Williams. Consider me properly chastised, just as you will be when you realize this is your last class."

"He didn't mean it." Noa's voice takes on a squeak of desperation. "Stone's hotheaded, but he's here for me. His mother couldn't be with me like we planned and I didn't want to lose my spot, so he graciously accepted to be my partner for these classes. My *silent* partner."

That last bit is directed at me.

The puff in my chest deflates at the shattered look in her eye, like I'm about to destroy her dreams once again.

It's with her expression in mind and not any chagrin on my

part that I turn to Saint and agree. "I'll keep my mouth shut. Please don't kick her out of the class."

After a pregnant pause where I'm almost sure the asshat is going to kick her out anyway, Saint says, "I bet that hurt to say."

I grit my teeth in an attempt not to rise to his bait. Noa trembles beside me.

"Consider that your final chance," Saint says. He turns to Noa, his eyelids softening slightly—such a small tic that I'm almost sure I imagined it. "Do the duck again, but correctly this time."

"Yes, chef."

Noa gets back to work, refusing to look at me.

In fact, for the rest of the evening, the only conversation I receive from her are curt words and brief instructions, and even then, it's not much. I'm relegated to stirring duty as I can't be trusted to cut vegetables evenly or work meat properly. They sufficiently wound my male ego as each minute passes with vague glances from Saint and pointed dismissal from Noa.

When the dish is finished and Saint approves of all but one, I know I'm in deep shit.

"The fat on the duck is charred along the edges, dry, and under seasoned," Saint says to Noa. "While the sauce is delicious, it will break by the time I'm finished this sentence. You didn't stir it enough."

I slant a look at him. *Ooooh, shot fired, asshole.*

"That being said, I'll allow you back next week because I see talent in your knife cuts and you've formed a perfect, delicious crust on top. You have potential, Miss...?"

Noa smiles despite the cutting criticism he'd wielded seconds before. Apparently, all this man has to do is add one compliment to five insults, and he's back to her good graces. Total toxic relationship.

"Shaw. Noa-Lynn Shaw."

"The guy gets your full name?" I blurt. She cuts a glare in my direction and I throw my hands up in surrender, muttering, "Sorry," before returning to scut duty and cleaning our station.

"It's lovely to meet you, Noa-Lynn. I look forward to seeing you rise to more challenges."

Saint finishes by gifting her with a closed-mouthed, dimpled smile before turning his attention to the other couples. To my utter horror, Noa grows a bashful flush under his attention. I momentarily pause in wiping down the counter, murdering the back of his head while a continues his natural criticism of the other tables.

"How is this meant to be a date night activity?" I ask. "I think it's more like if you're into masochism outside the bedroom."

"If you would stop excreting your big dick energy all over the place, you'd understand that he is *you* in the chef world. A James Beard award winner, one of the youngest in the nation, and a man who garnered critical attention by the age of eighteen. It's a privilege to work under him, nevermind be taught by him, and you of all people should not judge his success simply because he's currently living in a small town."

I have said it before, but Noa being smaller than me should naturally give me the upper hand in arguments. It doesn't. Her lively, beautiful eyes darken with a tempestuous storm, and if she could, she'd put me in the middle of her exasperated hurricane. If she could destroy me with a glare, she would.

"I'm trying to defend you," I reason. "Accomplished or not, he shouldn't speak to you the way he does."

"Like you do?"

I rear back. "I have never disrespected you like that."

"He's trying to make me a better cook. What have you ever done for me?"

My brows couldn't hike any higher, but they do. "Look at me, Noa." I splay out my hands. "I'm in a rented apron cleaning up food scraps in a restaurant when I should be reading for my next role. A role, I might add, I'm probably going to lose because I'm here, doing this, with you."

It's not entirely true, I'm here for Ma, but this is what happens when I'm cornered. I'm irrational and hurtful, and the truth is, it feels really good in the moment.

Noa recoils. She answers, "Don't do me any favors, then. Go back to Hollywood for all I care. I bet if I went up to Saint right now and asked if I could stay on as a single, he'd let me. You know why? Because I respect him. I listen to him. *I actually like him.*"

My lips peel back from my teeth as my gaze bounces between Saint and her. Sure, I call him *Saint* in my head, but that's because I refuse to acknowledge him as a human, never mind as a person with a title in my mind. But Noa calling him by his first name sends a swirl of fire into my brain so heated and so strong that I see red.

"Sweetheart, go fuck him for some cooking lessons. I bet that'll make you feel real accomplished and talented."

Noa doesn't gasp. Tears don't sparkle in those beautiful eyes. Her mouth thins. She reaches behind her and yanks at the ties to her apron. She pulls it off, lays it on the table with the utmost respect, then turns her back on me.

I'm forced to watch her approach Saint and touching the back of his shoulder to get his attention. When he turns to her, she leaves her hand there, smiling at him while her strawberry-pink lips ask him a question.

I can't hear what she says, but his answering, charmed smile is enough.

Blood clots burst in my vision. I pull at my apron's ties, but they don't give. Noa really did double-knot them. I yank so hard the threads strain under my temper, but they don't give.

Enough with this shit. I storm out of the back, away from Noa and her sweet smile and kind eyes and Saint with his bad-boy, talented chef flair.

I make a distinct and direct line for the hostess.

Eighteen

NOA

Stone stomps out of the open kitchen in my periphery, apron ties flapping.

With a rock lodged in my stomach, I drop my hand from Chef Toussaint's shoulder.

"I appreciate you giving me a second chance," I finish saying to him.

"And I'm happy to be your mentor, so long as I'm not used as a jealousy play again."

Shame inflames my cheeks until Saint softens the blow with empathetic, "I've had my share of passionate wildfires, and more than a few have ended in charred remains." He looks behind him to where Stone made his graceful exit. "Good luck with that one."

I sigh, staring in the same direction, but my thoughts are far away. In the past where they don't belong. "I shouldn't bring that kind of energy into the kitchen."

"Leave it behind next time and we'll all be just fine. I didn't offer couple classes thinking I'd receive a bunch of disassociated cooking robots. I can handle him if you can. The French are known for their passion, and it's accepted in the kitchen so long as it's transferred into the food."

Nodding, I retreat from the conversation, suddenly having nothing further to add. I can apologize for Stone all day, but if truth be told, I was just as immature in the moment. Stone has an innate talent for bringing my worst insecurities to the forefront and feasting on them with greasy satisfaction.

And I gave them to him on a silver platter.

Disgusted with myself, I leave the room without saying goodbye to the nice couples that are also submitting themselves to Saint's criticism. I overhear them agreeing to drinks at the main bar before going home. A part of me wishes I could join —I miss having cocktails with friends ever since Carly moved to the city and we both became so busy with our jobs—but I'm not in the mood. Maybe next time, if there is a next time, and if Stone doesn't piss me off to the point I want to flee this restaurant and curl up with Moo.

Unfortunately for me, my night isn't nearly over.

I burst through the double doors into the front room, now romantically lit and set up for a soft opening. The restaurant isn't populated with patrons yet, but it does have its first romantic couple.

Stone leans on the hostess stand, so close to her face that their noses nearly touch. He murmurs something to her and she giggles softly, running a long, taloned finger down the length of his arm.

He leans closer and tucks a blond strand behind her ear, sending her into another fit of unnecessary giggles.

Breath hisses from my clenched teeth so hotly, I'm shocked not to see steam billowing in front of my face.

Stone senses my presence. His eyes dart in my direction but refuse to lock on. His focus slides right off me like I'm nothing but a fangirl watching him hit on someone I'll never have a chance of becoming.

Then I wake up. For a stupid minute there, I thought I had to endure this. But there is nothing in our history to make me want to stay and watch him bed a girl simply because he can, so I storm right past, knocking into his shoulder as I exit.

The contact brings tears to my eyes, not because of the physical pang, but because of the intangible, unavoidable hurt deep inside.

The hostess laughs. "Wow, she seems great. Why do you hang out with her?"

I don't want for his response, as I'm sure it'll be something like, *yeah, Noa's a real fun-sponge*, as they both laugh at my expense.

I burst into the sidewalk, a frigid cold hitting my bare arms and sinking into my shirt with biting accuracy. My jacket is inside, but I'll be damned if I go back in and get it.

Thankfully, I tucked my phone in my back pants' pocket. I can pull it out and call for an Uber.

It's while I'm waiting for my ride that I hear the door behind me open with a waft of heated air before shutting again.

I don't bother turning around. I jolt when warm, weighted fabric covers my shoulders and a husky male voice says, "You forgot your coat."

My pride isn't so vengeful that I'll cast aside my jacket and refuse the warmth, so I shoot a curt, "Thank you," in Stone's direction before moving away from him to the street corner.

A moment of silence passes. Then he asks, "Are you getting in the car or what?"

I give a sharp shake of my head, refusing to face him. Terrified he'll notice the tear-tracks down my face, frozen into position by the shockingly cold night.

"Noa, come on, don't be like this."

"I doubt there's room for me if you're bringing the hostess back, too," I retort. Immaturely.

He gives an audible exhale. "She's not coming with us."

Us. I snort. As if there's an us.

"I'm good, thanks. I have an Uber coming."

"Cancel it."

"No. Drive home without me."

"I'm not leaving you out here in the cold."

"Why not? If I get too frozen, I can always go back in and get Chef Saint to warm me."

A dangerous growl sounds out to my right, but I cross my arms defiantly, staring out into the street.

Then my legs go out from under me.

"What—Stone!"

"Fuck this. We're not arguing on a street corner so we can be the town's fodder tomorrow," he grunts while my forehead nearly smacks against his ass.

"Put me down!" This time, I use my dangling arms to slap his ass. "This is humiliating, Stone! Haven't you done enough of that?"

There's a hitch in his long strides, then he resumes with more vigor. If he notices the cluster of townspeople out and about, pausing and muttering to each other as we pass, he doesn't give a damn.

But I sure do.

"Stone!" I try again.

At last, he drops me to my feet by the passenger side of his car. He smoothly transitions from plopping me down to opening the door and commanding, "Get in."

"N—"

After a brief eye roll, he shoves me into the car.

I wouldn't call it an aggressive push, or even a mean one, but it sure is effective. He uses his chest to navigate me inside, his large hands wrapping around my sides to bend me at the waist. His thumbs are uncomfortably close to the undersides of my breasts. The down of my jacket should protect me from feeling any *zings* or tingles at his touch, but I might as well be naked as he firmly places me in his vehicle, his face inches from mine.

His breath smells like salt and wine, like the sauce we made together, the very one I licked off the spoon.

In an unwelcome flash, I suddenly want that spoon to be him.

I push at his shoulders, my heart rate increasing with excited pumps. "Get off me, Stone."

"Gladly." His brows overcast his eyes in a line of frustration as he pushes off and makes his way to the driver's side.

I use the moment of being free from him to reluctantly cancel my ride. I'm positive if I tried to escape, Stone would hunt me down and we'd give the townsfolk an encore.

Stone gets in with a slam of the door, starting the engine and merging into traffic without a word.

We spend the entire trip home in tense silence, our mutual anger coming off our body in electrical waves that prickle against my cheek. I sense his body next to mine like I would a wolf crouched in the underbrush awaiting his moment to pounce on the poor deer who just wanted to take a cooking class and be happy for a minute.

Serves me right to think I could be content with Stone by my side. All he brings inside my comfort zone is trouble.

The house is dark by the time we pull up, Mrs. Stalinski long asleep. Stone gets out first and I follow, trekking up the shadowed patio and into the house without conversation. Neither of us bother to turn on the lights in the foyer since we're both so familiar with the layout.

"Good night, Noa."

Stone's voice rasps through the darkness and I pause on the first step of the staircase, my hand lingering on the banister.

"Night," I say.

Normally, I'd follow up with *thank you for tonight* or *thank you for coming to the restaurant with me*, but after his behavior and my reactions to it at the end, such a sentiment would be awkward and ineffective.

I pad up the stairs, my last image of Stone framed by strips of moonlight coming through the windows as he stands and watches me disappear up the staircase.

If he has any further emotion about what happened tonight, he hides it well behind an apathetic mask, his skin whitened into silver by the moon and his feelings just as far away.

Nineteen

STONE

I'm able to comfortably fall asleep on hard ground without issue. There was one time I had to stay on set overnight and we were in Yellowstone. I curled up in a tent, the weather turning below freezing, and conked out with the dedication of a coma patient, only rising to the mumbling and cursing of the film crew as someone tried to start a fire and warm themselves. My extremities were numb, but I slept through it.

Yet on Ma's pull-out couch in her den, I can't so much as close my eyes. I toss and turn, kicking the covers off then pulling them back on, tucking myself up to my chin, then discarding them again. I'm not hot or cold or physically hindered in any other way. It's my head that's the problem, full of images from this evening, except different.

Noa hanging on Chef Saint's every word while he teachers her to properly stir a mixture in a bowl (which is absurd. Obviously she knows how to stir). Him coming up behind her and showing her how to do it, pressing his chest against her, guiding her arm with his hand before her mouth parts and she turns into him...

"God*dammit*," I mumble, sitting up.

The sheets fall from my bare chest and I scrub my hands down my face, as if that action can erase these obtrusive thoughts from my brain.

It shouldn't matter if she has the hots for the tattooed chef. I want Noa to be happy, don't I?

Except, I think she'd be better off with me.

A *clank* rings out from the other side of my door. I finally notice the golden light drifting in from under the frame and shadows flickering as something moves.

Accepting that sleep will not come easy, I slide off the bed, thinking maybe it's Ma looking for a midnight snack and a chat. I could use the distraction and she could probably use the help, so I open the door and tiptoe into the hall so as not to startle her.

What I don't expect once I reach the kitchen is to see Noa in full cook mode, pulling out Ma's entire pot and pan collection, as well as a good portion of the pantry, all laid out on the breakfast counter like helpful soldiers.

Noa hasn't seen me yet. Her back is to me and she's dressed in a pink satin short and shirt combo with Ma's apron tied over it. The fabric shines over her curves—specifically, the curve of her ass as her bare feet pad around the linoleum while she prepares.

She's humming under her breath, her hair piled up on top of her head. Moo's joined her, threading between her legs and meowing his support as she deftly hops over him.

"What are you doing?"

Noa screeches and nearly drops the boiling pot she's

carrying from the stove to ... somewhere. She sets it down at the same time Moo yowls and his nails skitter across the floor as he seeks cover.

"Stone! You scared me."

"Kinda like what you're doing to me right now." I scan the mess. "You know what time it is, right?"

I check my watch just to be sure. Yep, 3 am.

"Did I wake you?" she asks.

To her credit, she appears contrite, her brows furrowed as she worries her lower lip.

I decide to be honest with her. "Nah. Couldn't sleep."

"Me neither." Then she laughs as she takes in her environment. "But I suppose that's obvious."

I inspect what she's pulled out. "Are you recreating what we made today?"

"Yeah." She sighs and massages the back of her neck. "I tried to fall asleep, but I kept hearing the chef's criticism in my head and how I could do it better. I don't want to endure that kind of humiliation again, so I thought I could practice and Mrs. Stalinski could enjoy the fruits of my labors." She smiles with a tired, lopsided, gorgeous tilt to her lips. "Because who wouldn't want French cassoulet for breakfast?"

I return the smile. "Does Ma even have duck for you to use?"

"No, but I'm trying to recreate it with chicken. See?" She steps aside to showcase what's sizzling on the stove. I move in for a closer look, conscious of her satin-clad body hovering nearby.

The woman is like a beacon of electricity, striking me whenever I get too close, and I both hate and love it. I'm her reactor, a role I took on at the ripe age of fourteen and never looked back from. I don't know why I figured the energy between us would die off with time. If anything, it's gotten stronger.

"Yeah, looks good," I say, huskier than I should. "Smells fucking amazing."

She smiles a little brighter. "Right? Say what you want about my browning ability but I have the seasoning dead-on."

I trace her face with my eyes, taking her in, memorizing her passionate determination and confidence so I can replace the one of her drooling over the chef.

Her smile falters the longer I stare at her. Her gaze slides away, at the sizzle and pop of her meat, then flutters back to me.

I shift closer.

"Stone," she whispers.

I dip my head. Chances are she could use that spatula she's holding against me, but I can't deny this subtle rippling inside me, an instinctive song pulling me nearer.

I want to put my hands on her.

She reads it in my eyes.

"Stone," she tries again. Then: "William."

My response comes as an exhale. "You use my real name, sweetheart, you better be prepared to meet the real guy."

"I know you. I've always known who you are. You can dress yourself up with a Hollywood name and Hollywood clothes and I'd still recognize you."

Our noses almost touch. "You haven't talked to me in ten years."

Noa tips her chin—her mistake. Her lips come dangerously close. So much so that if she weren't cooking a mouth-watering dish inches away, I'd smell her sugary lip gloss.

"Have you changed in that time?" she asks.

I have to repeat her question in my head. The colorful

flecks in her eyes are an unexpected distraction. She's stained glass up close, fragile and painstakingly put together, and all I can think about is shattering her in the best of ways.

"I'd like to think I have," I answer. Smoke drifts between us, putting her features in sorceress relief. That spatula becomes a wand and she can turn me into a frog if she wants.

I'd give in.

"You married during that time," she dares to say.

My lips quirk ever so slightly. "So you kept tabs on me."

"Not really." She breaks our stare-off and pokes at the chicken. "It's hard not to be updated when the entire town spoke of you like a God. That is, until recently when you—"

I put my hand on her arm and spin her. "I like your eyes on me. I'd prefer they'd stay on me while you try to eviscerate me with actions I've already accepted as part of my past."

She goes slack in my grip, allowing my hand to stay there. "I'd have to care about you to want to eviscerate you."

"You care."

"I don't."

"No?" My hand glides up her arm, catching on that tease of satin, running up her neck and tracing her jaw.

Noa closes her eyes and gives in to my exploration, canting her head. "You're insufferable."

"I've been called worse."

"We can't do this. I don't want this."

"Strong words," I say, my thumb snagging on her plump lower lip. "If only you meant them."

She tries to jerk out of my grip, but I hold on to her chin, preventing the escape. "Don't close off on me, sweetheart. Say what you gotta say. I'm open to hearing it."

Noa tries to snort. It's slightly difficult when I cup her jaw so her eyes handle most of the disdain. "You don't want to hear how I feel about you."

"Yeah?" I move my hand to the back of her head, using Noa's hair to angle her the way I want her while using my other arm to press her against me, holding her flush. "If you refuse to say it, then I'll just move onto other ways to prove you want me."

"You're a selfish, self-entitled prick," Noa hisses, yet she allows her head to be pulled back. Her neck to be exposed.

My lips peel from my teeth. "I'm aware. If I'm honest, you know me better than anyone I've ever met." I shut down the flash of triumph in her eyes by adding, "Just like I know that deep down, you're the same sweet, impressionable girl who has always had trouble getting this selfish prick out of her system no matter how hard she tries."

"And so you use that to your advantage? You're doing this just so you can put your mark on me before Chef Toussaint can. I'm not a part of your pissing contest—"

"If you think I want you because another man's sniffing around," I growl, surrounding her on all sides, "think again. I've wanted you since the day your turned up in class at school in over-sized jeans and that black halter top that made me want to cream my pants the minute I laid eyes on you."

"That was a long time ago."

"Yeah? Well, I'm the same man according do you and I self-ishly want to throw you on this counter and take you and make you scream. I want to know if you nipples taste the same— sweet with some tang. I want to know if you still shave or if you've gone bare. I want this Noa, the woman who has given up *everything* to take care of my mother, the woman who politely submits to an arrogant chef and saves her smart mouth for me, this woman who"—I pause to angle my head closer to her lips, short breaths escaping—"keeps a lot of secrets buried inside her and thinks I can't see them."

Her chest heaves against mine.

"You know me so well, Noa, sweetheart. I know you as completely. And I fucking need you."

She opens her mouth for more words, more wasted breath, maybe more denials. I don't let her. Can't. Not when she needs me, too.

I pull the pot off the burner, then seal my lips on hers.

Twenty

NOA

HE TASTES LIKE HOW I FEEL WHEN I SATISFY A craving.

Satiated. Sweetly addicted. Wanting more.

I shove that thought from my brain. My back presses against the edge of the countertop and my hands grapple for some leverage, an edge, a hold, an anchor to keep me from floating through the ceiling and into the night sky.

Stone's mouth has other ideas. His lips are hot, suctioned on mine, stealing all oxygen. He takes and takes until I dart my tongue forward and graze against him. Sensing my exploration, he dives, tilting my head back, angling it for the best kind of kiss, and finally, I take, too.

My fingers dig into his back. He came into the kitchen in his boxers, all cut lines and crinkled expression, like I'm just as confusing to him as he is to me.

I want to feel all of him, to see if he's different, and he is. His muscles are hills and valleys on his back, unlike the lanky, rebellious bad-boy I had in high school. Stone's kiss is the same, possessive and all-consuming, demanding my attention.

With that mouth and the way his body molds against mine, creating heat like flint creates fire, all my hurt drifts away. My worries and my pain. What's left is exactly the emotion he promised: *Need*.

Stone's hands glide down my body, supplicant at first, until he finds my buttons. He doesn't waste time unbuttoning each one. Stone breaks away enough to rip open my shirt, buttons scattering. I gasp, the heat from my core flowing up my neck and into my cheeks, as I wait for him to comment.

Stone's eyes are dark, dilated, and focused on my chest. His brow creates half-moons where the brightness of his blue eyes should be, and my exhales turn shallow as this beast studies his prey before he consumes me.

I whisper through my panting breath, "We shouldn't."

Stone rises. He takes his hands off me, my body aching from the lack of contact.

Instead of backing off, Stone says, "For once in your life, be selfish."

"What?"

"I'm standing in front of you, rock hard and desperate to pleasure you. Put your reservations aside and just *take*."

I hesitate. I feel a bead of sweat form on my collarbone, then trickle between my exposed breasts.

Stone watches it, then flicks his gaze back to me.

I could do the smart thing. Continue with the mantra, *we shouldn't*. My body says otherwise. I've deprived myself of life's most basic forms of finding ecstasy by burying myself in work and refusing to delve into memories. I left a lot of myself behind by doing that.

Here, now, Stone wants me to forget, but in an entirely different way.

My body remembers.

I mouth, *Take me.*

Stone buries his face in my breasts. I arch back on a moan when he captures one of my nipples and expertly bites down, then flicks it with his tongue. It turns my veins into electric wires, sending dangerous voltages up my body and sparking behind my eyes. I grip the back of his head, tangling my fingers in his hair.

"Don't stop," I groan to the ceiling. "Oh God, don't stop."

"Never. I could do this all night," he promises, before using the same skill on my other nipple.

I writhe against the countertop, the scent of bacon, onion, garlic and Stone against my nostrils. An aphrodisiac of epic proportions.

Stone's hand breaks away from my breast, traveling to the hem of my pajama shorts. The elastic is a poor defense against his deft fingers. Satin pools around my ankles and I kick them somewhere—as far away as possible because I want to be naked in front of this man. Fully exposed.

I haven't had sex in years and my vagina has taken over my brain, commanding attention and demanding the release of all this frustrated reserve of sexual energy.

Hiking my legs around his waist, Stone growls his approval, straightening and setting me on the counter. He grazes his lips across my cheek, his stubble prickling my skin, and murmurs into my ear, "With all these cooking supplies, I'd bathe your pussy in butter before I dine, but I know I don't have to because you taste like fucking honey."

Stone, being familiar with my scent and taste and having

deprived himself of it for years, takes the anticipation so much higher.

"I want your tongue on me," I pant.

Stone leans back to meet my eye. His are hooded, his pupils even larger than before. "Say it. Beg me to fuck you with my tongue."

I'm squirming on the counter, damp and throbbing between my legs. "Please, Stone. Fuck me with your mouth."

He smiles, predatory and sure, then lowers until he's nestled between my thighs. Stone's eyes flare at the sight of my bare pussy. He grits out, "Your wish, sweetheart, my command."

My hands slap on the granite behind me as I try to find some friction to keep from puddling onto the counter. Stone slides his velvet tongue from my anus to my clit, delicate and teasing as he collects the juices. His eyes flutter closed, and he groans.

"Damn, you're as delicious as I remember. More so."

Instinct has me thrusting my hips into his face, my body language insisting he go deeper, but he darts away with a wicked grin.

"You're on my timetable now, and I'm not getting you off until I re-introduce myself to every secret your pussy tries to hide."

"Please, Stone," I say, hoping if I keep begging like he enjoys, he'll devour me.

"Not gonna work, sweetheart. Now shut up and let me work."

Thighs trembling, I watch him bury his nose in me and inhale deeply. I should be embarrassed, but I'm not. No guy has ever wanted to scent me so thoroughly, except for him. This is the Stone I knew, the one I want, who prods me open with his tongue and spreads me farther with his fingers.

Then he thrusts.

His tongue is a cock in a different form, more dexterous and able to angle in all the right places. My hips meet him as he plunges in and out, his thumb flicking my clit and his other hand doing things I'd never imagined, like prodding at my anus and pushing in all the way to the knuckle.

My eyes pop open at the foreign sensation. I don't hate it. I *love* it. It adds to the ecstasy as he uses his mouth and fingers to bring me to unexplainable heights. I'm sure my juices would pool around me if they could, but Stone laps up every drop of passion, unsatisfied until I mewl, a vocal warning of my impending orgasm.

"I missed that sound," he says against my pussy, then mouth-fucks me harder.

The orgasm surges through me, shuddering my muscles and frying my nerves. I clutch his head to stay grounded because I'm sure if I let go, I'll sprout wings and fly.

"I ... I haven't felt this, anything like this, for so long."

I don't realize I've said it out loud until Stone rises, his mouth and chin as slick as his satisfied smile.

"That's great to hear, considering I'm not nearly done with you."

I look at him with trepidation.

Stone cups the side of my neck, his thumb tracing my jaw. "I wasn't lying. I need you. Need to be inside you, flying with you."

I nod against his grip, fully taken with desire.

Stone loses his boxers, his cock springing forth. It's so hard, it bounces painfully with its reveal, one side of Stone's face wincing at the movement.

"Your balls must be so tight," I murmur, kind of surprised at the dirty talk coming out of my mouth, but kinda loving it, too.

How long has it been since I stated my desires so simply? *As long as I've been away from him.*

"They're fucking blue balls, baby." Stone cocks his head. "What are you going to do about it?"

"Oh? You want this?" I spread my legs, forcing Stone to take a step back as I idly finger my folds, wet with his previous ministrations.

His eyes brighten with twin flames. "I wouldn't do that if you're not prepared for the consequences."

I bite my lower lip and meet his stare. "Damn the consequences."

Stone's chest rumbles. Then he moves.

I let him cover my body on the counter. Bowls fall. Dried white beans scatter. The logical part of my mind—the responsible, level, *you shouldn't be doing this part*—releases a quiet warning. My sex drive doesn't heed it and I cover Stone's lips with my own, wrapping my limbs around his lithe body and covering us in flour.

His fingers dive into my pussy, fucking relentlessly as I buck beneath him. He sucks out my cries and swallows them, the weight of him suffocating and addictive.

Air hits my cheeks when he rears back on a curse. "Condom. I need a condom."

"Get it," I heave out, then splay out like a starfish as he jumps off me and stumbles into the den, his dick jutting in front of him like a sword.

Stone returns in seconds, tearing open the wrapper with his mouth. He slides it on before climbing on top of me. I lift my knees and spread myself open for him and he growls his approval before slamming inside.

His entrance is slick, easy, and all the way to the hilt. I've never been more accepting of a man and his thrusts come immediately, our dance a familiar and desperate one as we reunite in the way we were always amazing at.

My back curves. My chin tilts up. My eyes shutter closed as I give myself into the way he stretches me and strokes the sweetest parts of my body.

"Yes," I whisper. "Harder. Please, harder."

Stone grunts, rising up on his hands, his abs undulating with his sure strokes. His jaw tightens, the tendons in his cheeks jutting, then releasing. His eyes won't leave mine.

"That's it, sweetheart. Give yourself over. Let me satisfy you."

My thighs tighten with glorious warning.

He adds, "I'm not coming until you do. I refuse. I want you to get there first."

My breaths come out shorter. I can't speak. I can barely hold his eyes with my own. My vision blackens.

Then his strokes slow.

My brows furrow as I cry out my displeasure.

His grin is slow and cat-like. "Did I forget to mention I'll have to torture you first the way you've tortured me?"

"F-Fuck you," I stutter.

He laughs before his eyes return to a sinful midnight blue. "You're so hot when you're mad and want to come."

In a spiteful move, I move my fingers to where we're connected and find my clit. "Allow me to help you help me."

Stone notices what I'm doing, then bites his lip in reluctant approval. "Resourceful little thing, aren't you?" He looks down again and stays there. "Damn, that's hot."

"Feels good, too," I say through a moan.

Stone pulls out, both of us fascinated with the slide of his dick and the furtive circles of my fingers. He can't contain his pleasure, groaning as he pushes in, then furtively pulls out.

The combined feeling of my fingers and him sent me over the moon and around it three times. I'm spinning, closing my eyes in wonderful bliss, our sweating bodies squeaking on the granite and clumping with flour.

Neither of us cares. We climb all the way to the top, Stone's balls tightening against my folds when he realizes I'm about to come.

"That's it, sweetheart."

Stone watches me tremble with my second orgasm, using one hand to hold my jaw so he can memorize each twitch and own every moan.

When I go slack, so utterly satisfied, Stone retakes the wheel and jackhammers into me, ensuring more of my pleasure and a third orgasm before he loses himself in his own.

Twenty-One

NOA

Hot air tickles the hair around my ear. I swat at it, thinking it's a fly, then nestle into my pillow.

It happens again.

Frowning, I roll onto my back, then come up against something hard.

Hard and warm.

Hard and warm, and moving.

And smelling like Stone.

Last night comes back in a wave, our spontaneous romp in the kitchen and the mess we made both in the kitchen and with ourselves.

"Shit," I mutter, trying to slide out from under the possession of his arm.

I don't regret what we did. Not physically. Stone made my body feel things I'd long forgotten were important, like pleasure and a satiating sleep. We'd showered together after in the guest bathroom, sudsing our bodies and unable to resist coming together again. And again.

Our bodies missed one another more than our minds allowed us to remember, and I couldn't control the innate need to have him fill me, carry me, and hold me.

Morning makes a difference, though, and as the golden sunrise peeks through the blinds, I sneak out of the couch's bed without disturbing him.

I pull on a T-shirt and thin robe before entering the hallway and going upstairs to do a quick check of Mrs. Stalinski's room.

Mrs. Stalinski.

Hot shame, more pink than the waking sun's rays, color my skin as I slump away from her door and down the stairs. Now that reality's set in, I realize what I've done.

Had sex with her son while she's upstairs.

Don't get me wrong. I'm no stranger to sneaking into Stone's room and enjoying the forbidden pleasures of fucking each other while our parents are asleep, but it's different this time. She's sick, and I'm her nurse. I'm in this house to take care of her, not myself.

It's a moment of weakness I resolve never to happen again. I plan on telling Stone the same, and for reasons beyond respecting Mrs. Stalinski, even though that's a top priority.

We're messy, he and I. Almost as destructive as we were to this kitchen, and this time, I don't want to throw my heart in the garbage disposal all in the name of becoming addicted to him again.

I stop in the entrance to the kitchen.

Blinking, I scan the room, wondering if I'm dreaming.

The granite counter gleams along with the stovetop. All

traces of spilled flour and escaped beans and baked-on sauce are gone.

Fresh lemon and vinegar wafts under my nose as I cautiously wander in.

Either magic cleaning elves came into the house last night while Stone and I were sleeping off our sex, or he came in here after I succumbed to exhaustion and did this all himself.

"Wow," I whisper, drawn to a folded note sitting near the sink.

I open it and read.

I'm sorry for being such a jerk last night.
Should've known you'd choose me over the saint. ;)
I hope this helps your regret this morning, because you and I both know you have nothing to feel guilty over.

x Stone

I don't realize I'm smiling until my cheeks communicate the ache. It's Stone's version of an apology. Not perfect, full of innuendos, and right on the money. He knows me too well sometimes.

"Wondering what to do now that you're up this early and have no kitchen to clean, huh?"

Stone's sleep-roughened voice comes from the archway.

Turning, I respond, "You've certainly put a wrench in my plans."

"I can think of an activity."

I huff out a laugh. "I'm actually considering it." Or more likely, my vagina is. "But your mom will be up soon and I can use this extra time to make us a delicious breakfast."

Stone pretends to consider it. "Hmm. We *do* need the calories."

"And your mom—"

"Don't," he says in a gentle tone. "I told you not to feel guilty over what we did."

"But she's sick and I'm her nurse. It was totally unprofessional of me."

"Listen, if Ma were healthy, she'd encourage it."

I roll my eyes. "I hardly think she would."

"You, sweetheart, were the perfect girl for me." His eyes widen. "What I mean to say is, she thought you were. She'd support any clues that we're back to—"

"We're not back together."

An indiscernible emotion flickers behind his expression. "I was going to say, we're back to being friendly."

"Oh." I scratch at the countertop, feeling like an idiot. "Sorry."

Though I'm not sure how I feel about his definition of *being friendly*. Then again, I didn't want him to say we were back together.

Conflicting emotions aren't my strong suit. I jump to attention, walking close to him to reach the cabinet above the fridge.

Stone doesn't shift.

I clear my throat. "Your mom needs her meds."

Stone continues to stare down at me, unmoving.

"We should talk later," he says softly.

I'd say anything to get us to move apart and reduce the electricity between us. "Sure. You won't have trouble finding me."

"I think we need more of an intimate setting. A dinner."

"A dinner?" I echo, retreating a step. He follows. "Like a date?"

"I wouldn't call it that. Just somewhere you won't run away. So you can talk to me."

Talk. He says it like it's so easy. "Maybe later. Can I get to the pills, now?"

"By later, you mean your lunch break. I'll make it easy for you and say we'll grab sandwiches at the Merc. I'll meet you there."

"If it gets you out of my way, then yes, fine, I'll see you there. If Maisy doesn't kick you out, first."

Stone turns to the cabinet and reaches for the container, pulling it down and passing it between us.

It's security in a way, a physical barrier between him and me.

My shoulders relax.

"She won't be able to resist my bad puppy look," Stone quips. "I have it down to an art."

He tries to deploy it on me. Stone's laugh lines turn into apologetic strokes and the usual witty slant to his eyes soften, his handsome features transforming into chagrined in less than a second.

I can't say it's acting that's given him this talent. He's been using this look on unsuspecting townsfolk, parents, adults, *me* since he could control his facial muscles.

"I'll go up, give Mrs. Stalinski her medicine, then come down and make breakfast," I say, ignoring the twinge in my gut. Damn him for making me want to go in for a hug.

Stone chuckles. He knows he's won. "Tell me what to do to get started."

"Really?"

"Yeah." This time, his smile is genuine. "I'm your sous chef now, right? Might as well practice at home. I feel bad for distracting you from your practice last night."

"No you don't."

But I give him instructions while ignoring the chemical

rewiring going on in my brain. If I'm not careful, I might actually start liking this man again.

"Start with pulling out the half-finished cassoulet from the fridge. Maybe we can make a breakfast skillet."

Stone's eyes light up. "I can definitely help with that."

And that's where I leave him, humming to himself while organizing ingredients in a way my brain only wishes it could categorize him.

BREAKFAST ENDS up being really enjoyable. Mrs. Stalinski comes down and joins, eager to observe us cooking in the kitchen together. Stone is the perfect assistant now that there isn't a third chef in the kitchen. He even insists on cleanup despite doing a midnight spray down of the kitchen beforehand.

If Mrs. Stalinski suspects anything went down last night, she's very good at hiding it. I spend most of my time studying her features for the slightest lip tilt or eye crinkle, maybe a frown of disappointment.

Her opinion of me means a lot, and I'd hate to be lesser in her eyes. Stone may be her son, but she's not oblivious to his behavior and wishes for him to sow his oats and settle down more than anyone. We both know it's not with me.

All I notice with Mrs. Stalinski is the pure joy at watching Stone and I bicker over how finely to slice onions and the perfect amount of salt to add to any dish. I catch her eye at one point, and she smiles over the rim of her coffee cup, her eyes alert and candid.

After the kitchen returns to its spotless condition, I leave them chatting over coffee. Saturday is any other day in my world. My shifts are seven days a week, and I have three patients to see.

I'm finishing up with my last patient, Mrs. Cavendish, when a text comes through.

Stone: See you in 10.

The phone drops to my side. I'm half tempted—no, entirely driven to respond with an excuse that I have a lunch date with Carly and have to cancel. Until Carly responded to my desperate text a few hours ago saying she was stuck in the city on a case and couldn't drive down.

If I didn't know any better, I'd say the two were in cahoots to have me sitting with Stone, fully clothed and without the excuse of naked fun to distract us. But, it's no secret Carly hates Stone, and if she were ever in cahoots involving him, it would be on where to bury his body.

I wish Mrs. Cavendish well and tell her not to use the stairs without her husband around, and after that, have no excuse to linger. The roads are clear on the way into town and a parking spot opens up directly in front of the Merc.

"Damn you," I say to the celebrity gods before pulling in, turning off the engine, and resigning myself to a lunch date with Stone.

I take solace in the fact that I'm in my scrubs and didn't dress up. Too many times, I wanted to look good for him, especially after a night of sex. I was one of those girls who sprinted out of bed before their man woke up to brush my hair, put on deodorant, and insist *I woke up like this* even though Stone clearly knew better.

"I like you messy and roughed up by me," he'd murmur into my lips before rolling on top of me.

The memory sends shivers down my spine. I shake it off, hardening my resolve by recalling the last vivid, terrible memory I have of him. That makes it easier to stroll into the Merc's cafe side with a straight back and closed mouth, scanning for Stone's broad shoulders.

I spot him at a tabletop near the back, surrounded by young fans. Two girls have their phones pulled out, and he's signing the baseball cap of the guy with them. Stone's all smiles, easygoing and happy to take pictures.

It's not hard to understand why he's famous and so well liked, despite his constant tabloid infamy. Stone is friendly, handsome, full of wit and humor. When he wants to turn it on, he's a goddamned florescent light.

"Your usual?"

Maisy's smoker's voice, louder than usual, flows into my ear.

She's at the register, staring at me with crossed arms and a knowing smile.

"Sure, Maisy," I say with an extra-sweet grin. "With extra mayo."

"I bet. Added some extracurricular to your lifestyle, eh?"

"What are you talking about?"

"Girl, I know a smitten study when I see one, and you're looking at that boy like you can pour him onto a plate and savor his taste."

"Maisy!" My mouth opens, horrified. "I am not!"

"Yeah, okay, I believe you." Maisy's accompanying look says, *Not*. "Your sandwich'll come up behind his. Go sit down and don't take any of his slick crap. You have a strong mind, my girl. Stone or William or whatever the hell he calls himself now likely still leads with his little head and zero brains."

Stone glances up at his name, narrowing in on Maisy suspiciously.

"Your order's coming right up, darling!" she trills at him

before her expression snaps back to flat and unimpressed as she turns to me. "You be careful with that one."

"I'm not doing anything," I defend.

"Uh-huh."

Eager to get out of Maisy's third-degree, I wind through the crowded tables to get to Stone. His trio of fans notice me coming up behind them, their faces falling with disappointment and envy as Stone extricates himself and greets me with a kiss on the cheek.

"Hey, sweetheart," he says.

I cut him with a look. "Don't be showing this town we're together."

Stone's unaffected by my warning. He gestures to the seat across from him. "Ladies, gentleman, it was a pleasure, but I must get on with my important, professional *meeting* with my mother's nurse."

I roll my eyes.

"It was so nice meeting you," one girl says.

The other adds, "You know where we're staying, so ... come over anytime, okay?"

Stone laughs, good-natured but full of *hell no, underage darlin'*. "I'll be seeing you around."

They drool over him a bit longer, then wave and depart, continuing to dart looks in our direction as they order more coffee.

"They're staying at Birdie's Bed and Breakfast," Stone says by way of explanation. "Came in from out of town. They heard I was here."

I lift my head. "Uh-oh."

"Yeah." Stone scrubs his face. "I knew it wouldn't be long until people investigated where I tucked tail, but my showdown in here didn't help. First come the fans, then it'll be the media."

"You'll be okay." I resist reaching over the table to cover his hand with my own. "Your reasons for being here have shifted. All that's important is spending time with your mom. The rest of them can suck it."

Stone responds with a tired, though uplifted, smile. "Thanks for that. But you don't have to do it, you know."

"Do what?"

"Make me feel better. I don't deserve that kind of treatment from you."

I lean back in my seat, my stare moving to the table. This was a long time coming. For months, years even, I'd imagined what it would be like to confront him and unleash all my pain. For Stone to feel a fraction of the hurricane going on inside me. But like everyone says, time lessens emotions. It doesn't get rid of them entirely, but the intensity of the pain, the vibrant red of my soul, is dulled now. Numb.

After a moment of nervous contemplation, I say, "Is that why you wanted to sit down with me? To talk about what happened?"

"You don't have to talk about anything you don't want to, but I'd like for you to hear me out."

I weave my fingers together, unable to raise my head.

Stone takes my silence as assent. "When you told me you were pregnant..."

I flinch.

Stone pauses. I'm not looking at him, but I feel him staring at me, assessing how far to take this.

"When you told me," he forges on, "it was like a gut punch. You saw me. I couldn't think straight for that entire day, because it was also the day they offered me my first real screen test."

"I remember." My voice is scratchy and not my own.

"Your news ripped through me." Stone's tone matches mine. "We'd always been so careful. I went through all the ways we could've slipped up, but nothing came back as the reason. And then I realized there didn't need to be one. It was happening, whether or not we were prepared. By that evening, I'd rationalized that I could go to LA, nail the audition, and get us enough money to raise this baby."

Baby. My hands clutch the edges of the table. I can't hear him say that word. My heart's empty enough as it is without an actual baby to hold, even all these years later. I turn the conversation back on him. I have to.

"You said all of this to me the day you left. Years separate that moment from now, but I can honestly say I can't handle hearing it again."

"No. Wait." Stone leans back, his corded arms tensing as he grips the table, too. "I'm not trying to make you relive my shitty, selfish self. What I'm saying is, I was a shitty, selfish kid who panicked. I freaked out, Noa. I rationalized my way to LA in order to make my real life a little less real."

"You saw me as a trap." My brows come down. My head still won't rise. "I was a trap to you, chaining you to this town, preventing you from reaching your dreams. Don't you get it? I've run through this all in my head a thousand times over. I know why you left, Stone. You don't have to ... I don't *want* you to keep—"

"You were supposed to come with me!"

Stone shouts it, drawing the attention of the other patrons.

I scan the crowded space through lowered brows, silently

pleading that everyone go back to their lunch and ignore Stone's outburst.

But that's impossible. Mr. Knox and his wife are by the window, frowning and murmuring their displeasure at the interruption. Stone's fan club titters at another table close by, one raising her phone to capture the uncomfortable moment until Stone's stern glance makes her friend smack the phone out of her hands.

High school kids on their lunch period eagerly feast on the rare moment of witnessing a celebrity without his professional smile. The order line houses Miss Amy, Luanne Smith, Priscilla DeWitt, Randy Berkins ... farmers, teachers, shop owners, residents of Falcon Haven who know me as well as they know each other.

My shoulders droop. I'm trembling in my chair.

And there's Maisy, standing by the magazine stand with Stone's handsome face taking up prime real estate on the front page, his arm wrapped around his ex as he poses for a movie premiere with **IS IT BACK ON??** as the headline.

I can't escape him. I can't run away from this moment. I was a fool to think I ever could.

I lift my head and stare straight into the eyes of the boy who broke my heart and the man who keeps on squeezing the pieces between his fists. "You don't get to say that word."

"What word?"

I tear past the open confusion on his face, snarling, "*Baby*. You have no idea what it was like for me to wake up one day, after weeks of feeling little flutters in my belly, of perfectly normal ultrasounds where I heard her heart, and feel nothing. Not a kick. Not a turn."

Stone grimaces. He rubs his face as if my words are hurtling toward him for a bull's-eye.

Good. I hope my aim is accurate.

"When the doctors told me I lost her, my hope ended. Do you understand that kind of world-ending hurt? Maybe you do now, because of your mother, but back then, I was seventeen. She was—that little baby was—" I choke on a sob that turns into a hiccup of sorrow.

It's hard to breathe.

"Hey." Stone's harsh, broken whisper reaches my ears.

I register his movement next to me, the way his arm slides around my back and pulls me in.

"Noa." My name is a hot exhale over my scalp. "I'm—I can't defend my actions. To know that I did this you..." He trails off, burying his face in my hair.

Then he jerks back, scraping his thumb under my eyes and scanning the Merc like he's suddenly conscious of where we are.

"I waited for you at the airport," he says, resuming his seat across from me, his expression more haggard than before. "I texted you. Called you. You didn't have to go through that alone. I wanted you *with* me in LA. You and the bab—*her*. I needed a fucking answer why you never showed, Noa, and I deserve one now."

I bristle. "Which answer would satisfy you the most? The one where I tell you that what you wanted was impossible, that we had no money, no plans, a baby in my belly, and no home to give her? Or how about the one where you expected me to leave my dreams behind and adopt yours, living under your shadow and raising our baby while you pursued your career?"

"That's not fair." Stone's expression darkens. He lowers his voice so I'm the only one who can hear. "We were in love. We were young, dumb, and fucking obsessed with each other, and I didn't want to leave you. I *didn't*."

"You couldn't have both," I say flatly. "You had to choose, and you did."

"Is that why you didn't show? Why you ghosted me at the last minute?"

"No."

I was ready and packed, willing to toss my carefully crafted future out the window and start a new and reckless one with Stone. Anything for him. I had fantasies of us living in one of those open apartments with a courtyard in the center, exactly like *Melrose Place*, where we'd meet our neighbors of a similar age and they'd become our *F.R.I.E.N.D.S.*, just like the show. Our baby would be celebrated. Loved. She'd grow up with both of us, whether or not Stone made it to fame.

Until my mother walked into my bedroom.

"No *what*?" Stone presses. "I was a dick who couldn't think beyond a one-way flight to LA, I can admit that, but I deserve more than a *no*."

I squeeze my eyes shut. "I'd packed my bags. I was ready to go with you."

Stone's silence is palpable. A thrum of tension seems to emit from us and into the atmosphere, sobering the lunch rush of the cafe. Conversation resumes, and attention is less on our table, but it's muted and concerned.

"I can't do this here," I manage to get out.

Stone pushes to his feet, helping me to mine by tucking his hand behind my arm. He leads me past the tables and the encouraging, "stay strong, hun," from Luanne Smith and "what does he *see* in some old people nurse?" from the fan girls.

I resist tucking my head into his chest because his wide shoulders and strong build are the perfect protection from the storm of judgment coming from either side.

I'm stronger than this. I've endured so much worse than

public opinion, yet I allow him to place his big hand on the small of my back and shadow me all the way out of the Merc.

He points at his car. I climb into the passenger seat, out of the nip of cold as wintry clouds encroach over the sun. Stone shuts my door and slides into the front seat, turning on the heat but remaining in park.

Stone's jaw juts out from grinding his teeth. He looks straight ahead. "You were going to come with me to LA?"

I nod, also staring through the windshield. Thanksgiving decorations are up, although the more enthusiastic shop owners have decided on Christmas lights and evergreen wreaths to decorate the street. Across from us, Beak's Hardware Store has flashing holiday lights, and a blow-up snowman battles for space against Feather's Flowers, who steadfastly commits to a turkey in a Pilgram hat, straw, and at least twenty different shades of pumpkins.

It's a years-long war of enthusiasm the owners are known for, and I risk a glance at Stone, wondering how ours has remained so passionate for so long, too. Shouldn't time have healed our wounds? Why do we have to rehash the pain to where I bleed?

"I had my duffel bag ready," I say. "Looking back, I can't believe I thought my hair dryer more important than a flash-light or any other form of utility that we'd probably need, considering we had nothing but the clothing on our backs."

Stone responds with a gruff laugh. It's hollow. "We were eighteen."

"Old enough to understand our lives would be forever rewritten." Sighing, I lean back, moving my focus to the side window where the Merc's mahogany golden glow cascades out the window. Comforting. Always warm.

"My mom caught me trying to sneak out."

"Oh." Stone draws out the word.

"With one leg out of my window. Complete cliché. I thought she'd found out about me, us, and the baby—the pregnancy. Her face sure looked like she did. I've never seen her so solemn, so straight-backed."

"Yeah, that would be a dead giveaway," Stone agrees. "Lynn was always the life of the party. Remembering everyone's names, chatting to everyone at all social events. She's so good at it, so genuine. I admired it every time I saw her. I modeled my red carpet behavior after her."

"You did?" A lightness lifts my heart, a feeling that hasn't occurred inside me in so long.

"Absolutely. Your mom's loved by everyone and I could only hope to emulate it."

"You did," I say quietly. "When she saw you on TV at the Golden Globes, she was proud of you for making it. She pointed out one interview in particular and how eloquent and charismatic you sounded. Nothing like the boy she'd shoo out the window with a hot curling iron."

Stone laughs. "I like to think I've grown out of escaping through windows."

I decide to absorb this moment of lightness, of feeling good, and use it to give me the courage to tell him the worst part. "She was diagnosed with stage four ovarian cancer. She didn't make it."

Stone whips toward me. "What? Are you kidding me?"

The parallels of our lives, first our fathers, now our mothers, swirl in his eyes. I never mention her death because it's too difficult to relive. She's the reason I went into palliative care. She's also the reason I want to do everything I can to soothe others' suffering—because I've seen the worst. I lived it through my mother's eyes.

"Noa. Sweetheart, I'm so sorry."

It means something coming from him. Stone's genuine sentiment brings tears to my eyes. "That night she came into my room, when I was going to sneak out to meet you, she told me she had cancer."

"Jesus."

Stone takes my hands into his lap and squeezes. I'm boneless. My heart is pumping blood into nothing but a sack of skin. Its beats amplify.

"Why didn't you tell me?" he asks.

"I couldn't. I could barely process what she was saying. And then it all came out. I told her about my pregnancy, sobbing that I needed her, that she couldn't go, she couldn't die, she couldn't leave me." I swipe my sleeve across my eyes. It comes back darkened and damp. "You say you're selfish and shitty. What does that make me?"

"A *kid*," he says vehemently. Stone palms my cheek, pulling me to face him. His thumb strokes my bottom lip. "A scared kid who found herself in deep shit and had no idea what to do. One who needed her mom."

"I did need her," I sob. "I needed her so much. I still do."

"I know." Stone shushes me, pulling me into his arms and keeping me there. I bury my face in his shoulder, inhaling the man he is while trying to remind myself of the boy he was.

"I thought of a thousand ways to tell you that night, but I was terrified of what your answer would be."

Stone's neck moves against my head as he tries to look down at me. "What do you mean?"

"If I told you about my mom and that I had to stay and that I..." I take a deep breath "... that I needed you to stay with me, you'd say no. You'd get on the plane, anyway."

Stone grips my shoulders and pulls us apart. He keeps his

hands where they are—gentle, firm—but his eyes boil. "You're serious? You think I would do that?"

"I know you would." To lessen the sting, I graze his stubbled cheek with my palm. "You did."

"I *didn't*. I didn't know what you were going through or what you needed from me, so I got on that goddamned plane. Had you given me a clue, I would've—"

"Would've what?"

Stone's expression washes out as my eyes fill with fresh tears.

"I texted you when I lost her," I say. "I called you and got no answer. I told you I'd…" An audible crack sounds in my ears as my heart breaks open wider. "But that was a few years after you left. What about when I sent news about the miscarriage? I never heard from you then, either."

Stone shakes his head, disbelieving. "You didn't talk to me for months. I wasn't just going to pick up the phone when I saw your number. I was mad at you, Noa. Pissed, because you'd left me at that airport without so much as a goodbye."

"And the voicemail I left telling you I lost our baby? What did you do after you heard it?" My voice grinds against my vocal cords, burning with the intensity of my words.

Stone's throat bobs. He doesn't look away, but the muscles around his eyes slacken like he's stunned with grief. "The first time I listened to it, I felt numb. The second time, the ache came. The third time, I cracked my phone wide open on the wall. The fourth time, I punched my computer. The fifth, sixth, seventh … I lost count. I lost myself. Went to booze. Drugs. Found solace in dark places where I didn't have to think of you crying and alone. I didn't deal with it well."

"I saw pictures of you partying and drinking, *laughing* while surrounded by girls. God, Stone, I hated you." I bare my teeth to repeat it. "*Hated* you and how you could move on with your life so easily. I don't care if you felt dumped at the airport. I deserved to hear your voice. I deserved *you* during the worst moment of my life when our baby girl died in my womb. And you ignored me."

Now, I want to punch him.

"You ignored me," I repeat, my voice a tremulous hiss.

"Noa—" He tries to stop my arms from reeling toward him, but then seems to give up, allowing the punches and slaps to hit his chest, shoulders, and face.

When I rise onto the seat, when I rear over him with tears and snot and a pounding, blood-filled face, he grabs my wrists and locks them against his chest.

"No!" I scream. "No, no, no! I lost her. I lost my mother. Lost you. Everyone left. *Fucking* everyone I cared about left me. And I had nothing. No one. You're a dick. An asshole. I hate you. I fucking *hate* you for doing this to me."

His eyes sheen over. He won't break my stare. My nose touches his as I turn feral in his grip, releasing the pent-up horror and agony that's laced my veins since the moment I was told my little girl didn't have a heartbeat anymore.

"I'm sorry," he rasps through my sobs. "I'm sorry, I'm so sorry, Noa, I'm sorry..."

I hear him, but I don't. I'm so wrapped up in the turmoil I've unleashed that I'm blind and deaf to reason.

"I just want it to stop," I sob. "The pain, it's..."

Stone pulls me into him, curling me against his chest, my knees bumping up against my chest as he cradles my body in his lap. He holds on so tight it hurts to breathe, but I have trouble breathing, anyway.

The weight of his arms, the strength of him as he rocks me back and forth, somehow grounds me enough to swallow the keening coming out of my throat and stem the flow of tears. Not completely, but enough that I can hear my stuttering breaths and notice the pounding of his heart against my arm.

"You're right," he says above my head, his voice barely above a decibel. "I wouldn't have stayed. I'd like to think I would've. The man I am now would knock that moron straight in the teeth for getting on that plane. But that kid ... all I could think of was finding a better life. When you didn't show, it hurt my pride pretty bad. I convinced myself you didn't think I was good enough. It never occurred to me you'd be going through something worse than figuring out how to be eighteen and a parent. I know it sounds so pathetic to say that to you now. And I promise to do better. I promise not to leave." He moves until his lips are against my hair. "I promise to stay this time, sweetheart."

I close my eyes against the pain of his vow, pulling my lips in to stop myself from uttering the truth.

I don't believe you.

Twenty-Two

NOA

Mrs. Stalinski asks me to make Thanksgiving dinner this year.

We're whispering in the kitchen so we don't wake Stone, who's slumbering in the next room. I'd crept down the stairs and noticed enlarged lumps on the pull-out couch. It's a twin fold out, yet Stone encompasses it like it's a toddler's mattress.

Tufts of his chestnut hair stick out from under the bedding, but otherwise, he's buried under the covers like a troll hiding under his bridge until an unsuspecting goat comes along.

He went hard last night. After our painful lunchtime confessions, he dropped me off at my car, then disappeared. Stone didn't come home that evening for dinner, nor did I find him sleeping on the pull-out when I came down for a 2 am glass of water. Thoughts turning over in my head and crowding in on one another kept me awake, memories, flashbacks, and wishes all fighting for space. I wonder if Stone was experiencing the same.

From the smell coming off the couch, I assume he found solace at the bottom of a bottle.

I'm glad Stone made it home. As much as I convince myself our lives don't have to intersect anymore, I worry about him. I care. And if I have to come down the stairs and smell a brewery while putting together a quick egg scramble, then I'll take it.

Stone's not sleeping it off somewhere else. He didn't find another woman. He didn't give anyone an excuse to press "upload" on their phones by being an idiot last night.

For all of those things, I'm thankful.

"So what do you think? Can you cook up a turkey for, say, six or seven people?" Mrs. Stalinski asks. She gestures for a refill on her coffee.

"Why seven?" I lift the carafe of hot coffee and pour. "Who's coming?"

"Well, I figure Maisy, Carly, and Mae, and Stone, of course, you, me, and I'm thinking of inviting Rome since he's all alone out on that ranch of his, and Stone said something about his agent stopping by next weekend."

"Next weekend?" My voice becomes high-pitched. "Oh my God, Thanksgiving is next weekend! I totally forgot."

Mrs. Stalinski reaches over the breakfast counter and pats my hand. "You've been busy."

I subtly frown at her, wondering exactly what she means by that. Mrs. Stalinski maintains her mysterious air as she leans back without a clue in her expression. It's not like Stone to open up and let her in on what we talked about yesterday or how we've christened this counter, but these are different times, and I know when my mother was at this point in her diagnosis, I told her everything I could and absorbed everything she had to tell me.

Then again, I think while staring through the archway at a comatose Stone, *denial is a wonderful choice, too.*

"Well?" Mrs. Stalinski asks, blinking like a patient owl.

"Um, can I think about it?"

"No."

"Oh." I pull the frying pan off the stove, buttery eggs sizzling nicely. "Then I guess I'm a yes."

"I knew you would be!" Mrs. Stalinski claps. "We'll do a traditional turkey fare and I'll help in any way I can. Maybe you can also prepare a dish from your new class."

"I don't know. I've only had one class with Chef Toussaint and he's, well, not exactly keeping up with the holidays. This week we're doing Choucroute Garnie à l'Alsacienne."

Mrs. Stalinski cocks her head. "What now?"

"Braised sauerkraut with mixed meat and sausages."

"Hmm. Not exactly Thanksgiving friendly, is it?"

I laugh. "No, but I'll come up with something fun to make. I'll enjoy looking through my old cookbooks."

"That would be wonderful. Surprise us. This will be fun."

Day brightened, Mrs. Stalinski slides off her stool. "Keep that warm for me, will you? I feel like a bike ride with my son."

"Is that a good idea?" I spin with her as she passes me. "It's getting pretty cold out."

"We go at a brisk pace. Don't worry." She flaps her hand behind her, waving me off, then approaches her son.

Hands on her hips, she studies him for a moment, then pulls the pillow out from under his head and whacks him with it.

Stone's groan rumbles through the entire house. He shifts,

then belly-flops back into position, face-planting into the mattress.

"This requires a more organized attack," Mrs. Stalinski muses. "Noa, grab an ice bucket."

"A—what?"

"You heard me. Fill it to the brim. That fancy sub-zero fridge he bought me should have more than enough to spare."

A surprised giggle escapes. I clap my hand over my mouth, horrified.

Mrs. Stalinski straightens, then meets my eye with a softened gaze. "It's okay to find joy in this house, dear. I still do."

I tentatively smile in response.

"Now, go get that bucket. Add some water in it, too."

I do as she says, filling one of the mop buckets. It's too heavy for Mrs. Stalinski to lift, which I'm sure she knew right from the beginning, so I'm tasked with tossing it onto Stone's prone, unsuspecting form.

A little part of me is excited about doing it.

Another is terrified.

Most of me is convinced this was a long time coming.

We left last night without a punctuation mark. It gave me the chance to voice what had haunted me all these years, yet I remain unsure where we stand. Scratch that—where we should go after a conversation like that. Do we continue like nothing has changed? Do we discuss it further?

One priority stays the same: Mrs. Stalinski comes first. So if she wants to throw ice water all over her hungover grown-up son, who am I to stop it?

"Okay, one, two..." Mrs. Stalinski watches me approach the foot of the bed. "THREE!"

Without hesitating, I toss the contents onto the bed, screeching as I do it. Mrs. Stalinski cackles beside me.

Stone roars, popping upright like an explosion has gone off. A streak of white and caramel fur flies out from the covers with a distinctly upset yowl. Little did we know Moo had bunked against the delightful warmth of Stone's body last night.

"Sorry, Moo-boo!" I call after him as he skitters around the corner.

Cold water drips off Stone's hair and face, his muscles undulating and straining with the shocking change in temperature. His nipples are small, hard, and directed right at me.

Lust builds inside me at the sight of him, angry, cursing, and half-naked. He stumbles out of bed, the slits of his eyes targeting first his mother, then me.

Mrs. Stalinski, damn her, is out of the attack zone, beetling back to the kitchen as soon as he tossed back his covers.

That leaves me, laugh-screaming and blubbering as I hold my hands up and tell him it wasn't me.

Stone's masculine presence freezes the hair on my arms as he steps close, studies me with a cranky scowl, then bends down to pick up the discarded bucket and plops it over my head before heading to the powder room and slamming the door.

"Good morning, son!" I hear Mrs. Stalinski trill from the safety of the breakfast bar.

I pull the bucket off my head, sputtering through a small smile.

TOO SOON, it's time for Chef Toussaint's class. I peel off my scrubs, lavender today, and dress in black denim and a black cotton T-shirt. I'd noted how the chef dressed under his coat and how the other couple, Danny and Ray, who I refuse to see as my competition but kind of do anyway, dressed in dark clothing, too.

It's been so long since I've thought about proper dress code in the kitchen, or prep, or knife cuts. It's coming back to me slowly. But it *is* returning.

I look forward to Saint's master class, regardless of how mean and picky he is. He's one of the most-watched chefs under thirty. We're lucky enough to have him in town, however he came to be here. Stone may not feel the same way, but I'm confident he'll behave this evening.

Well ... more like hopeful.

Or desperate.

I'm pleasantly surprised to find him waiting at the bottom of the stairs, dressed in jeans in a white cashmere sweater that hugs his muscles in all the right ways. I should recommend he dress in clothing less likely to stain, too, except I'm too distracted by how handsome this man is even while lingering by a staircase. I bet if I brushed up against him, he'd be as soft as Moo.

Eager to dissipate that feeling, I search around for Moo, noticing him curled up on the couch Stone folded back into place earlier. I make a dash for him without thinking, picking him up and cuddling his softness and hiding my blush in his fur.

Stone has always been handsome—gorgeous, actually. It's almost inhumane how he can be so effectively jarring, even when I'm supposed to dislike him or at the very least conclude we're not meant to be.

Moo squirms, licks my hand with his scratchy tongue, then uses his hind legs to push off my chest.

"Ah ... shit," I mutter, glancing down.

"Yup, you've definitely put yourself in a hairy situation," Stone observes.

I pull at my shirt and try to brush off the long, white hair.

"Stupid," I mumble, hating that Stone is such a distraction. I don't voice that part, but boy, am I disappointed in myself for not being immune to him by now.

"Lucky for you I have lint rollers in every bag I pack." Stone lifts a duffel from behind the couch and pulls out a black-handled roller. "I must be in pristine condition at all times. A requirement of my agent's."

He says it offhand, though I notice the downturn of his lips as he says it.

"It must be difficult to have to always be perfect," I say as he approaches me.

Stone peels off the sticker so I have a fresh one. "It was tough at first. I just wanted to dress in my beat-up jeans and faded shirts. Then the red carpets happened, Aaron hired a stylist, press junkets came along, and the rest is history, I guess."

Stone lifts the roller and glides it across the V of my shirt. I lift my face to his, ready to tell him I can do it, but I'm stopped by ... him.

He's not dangerous this close. He's lethal.

Stone's tanned from all the ranch work he's doing with Rome. From the worn cowboy hat I'm always picking up from the arm of the couch and hanging on the coatrack, he's using it often, but it can't compete with cloudless fall skies allowing the sun to beam down on him.

Even the sun has him in a spotlight, I muse as I trace his face with my eyes. His scruff is lighter than his hair, rough and auburn-streaked. His laugh lines are more pronounced by the permanent layer of grit he can never seem to wash off completely. Stone angles his head, focusing on the direction of the roller, and the carved structure of his face hits the overhead lights with breathtaking accuracy.

His clear eyes dart to mine, and there they stay as the roller moves over my breast. When he hits the peak of my nipple, Stone slows his movements, his brows furrowing in silent question.

My lips part. My eyes stay on his. When his free hand comes up and cups my other breast and he pulls me closer, my breath hitches.

Our lips are an inch apart. Stone's head is at the perfect angle to seal his on mine. The roller moves, back and forth, against my breast as he massages the other, the varying sensations becoming too much.

I lift my hand to slap the roller out of his, grab the back of his neck, and kiss him until I can't breathe, until we're interrupted.

"You two ready to go? You'll be late if you don't hustle."

Mrs. Stalinski hasn't wandered all the way around the corner, giving us enough time to break apart and for Stone to shove the roller in my hand.

Jesus, who knew such a benign tool could be so stimulating.

I busy myself removing the rest of the hair since Stone did such a poor job by becoming so easily distracted by my breasts. Stone clears his throat.

"Just about ready, Ma. Noa decided to say bye to her cat by hugging him until he porcupined her with hair."

Mrs. Stalinski nods her head with a smile as if she believes him, though when she gets to me, her eyes have a knowledgeable slant, like she knows what we were getting close to doing.

"Well, get on, then. Moo and I will entertain ourselves with a movie."

"You'll be all right?" I ask her, handing the roller to Stone, who deposits it in his bag.

"I'll be fine," Mrs. Stalinski assures. "I noticed the pills you left me if I need them and the plate of dinner I can warm up when I'm hungry. I've also noted the fresh bath salts on the side of my tub and a wonderful new candle and headrest to go along with it." She pats my cheek as she passes me and makes herself comfortable on the couch. "I am properly taken care of, my dear. You two go have fun."

"If you're sure," I say to her, "because I'm here for you."

Stone pauses in palming his keys from the sidetable. The glance he sends my way is both sweet and uncomfortable. It's the type of loving gaze he used to give me during our post-coital glow, rested and content in each other's arms. It communicates his gratitude for how I'm putting his mother first, but I shift on my feet, the similarities between our past innocence and our current grief hard to swallow.

"If we're not back by curfew, Ma, don't wait up for us," Stone jokes.

"I'll try not to look at my watch every hour," she retorts. "Stay out of trouble, my darlings."

We say our goodbyes and take Stone's car into town. He's not as lucky this time around and has to park around the block, but the short walk to the restaurant is nice and chilled.

The frosted air against my cheeks brings a smile to my face and I bite back a chuckle.

"What's so funny?" Stone asks beside me.

"Oh, just remembering that one time your mother woke you up by tossing ice cubes in your face."

"Ice *cubes*? More like you two half-drowned me in a reverse Polar Plunge."

That sends me into a fit of laughter. He lightly punches my

shoulder to stop me. "Glad you enjoyed seeing me shrivel up so much, sweetheart."

"It wasn't my idea, I swear. But I did kind of enjoy it."

"I bet," he says, grinning while he shakes his head. "I hope you're ready for payback."

"Excuse me?"

"Oh yeah. I have plans for you."

"Don't you dare."

"You won't see it coming."

We keep going back and forth, joking and keeping it light-hearted, and I have to admit, it's way more preferable than the alternate version of us.

It's how we are when we walk into Chef Toussaint's kitchen, where he waits for us with folded arms and a frown.

"The last ones here again," he says.

That promptly shuts me up. I hurry to our table, noting that we are one of three couples in the room. The younger, college-aged couple aren't here.

"Is it just the three of us, then?" I ask while tying my apron.

Saint responds with a curt nod. "Claire and Graham have decided not to continue."

"I suppose this wasn't their idea of a fun date night," Stone mutters beside me.

I elbow him to shut him up.

Saint stands in the middle of the kitchen, demanding our attention. "Today, I'll begin with a demonstration of how to create Choucroute Garnie à l'Alsacienne. This is a true winter meal that can feed your family on the chilliest of days and keep their stomachs warm. After that, we'll dive into French desserts. Specifically, crème brûlée. American Thanksgiving is next weekend and I consider it my civic duty to equip you with a true delicacy rather than that abomination you call pumpkin pie."

"I fucking love pumpkin pie," Stone obstinately states. He mirrors Saint's folded arm stance while saying it.

Saint either doesn't hear him or chooses not to care. He stalks to his chef's station and prepares ingredients, talking over his chopping as he explains our steps.

Danny and Rad jump into action, cooking along with Saint and following him in real time. Stone notices them, too, and moves to catch up, but I lay a hand on his arm, stalling.

I want to watch everything first, take notes, and then begin. I've been practicing the chef's dishes every night when Stone and Mrs. Stalinski go to bed, and I've noticed I do better with all the steps laid out before me rather than jumping into it and learning as I go. It's a cautious gene, one I don't believe I inherited from Mom and probably came from my father, who I never met. Because of that, I've been nurturing it with pride. It's a special rarity when I notice similarities between my late father and myself.

Stone sees me pull out the notepad from my apron and relaxes, letting me take the lead.

When Saint finishes his instructions, I start. With renewed focus, it's easy to delegate to Stone and organize our pantry items, produce, and meat. Stone doesn't question what I say, following my requests smoothly. Soon, we're moving in sync, passing each other what we need and moving at a nice clip.

"Behind," he says as he walks around my back with a hot pan.

I meet his eye and smile, impressed at how quickly he's picking up the lingo.

"Never played a chef before," he says while he sautées onions in goose fat. "Now I kind of want to."

I snort, reaching around him to add wine to his pan. "Yes, you'd get along really well with the kitchen staff."

"You don't think so?" He peeks at me from the side and winks. "I'm as charming as they come, sweetheart."

"When you want to be."

Stone considers this. "True."

Saint walks by, critiquing our preparations. "You're not there yet, Noa. Before you finish, I recommend you visit Danny and Rad's table. They've gently poached their sausages, whereas you have thrown yours directly into the pot where they will burst from the heat."

"Don't blame her," Stone interjects. "That was all me."

Saint regards him with a flat gaze. "I consider your plates as a team, so your mistakes are hers and vice versa. Perhaps you should keep that in mind the next time you watch your teammate take down copious notes while you simply stand there watching everyone else attempt to learn."

Stone sneers. I lay a hand on his arm hoping to cut off his retort.

"I told him to wait while I took down notes," I defend, to my surprise. "It's not Stone's fault."

Saint didn't expect my defense, either. His brows jump. He takes a moment to study the two of us. "While it's admirable that you protect each other, that's not what you're here for, is it? I'd prefer not to take part in whatever healing journey you two are on..." Saint's stare slides to the stockpot on the burner "... as my three-year-old daughter wouldn't eat those potatoes even if her healing journey would take her to Disney world."

Stone idly follows Saint's stare, then jumps to attention. "Shit!"

I slide out of the way as Stone struggles with the over-boiling pot, book-ending his curse with one of my own.

"Overcooked, mushy, and tasteless, I would venture to guess," Saint muses before heading to the next table, where Mr. and Dr. Stanton wait patiently.

Chest tight from another round of the chef's criticisms, I devote myself to serious study for the rest of the evening. I don't register Stone's actions until he asks me for a spare pen.

"Sorry," I say. "I only brought one. I didn't think you'd want to write anything down."

"Fair enough." Unaffected, he strolls over to the Stanton's station and asks for an extra pen, which Dr. Stanton is delighted to give him.

It's his way, but I'm always amazed when I see people so easily sidle up and make conversation with those they don't really know. Stone has a talent I'll never possess, an ability to get anyone on his side, which I suppose is why so many have let him get away with so much.

When he says something that makes both Stantons laugh, I have to force myself back to the task at hand, otherwise I'd just keep staring at him.

I'm busy redoing the potatoes when Stone returns.

"I figure the Stantons are safe," he says to me. He places a wad of bar napkins on the table in front of him. "They mean well. It's Danny and Rad we have to look out for."

I risk a look at him, fighting a grin. "You felt it, too?"

"Hell yeah, I felt it. They're out for blood and they're not gonna get it, because we'll win first place. That fucker over there wants me to take this seriously?" Stone notches his chin to include Saint, who is busy discussing brûlée techniques with Rad, "then I'll fucking give it to him. I'll write a damned novel by the end of this session."

Stone poises his pen above the napkin stack and starts copying the notes from my notepad.

I can't help it. I laugh. "I could've ripped you out a piece of paper to write on."

"Nuh-uh. I'm coming from the bottom and I plan on working my way up. You with me?"

"You know I am."

Stone gestures to the boiling potatoes. "Then let's go."

And that's how my classes with Stone suddenly became enjoyable.

Twenty-Three

STONE

TIME MOVES WAY TOO FAST.

One minute I'm at the top of my game and then I'm not. One month of good behavior and I'm yesterday's news. *Cascade's* director will give me my role back. I should be thrilled, and I am, at least for my career. *Cascade* will be all that it promises and is the most Oscar-worthy role I've ever taken on.

But.

My mother isn't getting better. The results of her latest PET scan came back, and she's worse than ever. The cancer's spread. If I wasn't convinced she was on the placebo before, I am now, and by the look on Noa's face when Ma told us her results, she agrees.

Yet, Ma presses forward, demanding our Thanksgiving feast take place despite the bad news and that we enjoy each other as friends and family.

I kept the information of *Cascade's* renewal to myself,

mulling it over for over a week, then determined to put it aside as the holiday approaches. Aaron's convinced my lack of answer will kill my career, but that's him in a nutshell. Panicky, bull-headed, annoying, and brilliant. This is partially why he's headed to Falcon Haven, uncaring of Thanksgiving since he has no family of his own and is too busy for friendship.

Another reason I'm delaying the decision to go to Madrid to film is *her*. The girl standing across from me right now, humming as she writes the final notes to her holiday food plan, bent over the counter with her ass waggling side to side, beckoning me to part her and slide my dick in.

The thing about medical scrubs is that elastic waist. So easy to slide down her hips and expose her, so tempting to wrap her ponytail around my wrist, put my other hand on the small of her back, and ride her.

Prudish thoughts aside (grin), there's more to Noa than her looks and allure. She's the sweet girl I remember, but now with a little ginger snap thrown in. Spicy and hot on the throat. Her confession that she'd given up everything to take care of her mother and then fell into the position of caregiver so others wouldn't have to go through what she did rocked me more than I expected.

And if she thinks I don't know how she stays up every night to refine the chef's dishes, she has it wrong. I spend those nights with my arms folded behind my head, listening to her quiet patters and gentle humming as she goes, noises I'm coming to rely upon to feel comfortable and drift off to sleep.

I may not be the boy who left Falcon Haven without a second glance anymore, but even now, with the wisdom I've accrued, I still wouldn't give up my dream the way she did.

If it were my mother diagnosed with cancer when I was eighteen with Hollywood beckoning, would I have stayed? I'd like to think so. I love my mother more than life. But I wonder, and I'm relieved, that I never had to make that kind of decision.

Where Noa is selfless, I am selfish. Where she is polite, I'm brash. And where she is devoted, I'm paying penance for my bad actions.

Our opposites are glaringly present, yet I can't look away despite the warning so bright it's blinding.

Noa, sweetheart, what am I going to do with you? With us?

She lost our baby, and I left her to deal with it alone. I never contacted her because I thought she hated me and wanted nothing more to do with me. I assumed her mother and the entire town supported her through the crisis. Christ, we were so young. I figured she'd pick herself up and move to Paris like she'd planned before I begged her to follow me instead.

I didn't know.

I didn't fucking know.

But is that enough of an excuse?

Watching her tuck an errant strand of dark hair behind her ear as she completes her planned feast for my mother makes me think it isn't.

I could stare at her all day. I clear my throat to shake myself out of it. "What have you decided on?"

"Hmm?" Noa looks up, her eyes glazed over with inward focus.

A strand of hair she tried to tuck away is stuck in her lip gloss. Christ, how badly I want to touch her cheek and brush it aside.

"Your special side dish," I say instead. "Ma said something about you wanting to cook one of your famous recipes."

Her gorgeous eyes become more gorgeous as enthusiasm trickles in. "Actually, I'd love your opinion on it."

"Really?" I wonder if my eyes are doing the same.

"Yeah." She laughs, pushing off the counter and straightening. "You've been my sous chef for a few weeks and in the trenches with me. I'd say you're entitled to an opinion."

Her flattery tightens my chest more than scoring the sexiest man alive title ever did—and I was fucking proud of that award.

I straighten my grin so as not to appear too eager. "Okay. Shoot."

"I'm wanting to use some skills and techniques we've learned from Chef Toussaint."

I stifle a sneer and turn it into a resigned twist of my lips instead. "Good plan."

"What do you think about creamed leeks and asparagus in a puff pastry for the appetizer and a cranberry crème brûlée for dessert?"

That sounds fucking delicious, but I stare at her suspiciously. "Is pumpkin pie also on the menu?"

This time, her tinkling laughter lifts the surrounding air, if that's even possible. But it has to be, because the hairs on my arms stand up and there's a tangible shift of the atmosphere against my ears.

It's at this moment I realize how heavy the environment is in Ma's home, filled with negative anticipation, dread, cautious hope. None of it feels like Noa's unhindered laughter. Nothing sounds like her, either.

"I'd never deny you America's dessert," she says.

"Good." My approval comes out tight with restrained emotion as I wrestle with the reality of our relationship. "It's the one holiday where I get to cheat on my nutrition plan."

"What do you normally do for Thanksgiving?" She cocks her head. "You haven't celebrated it in Falcon Haven for a long time."

Noa doesn't ask it with judgment. She's curious, which, after our heartfelt gushing of pain in the car, she's entitled to ask.

"Usually, I'm on location somewhere, and craft services would treat us to a spread between filming. Thanksgiving isn't really celebrated in countries other than North America, and a lot of our production team isn't American, so ... sometimes nothing happened. Or when I was in LA, I had Ma join me. I'd take her to a fancy restaurant that had a Thanksgiving meal as their special." I feel the need to add, "I'm talking five-star special, like maple squash gratin and lamb chops sizzled in garlic ..."

I shut my mouth because I'm embarrassingly close to trying to impress her.

She smiles. "Sounds delicious."

"It was." I jerk upright. "It won't compare to what you cook, though."

Noa laughs again. "Relax, Blue Flood. I appreciate the flattery."

I ask through a smile, "You've seen my movies, huh?"

"What? No." Noa busies herself collecting her pens and notebook and clutching them to her chest. "But I'm not your target audience."

"You damn sure are." My statement comes out husky with lust.

Noa fidgets, a light blush creeping along her cheeks.

All I want to do is make it bloom.

She says, "Falcon Haven goes nuts when your movie releases. It's practically a holiday. Signs everywhere, lines around the block to see it in our theater." She peers closer at me. "You realize how much this town supports you, right?"

"Yeah, sure." I stand from my spot at the dinner table

nobody ever eats at. We're always crowded around the breakfast counter, elbows knocking into each other.

She notices. "What's wrong?"

I want to jump you and make you smell like the ingredients you've laid out as I grind you into them. "Nothing. You need help shopping for this stuff?"

"Stone. You can talk to me." Her gaze slides away and then comes back. "Especially after I unloaded on you. I admit, it felt good to do it."

"I bet." I give a sad smile, then scrub my face with one hand, reminding myself Ma is awake in the other room. The desperate battle makes it all too easy to be honest with her about personal stuff.

"That's what makes it so hard sometimes, all the love," I say. "Like I'm on a pedestal and nothing can get to me. It's hard to explain, and I may sound like an ass saying it but, once you reach a certain level of success, all that support can turn into determination to knock you down. And I balance that love/hate relationship with the public every day."

A line forms between Noa's brows. "I never thought about it like that. The pressure you must be under. You're always so carefree and confident."

"I'm a great actor." My grin widens, but there's no energy behind it.

Noa pulls her lips in, regarding me—differently. My jaw works under her study, my tongue ready to peel off the top of my mouth and ask her what she's thinking. If she has any positive emotion left for me at all. If, without my mother keeping her here, she'd give me the time of day.

I stroll around the counter and pluck the list out of her hands. "Let's get these groceries before the Merc sells out."

Thankfully, Noa allows the subject change. "You really are

rusty on the holiday. We'd be in big trouble if we were shopping for all this now. I pre-ordered the groceries a week and a half ago. Our bags should be ready in an hour."

"Of course you did."

Noa follows me out the door.

I know this because I look back at her to make sure.

AFTER WE PICK up the groceries and dump them in the kitchen, Noa gets to work. Thanksgiving is tomorrow, and according to her, we can make most of these recipes ahead. I'm not one to argue and fall into her sidekick role like I was always meant to be there, chopping and stirring and station cleaning.

During the arduous prep, I make a mental note to thank Roderick, the actor who plays Blue Flood's sidekick Splash Boy. Who knew they had to work so damned hard?

Ma joins within the hour, perching on the stool and observing Noa's and my dance with food.

At one point, I lift the twenty-pound turkey and make it do a little jig. Ma laughs out loud while Noa does her usual swat against my arm to stop me from damaging the wings.

Somebody breaks out a bottle of white wine and we all pour a glass, Ma's being the heaviest. She side-eyes anyone who tries to tell her otherwise, reminding us that during this holiday, she will drink and dine all she damn wants.

I sneak glances at her more than once, enjoying her alertness and constant questioning of Noa's culinary decisions. Our bike rides are way more enjoyable than I thought, and I look forward to them every morning. It doesn't matter that I'm at Rome's ranch before dawn, hauling hay and mucking stalls.

When I return home in the morning, I turn right around and take my mother for a ride around the block.

She was slower this morning. We made it maybe one block before she asked to turn around, but I put that worry out of my mind as she sips on her wine and asks questions about Noa's leek preparation instead.

Noa gives one last look-see at my plastic wrapping skills to cover our prepped plates and put them in the fridge, then says, "Okay! We're done."

"Yeah?" I can't keep the excitement out of my voice. "Can I go watch sports now?"

"Are you calling out the gender differences during Thanksgiving preparation, my poor, unsuspecting son?" Ma's eyes turn into slits.

"Hell, no," I say, and mean it. "I just honestly want to kick back and watch ESPN updates on the NFL triple-header tomorrow, and I'd love for you ladies to join me."

Ma smiles over the rim of her glass. "Good boy."

"Uh-huh," I say, fully aware of the hell-storm I'd dodged and hold out my elbows for my two women.

Noa gives an amused shake of her head and takes my arm with Ma on the other side. Noa's on her second glass, her cheeks flushed with the ruby glow of fermented grapes and her lips loose and easy in the corners.

It occurs to me I haven't seen her this relaxed since returning to Falcon Haven. She's always either tending to Ma or checking on her other patients, constantly in professional mode. The holidays must mean a lot to her for these needed days off, and I want to kick myself for not noticing it earlier.

Ma leans into my side, redirecting my thoughts, and I glance down at her with concern. The energy it took to stay with us all afternoon seeps out of her, and she sags against the sofa chair as I gently help her into it.

Noa notices at the same time I do. "I'll get a patch for her."

"No." I hold out a hand to stop her, observing how fast Noa's expression switched from tranquil to anxious. She's snapping into nurse mode on Thanksgiving Eve, and I won't have it. "Let me do it. I know where everything is."

After a second of consideration where she holds my stare, Noa gives a single nod and steps aside to let me pass.

While pulling the drugs out of the cabinet, I see Noa out of the corner of my eye pull a throw blanket from the couch and lay it around Ma's legs.

"Don't you dare tell me to go upstairs to bed." I hear Ma warn. "My butt is staying in this chair to watch sportsball."

"I wouldn't dream of it," Noa says. She pats Ma's hand and sits on one side of the couch.

One side of my mouth tilts up after witnessing that gesture. Looks like Noa's learned from the best.

I head into the living room with a patch in hand. I've watched Noa do it enough times to ask Ma to lean forward so I can put it on her back. She does without protest, meaning she must really be hurting.

My eyes go hot. The surrounding skin tightens painfully. But I remain silent as I help my mother, and Noa watches me with gentle empathy.

All at once, it's too much. Noa's losses, my impending heart amputation, Ma's struggle. I bite the side of my cheek to stop the overflow and go to the other side of the couch, flicking on the TV to ESPN and listening mindlessly to talking heads discuss tomorrow's roster.

It doesn't take long for Ma to fall asleep, her soft snores

reaching my ears seconds before Noa stands and gestures for us to help her to bed.

I wave her off, whispering something to the tune of, "I got it. Pour another glass, and I'll be right back." My heart wrenches at the sight of my mother, her tiny body disappearing into the sofa cushions.

The reality of my chest twisting every time I look at my mother from now on is like a sucker punch. I attempt to think back to all the times I regarded her with joy, all those moments I took advantage of my healthy, devoted mother as a snot-nosed toddler, bratty kid, then asshole teenager.

And now, an absent son.

It takes one slow, deep breath, and then another, before I'm able to go to my mother and cradle her to my chest. She murmurs nonsensically through her snores before going slack in my arms.

If Noa notices my difficulty, she has the decency—or kindness—to say nothing as I turn in the center of the living room with wet eyes and trembling limbs.

If anyone understands, it's her.

I should talk to Noa. Any therapist would be on board with sharing my grief with someone who truly understands this kind of suffering.

But I can't. I don't know how.

I lay Ma down in her bed, covering her from chin to toe and shutting the door softly behind me.

When I reach the living room, Noa's poured us two fresh glasses.

"Red this time," I observe since I can't think of anything else to say.

She responds gamely. "A good one, too. I had Maisy put a couple of bottles aside for us because it goes so well with

Thanksgiving spices, but I thought we deserved a glass tonight."

"Not gonna argue with that."

The couch sags with my weight. I grab the wineglass and down half of it.

The warmth hits my throat, the peppery remnants coating my tongue and the heavy tannin sucking up the rest of my saliva.

In my days of shmoozing directors and impressing studio execs, I've become a good study with wine. Noa's right. I finish it in two gulps.

"Fucking delicious," I mutter, swiping at my lips, then slamming the wineglass down.

"Hey," Noa says softly. She shifts closer, lifting her hand and thumbing a droplet from the corner of my mouth.

I stiffen under her touch. "I wouldn't do that if I were you."

Her thumb lifts off my skin. Her hand hesitates in the air.

I whirl, catching her wrist and tunneling my vision until all I can see is the teary-eyed warmth of her gaze.

"It's not because I don't want you to touch me," I rasp out. "But because I do. Deeply. Badly. Uncontrollably."

Noa allows my grip to stay, though it must be painful with how tight I've wrapped my fingers around her delicate bones.

"I won't tell you it'll be all right," she says softly, holding my gaze. "It's only going to get worse. And it hurts, and time will help, but you'll never be the same. You'll have to take pleasure in the small things to get your mind off it, to make you remember what the world's like when it's good."

"You're no small thing, Noa."

Her mouth works, her thoughts needing to catch up with

my words. Then she leans forward. "If you need me right now, I'm here."

My teeth grind together. "Are you sure about that?"

The question comes out of me with considerable warning, rough and husky.

She gives a slow nod, her stare unmoving. "I wish I had someone back then. I wish I could forget."

My free hand finds her jawline, then her cheek. My thumb pulls against her skin until her plump lips stretch, then bounce back.

She's beautiful. Pristine. Open and loyal.

"I don't know what I've done to deserve this moment," I say tightly, "But I'm fucking taking it."

The moment her lips part, I grab the back of her head and yank her against me.

Twenty-Four

NOA

Stone's tongue plunges into my mouth, almost reaching the back of my throat as he tilts my head to get the best angle to devour me.

I let him.

He smells like fresh cotton and cologne. He tastes like expensive wine and salted memories. Without breaking our kiss, I climb on top of him, my hands digging into his hair the same way he tangles his fingers in mine.

I grind into him, feeling his rigid stiffness through his jeans. We rub ourselves up on each other, almost viciously, our teeth coming out, too, nipping, biting. Possessing.

In a single maneuver, Stone stands, gripping my ass to keep me where I am. He spins as if to drop me onto the couch so he can crawl on top, but I pull away, laying a finger on his mouth, wet and shiny with my thirst.

"Take me to bed, Stone."

Somehow, his brows lift over his darkened, lust-filled eyes.

"You deserve a real bed," I continue, my lips brushing against my knuckles.

"Only if you're in it," he says.

Stone stalks to the stairs while I cling to him. He growls and claims my lips, even as he takes the stairs.

Stone's never been clumsy. He shows that off as he smoothly takes the stairs with his tongue tangling with mine. We round the banister and make it to the guest bedroom without a single stumble, and Stone kicks the door closed with his heel before heading to the bed.

"Wait," I say breathlessly, my lips tingling from his scruff. They're swelling, and all I want is more of him.

Sliding down his toned body, I back up enough to help him pull off his shirt and unbuckle his belt. After unbuttoning and unzipping his jeans, his cock springs free, pulsing and hot in my hand.

"I want to take care of you," I say, unable to take my eyes off the piece of him throbbing in my grip.

Stone's answer is to groan while his head falls back. "I can't say no to you, sweetheart, not in this position."

Smiling, I push at his chest until he falls back on the bed, naked and divine.

I get down on my knees between his legs and take him in my mouth.

Stone's salty pre-cum hits my tastebuds, and I purr with satisfaction. The noise makes Stone buck, shoving his dick deeper in my throat, but I relax my muscles, opening for him.

If I remember right, Stone loved a good deep throat, and though it's been a while since I've done that for a man, my body remembers what to do. Tipping forward, I lower my head until my chin hits his ball sack.

Stone gives a muffled curse, wriggling and straining with the rapture he must feel from being so fully consumed by my mouth, my tongue grinding against his underside, and my teeth grazing across his delicate skin.

His balls tighten with an impending burst of cum. I massage them while bobbing my head, twisting my mouth, then going down on him again, the movements sending him into a frenzy.

"God—*fuck*—Noa—stop. If you want me to fuck you, you gotta st—" His warning is cut off by a tight moan as he explodes in my mouth. The taste overflows, like salty seawater and *him*. There's so much of it I can't swallow quick enough, and it dribbles from my lips.

Leaning back, I reach up to wipe it with my sleeve. Stone stops me by grabbing my wrist.

"Oh no, you don't," he says, his pecs and abs straining as he moves into a half sit-up to grab me. "That's my mark, and it's staying on you until I say you can remove it, and let me tell you, sweetheart, it looks too fucking good on you to ever leave your lips."

I glide my tongue over my lower lip, collecting droplets of him. "You do that a lot, you know, grabbing my wrist and making demands."

He arches a brow, nonplussed. "Do you like it?"

"When you tell me what to do?" I clarify, a bubble of embarrassment clogging my throat. "Not in the day-to-day, but here ... in bed ..."

Stone's lips move in a slow grin, made more predatory by the moonlight filtering over our bodies. "Then stand up, sweetheart, and strip for me."

He releases my wrist.

Biting my lip, I get off my knees, unbuttoning my shirt and

peeling off my jeans. Stone doesn't help. Just watches while resting on his elbows as I take off my clothes between his legs. His satiated dick jerks at the sight, readying for another round.

"I like you dressed in nothing but my cum on your lips," he says through the shadows.

His tone glides over me like a shiver, my nipples peaking at the compliment and my hips moving toward him.

Stone lifts off his elbows, sliding off the foot of the bed and to his knees. He cups my butt cheeks and brings me close. So close that he's able to bury his nose in my slit and inhale.

Natural instinct makes me want to push his head away. As a female, I've always been worried about how I smell down there and what guys think of it. Stone never made me feel gross or humiliated in any way, but we're older now, and things change ...

"Noa," he says in a bid for my attention.

I force myself to meet his eyes over the horizon of my stomach. His hand moves over my belly, nearly spanning my stomach from breast to apex.

"You're perfect." His eyes sparkle glitter white stars and shadows. "Every part of you amazes me, and I've never kicked my addiction to this pussy."

He laughs at my mortified squeak, his amused rumble coursing through his hands and into me.

"I'm just being honest," he says with an innocent quirk of his lips.

"I appreciate the—oh God. Oh *fuck*."

Stone stops any further conversation by licking my slit from top to bottom, then spreading me open and feasting with purpose.

If it weren't for his hands holding me up, I'd buckle. No,

I'd lose my bones and turn into a puddle before him, one his tongue would lap up.

I move in circles against his expert mouth, arching when he sucks on my clit and slips his fingers in, curving them until they grind against my G-spot and an explosion builds.

Stone holds me during one of the strongest orgasms of my life, so stimulating and effortless that tears come into my eyes.

He rises as I recover, his hands gliding up over my body as he does so and coming to a stop against my neck. He uses both thumbs to tilt my chin up.

I'm greeted with a majestic sight, moonlight cruelly assisting in highlighting Stone's angular beauty. His dimples flash as black crescents in his face.

"Hi, beautiful," he murmurs.

Stone greets me so sweetly, holds me so tenderly, that if tears weren't already pooling, they'd flood my eyes.

When they puddle against his hands, his brows draw down in concern. "Noa..."

Stone loses his smile.

This isn't what I intended. I meant this time to be for Stone, to take his mind off sad things and maybe mine, too. Neither of us needs more cracks in our hearts, more agonized confessions, and it's with that in mind that I palm his chest and push him back onto the bed.

"Hey now," he says with surprise, but splays his arms out in welcome as I crawl on top of him until my lips meet his.

Stone kisses me with passion, his hands tangling in my hair. I lose myself in the swollen suction, the rasp of his scruff on my sensitive skin, the feel of his tongue in my mouth.

Breath hitching, Stone pulls back and asks, "Do you have a condom in here?"

I freeze. "Um. No. I don't normally have men over and never planned for this ..."

Stone chuckles. "Don't finish that sentence. I like how it started. I can go downstairs and get one from my bag."

It would be the smart thing to do, but that would require him to get up and put space between us. Distance neither of us needs because it would leave room for thought and consequences.

"No."

"No?" Stone echoes.

"I'm—I have an IUD. And no STDs."

Stone's amusement jostles my body. "I never assumed you had some. I don't have any, either. I have regular—"

"Nope." I clap a hand over his mouth, reluctant to hear about his regular checkups because of his constant exploits. "Don't finish that sentence. I like how it started."

I feel his grin on my palm. He playfully licks it, and I squeal, pulling my hand back.

As soon as his full face is back in my vision, I soften. He's so incredibly handsome, so soft and sweet when he wants to be and surprisingly sensitive despite the mask he puts on for the world.

Without breaking eye contact, I line him up with my entrance, then slide onto him excruciatingly slow. I want to watch every second of taking him and see him transform into a man who fits me. Who's meant for me.

I lower to my elbows on either side of his shoulders. I start moving, our faces close together. He keeps our eyes locked, his hands cupping my ass but not taking control. Stone undulates underneath me, meeting my pleasure but not overtaking it with his own. Our sex is gentle, sweet, and astonishingly heart-wrenching as we watch each other come apart.

The tears aren't dry on my cheeks before more appear, but these aren't from sadness.

They're from the pure pleasure of rediscovering what it's like to make love to the man you were in love with.

Twenty-Five

NOA

THE FROSTED LIGHT OF A WINTER SUN PEEKS through the translucent curtains of the bedroom.

I crack my eyes open and stretch, my arm bumping into Stone's bed-warmed side. Pushing a tangle of hair out of my face, I study him in slumber, peaceful and boyish.

I don't regret what we did last night. If this time with Stone has taught me anything, it's that we are each other's escape, and escapes always feel like the right decision at the moment. Against my better judgment, he's endeared himself to me during these several weeks, gamely attending cooking classes taught by a chef who fast became his mortal enemy, helping me with Thanksgiving, adjusting to his mother's illness by being present, spending time with her, and lessening his denial until nothing but a droplet remains.

I'm watching the boy who never grew up mature before my eyes, and while I don't count myself lucky, I consider it to be fate.

The house is silent. I lift enough to check the clock. 7:00 a.m. Mrs. Stalinski won't be awake for a few hours, and I should've put the turkey in an hour ago.

I flop back on my pillow, considering.

I'm all tingly and relaxed from our sex last night, and a part of me doesn't want it to end. Too soon, this house will fill with company and holiday scents and the sound of football on a loop. It'll be noisy, an amazing distraction, and brimming with social pleasure. We'll all have fun.

Right now, though, all I want is him.

I tilt my head to study Stone again, biting my lip against a mischevious smile.

It's so unlike me, too spontaneous, but I'm certain we'll both be game.

Sitting up, I peel the covers off me and straddle Stone.

Around his head.

I knuckle the headboard as I press my pussy onto his lips and make tentative circles.

Muffled surprise comes from down below. Stone's lashes flutter.

My heart skitters with embarrassment. Maybe this was too much. I've never woken a man up like this. Last night, he said he liked my pussy, but he could've just been saying it to be nice. I should pull back and pretend this never—

Hands clap onto my butt cheeks. They push against me at the same time his tongue darts out, and he groans inside me.

My head falls back on a sigh, my balance against the headboard assisting in my fucking his face like his tongue is his dick.

When he circles my clit and sucks, I lose any reservations. I come against his mouth, and he licks up every drop, ensuring no place is unattended as he parts my folds and finishes his breakfast.

Then with a determined grunt, he flips me onto my back and plunges into me with his morning wood.

Our sex this time is hurried, meant for quick pleasure, and while his girth and length are always pleasurable, I want this to be for him.

Stone seems to notice something's off when I wrap my legs around him. He stops while buried inside me. "You okay?"

"Yeah, fine. Why?"

"You're not about to come."

"No, well, I just did. I don't have to come every time."

"Uh, yeah, you fucking do."

If pillows weren't underneath my head, it would've jerked back with surprise. Other than Stone, no man has ever been so determined to make sure I'm satisfied first. Even the teenaged Stone wasn't this adamant.

"I don't come until my woman does." Stone must see a flicker of reservation in my expression, because he adds, "Right now, you're my woman, Noa. And I'm not coming until I see you explode. Plus." He nips at my lower lip. "The sounds you make when I bring you to orgasm help me get off, too."

"Okay," I whisper, unable to fight the flush in my cheeks.

"Good girl. Now, touch yourself while I fuck you."

"H-Huh?"

"You must not remember how much I loved seeing you get yourself off when we were one the counter." He tilts his head and gives me a mischievous look. "Let me see you massage your clit."

His dirty talk has the intended effect. My vagina swells with want around him.

I skate my hand down my clavicle, between my breasts, and

over my navel. He watches the whole thing, his eyes hooded with the dark dare.

When I reach my slit, I rub two fingers over my small nub, made larger by his presence and my prodding.

I arch underneath him at the instant zing of pleasure I bring to myself.

With a cocky smile, Stone repeats, "Good girl," and thrusts with my swirls.

I bite back a moan until Stone encourages me to unravel, eager to hear my moans and pleas to go faster, harder, more.

He does, rising on his hands so he can watch his cock slide out of me, then in while my fingers work on myself.

Stone likes what he sees. His jaw cuts through his skin. Tendons and muscles pop in his cheeks, and his skin has a strained flush.

"I'm not coming until you do," he grits out.

I'm beyond comprehension. I'm writhing against the sheets, angling so his cock hits me just right, and pleasure builds beneath my hand.

"I'm coming," I gasp.

"Hal..." he stutters between thrusts, "le-fucking-lujah."

We come together, our sweat-coated bodies meeting, sliding against one another and taking all the other has to give.

I release my clit and scrape my nails down his back, marking him more permanently than he did me last night and taking from him all that I want.

We end on mutual gasps, flopping onto our backs side by side and catching our breaths.

After a few beats, Stone's head turns to mine. "I'd say this warrants a giant feast, don't you?"

I laugh up at the ceiling. "I'm *starving*."

Stone rumbles with a pleasured growl before climbing on top of me again.

MOST OF OUR guests arrive on time.

It's a good thing because I've timed the appetizers for their arrival and would love it if everyone ate them warm.

Maisy, Carly, and Mae arrive first, laden with flowers, pecan pie, and a local cheese plate.

"Happy Thanksgiving!" Maisy greets brightly as they wander in. She kicks at the doorframe, dislodging the buildup of frost and dirt on her boots. The weather has turned into November's gray skies and frigid wind, but no snow. November likes to greet us with dead, slimy leaves and hard-packed earth. The whole white Christmas thing doesn't really apply to Falcon Haven—we really only see it come February.

"Where's Judy?" Maisy asks after scanning the entryway.

I glance at Stone, who greets everyone with his trademark smile, his eyes dulled with concern. "She's not feeling well and says she'll come down when dinner's ready."

Maisy hums in sympathy. "Mind if I go up and say hello?"

"She'd demand it," I say before Stone can deny her. Mrs. Stalinski is already upset about not being able to join in the early festivities, so I don't want her to think we're keeping her isolated.

Stone and I have been switching off all day between Thanksgiving prep and taking care of Mrs. Stalinski, a woman who threatened to smother us in our sleep if we tried to cancel today after we noticed she wasn't doing well.

Stone catches my drift. "Just let me know if she needs anything," he says to Maisy.

"Will do, doll." Maisy sets her boots near the door, then climbs up the stairs.

"Hey, girl."

Carly envelops me in a hug, her long, auburn hair cold against my cheek from being outside. She's dressed in a maroon cap-sleeved dress under her plaid coat, appearing refreshed and beautiful despite her commute.

"Hi," I say, a little too emotionally. I didn't realize how much I needed a hug from my best friend until she gave me one.

Carly senses the change and pulls me in tighter.

"Everything good?" she murmurs into my ear.

"Yes, of course." I blink back my emotion. Now's not the time to tell her about Mrs. Stalinski's failing health and my growing feelings for her famous son. "I've missed you."

"I've missed *you*. Like miss missed. I'm so glad I'm here and I'm ready to catch up when you are." She kisses my forehead before pulling away.

"Stone," she says while brushing past him to the living room.

"I suppose that's her hello," he muses as she flounces away.

I shrug. "She hasn't had as much time with you as I have."

"You've got that right." His voice fills with promise, but he's distracted and returns to reality when Carly's younger sister, Mae, steps between us.

"Hi, guys. I'm so sorry about your mom, Stone."

"Thanks, little sweets." Stone regards the younger, blond version of Carly. The last time he saw her, she would've been thirteen. "Jesus, you've grown. Probably shouldn't call you little sweets anymore."

"Are you kidding? That's my claim to fame—Stone Williams has a nickname for me because he's known me all my life. Well, half my life, I guess. But I remember you in a lot of it, and I use it as pull when I'm out in bars."

Stone's forehead wrinkles. "I ... don't know how I feel about that."

"Just hug me." Mae laughs as Stone brings her in for a hug and tousles the top of her head.

I make sure Carly and Mae are settled in with drinks and surrounded by appetizers before I ask Stone, "Where are Rome and Aaron?"

"Coming, I assume." Stone answers me, but his focus is clearly somewhere else. He keeps glancing up the stairs.

Our explosive, amazing sex is long forgotten as Mrs. Stalinski deteriorated throughout the day. I do my best to keep his spirits up, but honestly, cancer is so fucked up and unfair, and I let him go through the emotions of it.

Thirty minutes later, Rome ambles through the front door carrying a cooler of God knows what.

"Hey, farm boy," Rome drawls as Stone comes into the foyer to meet him, holding two beers. Rome's in a black Stetson hat, black button-down, and black jeans.

"Dressing up for the holidays, I see," Stone says, then points at the cooler. Stone's dressed in what has fast become my favorite white cashmere sweater and jeans. "The hell is that?"

"Fresh venison. I had little else on the farm to bring and figured you'd do with my latest hunting. Noa's a skilled cook now, I hear."

"I wouldn't say that," I say, though I'm flattered. Anyone immune from a man like Rome with his stormy eyes and rugged good looks isn't someone I'd like to meet. "But thank you. Truly. I haven't cooked venison in years."

Stone eyes the cooler like what's in it is still alive.

"You should come hunting with me next time," Rome suggests to him.

"Fuck no." Stone passes Rome a beer before making a quick exit.

Amused, I gesture to Rome. "Bring it into the garage. There's a freezer I can put it in."

"Lead the way."

I open the attached door to the garage, and Rome passes through it, carrying the cooler with ease. He sets it down by the freezer and opens it.

Rome's butchered the deer into separate, edible parts and wrapped them, too.

"Wow, you didn't have to do all that," I say as I open the freezer for him to drop them in.

"It was my pleasure. The least I could do after Judy offered up her son as sacrifice to my ranch."

I take the carrot he dangled and bite into it. "How's Stone doing over there, anyway?"

"Fine. Good." Rome tosses a tenderloin into the vacant freezer and moves to the wrapped brisket. "I think it's been helpful for him to unleash his buried emotions."

Rome doesn't have to elaborate. Stone's kept his feelings about his mother on such lockdown, the only thing stopping me from wondering how he hasn't exploded is the fact that he can deal with a lot of his anger and distress through physical labor and sex.

Lots of sex.

"You help, too," Rome says.

I blush as if he read my thoughts. "Huh?"

Rome straightens after throwing the last of the loins in. His eyes crinkle with amusement. "Don't think I haven't noticed the change in him over this month. He started off snarly and prissy but came to work this week willing to *finally* listen to instructions and with a pep in his step. If he keeps it up, I might even let him play with the big boy power tools."

"Oh, that has nothing to do with me." I laugh uncomfortably.

Rome gives me a careful study. "Why do I feel like I'm flashing back twelve years to when you two were first getting together?"

"We're not together." I say it a little too defensively. "We're just ..."

Rome raises his hands in surrender. "That may well be, but whatever you're doing, keep it up. It's helping him, and knowing you the way I do, that's helping *you*."

Not being one for heart-to-hearts, Rome ends the conversation by spinning on his cowboy boots and clomping back inside. I doubt he'll take them off throughout dinner. He doesn't seem like a walk-around-in-socks kind of man.

Shaking my head in bemusement, I follow him, shutting the door and joining the small party in the living room.

I notice our new guest instantly, as he stands out more than Rome. Some people are born to wear a suit, and this guy's one of them. Dressed in an expensive, tailored charcoal suit, with professionally styled golden-blond hair and eyes the color of brushed copper, he stands almost as tall as Stone and Rome, dwarfing all the females except for Carly who matches his height with her three-inch heels.

"You must be Mr. Golde," I say, drawing closer with my hand held out.

He takes it, his hand warm, dry, and firm. "Aaron, please. And you must be the famous Noa."

I tilt my head in confusion. "Famous? I don't think so."

"From what Stone tells me—"

"Aaron." Stone appears beside me, unclasping our handshake by pulling my arm back by the wrist. Gentle but possessive and firm.

That stupid move of his. I squint at him in warning. "What have you told your agent about me?"

"Nothing, and that's the point. Noa is invisible to the public eye, isn't she, Aar?"

His protectiveness is a pleasant surprise at the same time his calling me *invisible* is jarring. Aaron doesn't give me any more time to process.

He placates Stone by saying, "Of course. Noa isn't known to anyone but me. I only meant to say it's a pleasure to meet Stone's high school sweetheart, the one who got away. He talks about you with a certain wistfulness, a joie de vivre, I should say..."

"All right." Stone grunts, turning me away by the shoulders. "That's enough, jackass."

Aaron laughs behind us. That short exchange gave me enough intel to understand the playful joviality between the two and that Aaron means nothing by it.

And that I'm disappointed he's not serious is something to be cast aside, too.

I should be glad Stone has someone he can trust that much.

Stone leans close to my ear as we walk. "Everything okay with you?"

His breath tickles the small hairs around my temple. Quick and pleasurable. "Absolutely. I'm going to make sure everything's ready in the kitchen. Why don't you go check on your mom, see if she wants to come down and join us at the table?"

Stone nods, his hand straying up my back and squeezing the nape of my neck before releasing.

Fast and pleasing.

"Care to share?" Carly sidles up to me, following my line of sight. Her eyes narrow in suspicion.

"It's nothing." I make an about-face into the dining room. Not that Carly would stay where she is.

"Doesn't look like nothing to me."

Sighing, I focus on straightening the place settings. Multi-colored pumpkins decorate the maroon tablecloth, nestled in small bushels of straw. Cream candles stand at varying heights, their flame reflecting off Mrs. Stalinski's gold-rimmed china plates. I've dimmed the small chandelier above, and while the sun sets, a soft glow encases the entire room.

It's beautiful. Perfect. I wish Mrs. Stalinski could see it.

"Turning into Martha Stewart won't get me off your case," Carly says behind me.

"I'm figuring out what to say and how to say it." I straighten the forks beside each plate unnecessarily.

"Are you sleeping with him? No, don't answer that." Carly peers closer, her proximity tingling against the side of my face. "You're totally fucking him."

"Okay, fine." I throw my hands up and face her. "I am. And I'd love your support while I do it."

Carly cocks a manicured auburn brow.

"You don't have to say it," I continue. "It's not a good idea since we have so much history and baggage. He broke my heart and left me. But I'm older now, and I'd like to think wiser, too. We need each other's bodies to forget the harder parts of our lives, and it feels *good*, dammit. This time, there's no unbreakable connection. No hope. I'm not in love with him anymore, which means it doesn't hurt to use him for my pleasure."

It's hard to catch my breath after that speech. Difficult to hear myself over my rampant heartbeat.

Carly takes my hands in her own. I expect a lecture to

come, the requisite best friend insisting she must protect me from my demons.

Instead, she surprises me. "Noa, if it makes you happy, then that's all I care about. I'm not here to judge." Carly's gaze darts past my shoulder, her eyes widening. "But ..."

I stare at her, perplexed. "What?"

Her eyes come back to mine. "Stone's behind you."

My heart ratchets up my throat. I release my hands from hers. I have to face him, but I won't lie and say my slow spin wasn't painful. It takes extra effort to raise my head and see his expression and if he heard what I said.

"Stone, I—"

"It doesn't matter."

His curt interjection eases my turn into his spotlight. But when I meet his gaze, my chest twinges with sick agony.

Worry lines frame his eyes and mouth. His blue eyes, as warm as a summer sky, have dulled into gray clouds. Those lips of his, always ready for a quip or wry comment to release humor to make any situation better, are closed and flat. Maisy stands next to him, her lips thin and white around the edges.

My attention returns to Stone. I've never seen him this closed off.

It makes me nauseous to think I caused it.

I step forward, wanting to grab his hand and assure myself he's still warm. I only said what I thought he'd want in this situation. No strings, no involved hearts, just sex. If I'd told Carly the truth, that Stone was curling under my skin again, and this time, I wasn't confident I'd be able to cut him out, she'd surely give me the best friend demon speech.

I open my mouth to tell him all of this, hoping to reverse what new, deep cracks I've put in his expression, when he recoils from my touch.

His scowl deepens. "Ma can't come down. As in, I can't get her out of bed without her crying out in pain. I can't do this. I can't have a huge feast in her dining room with her in agony upstairs."

I clasp my hands together. The backs of my eyes heat, but clenching my teeth together and swallowing hard keeps the tears at bay. I nod, acknowledging his anguished revelation.

"I have an idea," I say. It feels like I'm talking through the spaces in my teeth. "It's something I did with my mom. Maybe Mrs. Stalinski will be up for it."

Stone's already shaking his head. "You've seen her. She can't roll to her side without suffering."

"Let me talk to her," I say, too brightly, too eager to escape what was once a warm, inviting, family-centered room.

I brush Carly's shoulder during my escape, giving her a chance to glide her hand down my arm in support. I'm thankful she's here as much as I hate that we're observed by a crowd. Stone's worked hard to keep his mother's sickness out of the media, and it's not that these carefully picked close friends would leak her condition to the press, but no one knew how badly she's declining. Not even them.

It doesn't matter anymore.

I sprint up the stairs and push Mrs. Stalinski's door open. It's about memories now, more for Stone than for Mrs. Stalinski, but benefiting them both.

"Mrs. Stalinski," I whisper into the darkened room.

"Noa." Her croaky voice comes from the vicinity of the bed. "How many times must I tell you to refer to me with less formality?"

I crack a smile. "The first time I met you outside of a school environment was as Stone's girlfriend. It was terrifying, and I

253

wanted to do anything to make you love me. It's ingrained at this point. Unless you'd prefer ma'am?"

"You insolent child," Mrs. Stalinski mutters, but I hear the smile in her voice. "Call me that and I'll whack you with this lamp."

"Speaking of, can I turn it on?"

Her voice becomes tired. "I suppose."

I flick the switch, bathing her exhausted form in a golden hue. Chronic pain has a way of leeching all life from a person. But she lays above the covers in a festive tunic of gold, red, and white, with comfortable black leggings underneath. She's capped off her outfit with a matching scarf tied around her head to hide her thinning hair. I note the blush she's applied to her cheeks and the gloss on her lips.

Mrs. Stalinski was ready to come join the party. She wanted to. Now, she can't, but I'm here to remedy that.

"How is it going downstairs?" she asks. "I hear Rome's deep baritone and a posh, obnoxious male voice sounding suspiciously like Stone's greedy sidekick."

"Aaron?" I laugh. "Yes, he was the last one to arrive. Everybody's here."

"That's good. It's good for Stone to be surrounded by people he loves and trusts."

"I agree." I perch on the edge of the bed. "And you deserve the same."

"Oh, honey." Mrs. Stalinski lays her hand on mine. "I appreciate the effort and how hard you've worked for this—all because I asked you. But as much as I try, I cannot get out of this bed."

"I know. Which is why I'll bring everyone to you."

Mrs. Stalinski stares at me in confusion.

"I saw TV tables in the garage when I was helping Rome put an entire butchered deer in your freezer."

Mrs. Stalinski nods, unfazed by Rome's gift. Rome's and Stone's antics and strange decisions have stretched long and wide into Mrs. Stalinski's life.

"I'd love to bring the feast to you and all the people who love you. We can fit in this room, easy. If you're up for it."

Mrs. Stalinski scans the room with a frown. My heart sinks.

She won't agree. It's too much on her. I'm fully aware it's a lot to ask and will deplete the little energy she has on reserve, but I'm not sure how many holidays she has left. And when it came to my mother, spending the holidays with me, her only family, was so important to her toward the end.

"Stone bought me this house because of the size of the main bedroom. Have I ever told you that?" she says.

I shake my head.

"I always thought this room was better served as a rich bitch's ballroom. Send them in."

My smile reaches my ears. In a burst of affection, I lean forward and kiss her cheek.

She uses my momentum by catching my hands, bringing them to her heart, and squeezing hard.

It stalls my retreat, and I look down into her watery eyes.

"Thank you for this, my dear. I love you. If I've never told you that, then that is my mistake."

Now it takes clamping my teeth against my lips to keep from crying. I give a jerky nod, squeezing back and whispering, "I love you, too," before departing and heading downstairs to tell everyone the change of plans.

STONE HELPS BRING the necessary TV tables into Mrs. Stalinski's room without a word. Aaron and Rome are happy to help, with Maisy joining in and Carly, Mae, and I transferring the plates upstairs.

Mae jokes she knew she worked at the Merc's cafe for a reason when she balances four full dinner plates up at once. Carly agrees that the Merc's wine cellar has given her the same experience as she carries four pinot noirs in her long arms.

The sisters' banter travels all the way up the stairs and lightens the mood as we crowd in.

Stone carved the turkey downstairs and the cacophony that began in the kitchen as everyone shouted for their preferred cuts to be dropped on their plate traveled into Mrs. Stalinski's bedroom with equal fervor.

Maisy and I teamed up and brought the table decorations into her room, too, decorating her vanity, side tables, and wardrobe.

I sit cross-legged on the bed beside Mrs. Stalinski, my plate balanced on my thighs. The rest form a half circle around the bed, Stone the closest to his mother and Aaron on the other side, nearest to me.

Conversation flows as Mrs. Stalinski picks at her plate, then nonchalantly pushes it aside, nestling it beside me. Her appetite wasn't the point of this dinner, and nobody says a thing as she folds her arms against her concave stomach and joins in on the conversation, her smile permanently in place.

Scrapes of cutlery against emptied plates soon join into the flow. Aaron makes what I hope he considers a joke when Carly stands up for seconds. He fast becomes one of Carly's many victims under her lethal stare.

"City boys," Mrs. Stalinski says. "They never learn."

"Just for that," Carly says to Aaron, "I'm stealing your cranberry crème brûlée."

"Wait—there's crème brûlée here?" Aaron truly appears perplexed that such a dessert would appear in a small town like this.

I laugh. Mae and Maisy join in, with Carly following (though Carly's is more of a *I'm making fun of you, stupid city boy* laugh).

"Noa made it, and it's fucking divine, so you better shut your freshly waxed mouth and respect my women," Stone adds.

It's the first time I've heard his voice over the others, and I look over at him in surprise.

He catches my eye and winks.

And just like that, my heart floats.

It's okay. We're okay.

Twenty-Six

STONE

NOA SAVED THE DAY.

I shouldn't be surprised. The woman has a superpower in bettering a situation simply by being present.

Ma got the Thanksgiving she wanted, and while her condition is no longer a secret, I'm bowled over by the amount of support this close circle of people gives me.

I shouldn't be surprised at that, either, but Hollywood changed me. I'm suspicious, cautious, and constantly searching for a person's true motive. Falcon Haven is as static as a storybook, unchanging and picturesque with its down-home country vibe. The residents have grown, but the sentiment remains the same: we lift up our own.

The love my mother received tonight was almost too much to witness. She deserves love like this every day, and she gets it. But to see it so concentrated in one room, to watch everyone do their damnedest to keep that smile on her face? I'm about ready to bawl, and I can't readily do that in front of a crowd.

I excuse myself while Rome is deep into one of his ranch stories involving a barn owl and his feed supply, exiting with little notice—except for Noa.

She watches me depart, and I don't feel her eyes leave me until I pass through the doorway.

Her confession to Carly rings in my ears, louder now that the worry over my mother has settled into a low ache. Before I heard her, I was convinced last night was different. We didn't have sex; we made love. I've never in my life kept eye contact with a woman well past orgasm. Noa was so soft and supple, butter in my hands. Her soft cries echo in my head, sounds of true devotion. Proof that I'm hers.

Fuck. I didn't read any of it correctly.

I can't read her anymore, not the way I used to.

That truth rattles inside my chest as I push outside onto the front patio, where my exhales turn into icy clouds. The glow and warmth from inside don't follow. I'm plunged into midnight blue with white casts of electric light from the outdoor lamps.

In my haste, I'd forgotten a jacket, goose bumps blasting across my skin and my teeth turning cold.

I embrace the numbing freeze, preferable to the heated conflict inside my head. Leaning on the railing, I look up at the moon, full and gray, coated in winter as much as I am.

"Thought I'd find you out here."

The snick of a lighter follows Aaron's voice. I half turn to greet him.

"Want one?" he asks as he comes up beside me, holding up a cigarette.

My cloudy exhales coat his offering. "I shouldn't."

"For so many reasons," Aaron agrees. He sticks it into the

corner of his mouth, dips his head, and cups the lighter before saying, "But I won't tell."

He inhales, puffing out the smoke, then hands it to me.

I take it, closing my eyes as I take a deep inhale, the nicotine doing its work. I take my time blowing out the smoke. "Thanks, man."

"Did it help?"

"Not a bit."

Aaron chuckles. There's no mirth in it. "I knew it was bad, but I didn't know how bad. I'm sorry, my friend. Truly."

I nod, staring out into the road. "Thanks."

"I'll be honest, I was worried you wouldn't be able to handle coming back here. With the way your mom is, I was sure you'd act out your anger somehow and do something stupid. No offense."

"None taken," I say wryly, yanking the cigarette from him again.

"Your ex, though. Noa. She's keeping you level. Anyone can see it."

"What, I can't do it all by myself? I need some sort of anchoring force to keep me from doing bad things?"

"Yup."

"Thanks for the support."

"You understand where I'm coming from, Stone. During the worst times of our lives, we need someone who cares about us to keep us from going under. In my fucked-up way, I'm telling you I'm glad you have that woman. You and I both know without her, I'd be here for different reasons."

I'm silent for a moment. "Yeah, I guess I can't argue with that."

"Do you regret letting her go?"

"Jesus." I hand the cigarette back. "I'm not in the right mind to get into it."

Not since Noa explained we were nothing but good sex.

"I think she regrets it," Aaron continues.

"You wouldn't if you heard what I did." I push off the railing. "We should get back."

But Aaron's relentless. "But if you saw what I did, you'd believe me. You know what it means when a woman is in a room filled with handsome bachelors and she only pays attention to one?"

I roll my eyes. "Let me guess, it means she's obsessed with your good looks?"

"Nope." Aaron flicks the butt over the railing and into the frosted-over grass. "It means you're her boyfriend."

EVERYBODY STAYS to help with the cleanup. Ma falls asleep as soon as we leave her bedroom, Noa assisting with that by giving her nightly pain meds.

When the last plate is rinsed and put in the dishwasher, our guests say their goodbyes.

Aaron, unsurprisingly, is the last to leave, taking a bottle of my best whiskey with him to the B&B he's staying at in town.

"I'll be here until Sunday evening," he says as he heads out. "Let's have a meeting that morning for brunch. We can discuss your next steps."

It's unavoidable and a large reason he's here—what I'm going to do with my upcoming movies. *Cascade,* in particular. The deadline is fast approaching, and I don't feel any closer to finally deciding. I'm risking millions by delaying the role and practically guaranteeing I'll miss my chance at an Oscar. Every drop of sweat I've put into my career, every sacrifice, every *reason* to leave Falcon Haven and Noa behind will be for nothing.

That alone should spur me into action, but the next morning, after a night on the pull-out instead of beside Noa, I remain conflicted.

It's no great shock to see Noa fussing around in the kitchen when I wander in, rubbing the top of my head and scraping the sleep out of my eyes.

"Is it even morning yet?" I ask, my voice thick with sleep.

She turns, and I take her in. She's in running gear, tight leggings, and a form-fitting zip-up. I'd call the color bluish-purple, a spectacular complement to her dark hair and pale complexion.

Her breasts are squished up and held in the exact position they need to be for me to hold them in both palms and lick between the crease.

In fact ...

Her gaze lowers to my midsection, where my hard-on is visible through my briefs.

"Stone," she says, her attention staying on my cock.

I respond by crowding in on her and placing my arms on either side, pressing her back into the fridge.

"Mm," I say, grinding my dick against her stomach. "You look so fucking sexy right now."

A small smile tickles her lips. "I was about to go for a run."

I lower my head, sucking on the side of her neck. "I can think of a better way to burn calories."

She moans, her head tilting so my tongue can have better access. "Stone, I don't think this is a good idea."

"Isn't this what you want?" I murmur into her warm skin. "Good sex? That's what we do, right?"

Her head straightens. "Um. Yes, sure, but—"

"Then let's fuck."

I cup her ass and lift her until her legs wrap around my torso.

She lets me kiss her and mewls softly when I massage her ass cheeks, but she pulls away and wriggles out of my hold. "I can't. Not right now."

I release her, backing off, but her dismissal rubs me the wrong way. "If I can't fuck you, then what am I good for, anyway?"

Her brows crinkle. "What are you talking about?"

"Use me." I splay out my hands. "For your pleasure. That's what you said, right?"

Her expression ripples with hurt. "That's not what I meant, and you know it."

"No? Because those were your exact words."

Noa sighs, her shoulders sloping. "I wanted to get a run in before your mom wakes up. I'm sure she will need extra care today after all the activity yesterday. I heard her rousing a little while ago, which is why I said no to you right now. She'll be up soon, and I have pent-up frustration to release, too. It's not just you."

Point made. I deflate. "You're right. I'll watch her. Get a run in."

"Thank you."

"You don't have to thank me. I'm acting like a jerk."

She pauses halfway through her turn to the door. "You're not being a jerk. You're a person in pain. There's a difference."

Is there a difference in us? I want to ask her but keep my mouth shut and let her go.

The last thing either of us needs is to complicate our current situation with more feelings.

I wait for the front door to open and close before slamming my palm into the kitchen door, keeping my hand there as I lower my head and rest it on the inside of my arm, my pent-up frustration having nowhere to go.

Twenty-Seven

NOA

THE DYING GRASS SPARKLES WITH FROST IN THE rising sunlight, telling of an incoming snowfall. I look up at the sky as I stretch, as if the gray-blue sky can tell me when it'll burst open with snowflakes.

Snow on Christmas would be amazing. Mrs. Stalinski would love it. I send a prayer into the morning sky asking for a snow day before picking up my feet and taking off.

It takes at least a mile before I find my breath and can focus on the audiobook I have playing in my earbuds. The tightness in my chest changes from a burn to a tolerable ache and my muscles warm, pulsing with action as I jog through the neighborhood.

I'm in the zone, relaxing into my thoughts and allowing my subconscious to work through the tougher aspects of my life, when a flash catches my eye.

I blink, and it's gone. It occurred in my peripheral vision, and I'm thinking I imagined it when it happens again.

My steps slow. When I notice movement behind the hedges bordering the nearby park—deserted at this time of day because of the time of day and chilly weather—I pull my earbuds out.

"Noa-Lynn Shaw!"

I jolt at the unfamiliar, *loud* cry of my name.

"Miss Shaw!"

Someone else shouts my name from a different direction. My head jerk toward it.

Rushing feet follow, and suddenly, I'm cornered in the middle of the road.

"Miss Shaw, do you care to comment on the status of your current relationship with Stone Williams?"

"Can you confirm you're back together?"

"Are you aware of his playboy status and choosing to commit to him, anyway? Wouldn't you call that once shamed, twice burned?"

Cameras flash. I wince.

Men in dark clothing surround me. Not one of them sounds nice.

I do a slow spin, my eyes stretched wide in both shock and terror as phones focus on me, cameras zoom in, and voices shout over each other.

"How do you know who I am?" My question is shallow and breathy from my run. At least, that's what I tell myself.

"An anonymous tip came in."

"I can't disclose my source."

"Fact remains, someone has outed you as Stone's new fling and the reason he's not resuming his role in *Blue Flood 2*. The fans will send you some hate, girl, so get ready."

"Yeah, the Blue Belles will want to set you on fire. Smile!"

Flash.

"N-No comment," I stutter out while holding an arm up over my face. I try to break out of the circle, but I'm held back as they crowd in. "I said no comment! Leave me alone!"

"One last question. Is it true he asked you to abort your pregnancy so he could avoid a scandal and become famous?"

I freeze.

My ears lose all sound.

My mouth stops working.

Trembles overtake my body, and my knees buckle. Rapid blinks won't stop the sudden onslaught of fire.

"Well? Can you answer me?" the same asshole asks.

My lips peel back from my teeth. "*Fuck* you!"

I rear forward to push him or claw at him; I don't care which, the moment he presses record on his phone. "I take that as a yes."

The last thing I see is his satisfied smirk before he's ripped out of my eyesight and tossed to the ground.

"Stay the *fuck* away from her!" Stone's yell echoes down the street.

Stone comes barreling toward me, his chest heaving and his lips twisted in a smile. He whirls, pressing his back against my chest and covering me from the cameras.

Behind his protection, it's safe to sob. I tangle my hands in his coat, bury my forehead in the fabric, and let it out.

He stiffens at the sound. The muscles in his back spasm, his body vibrating with renewed fury.

"I said back the *fuck* off! Move!" he roars, wrapping one hand around me as much as he can to keep me pressed against him. "If you want to keep those cameras and your noses, step away."

"Hey, we're on public property, man!" one says.

"We're free to film you now that we know where you're at!"

"She's pretty, ain't she? You think I can sell these photos and they'll do a side-by-side of Miss Small-Town and Ravynn? Who did Stone do better?"

Air flies into my face when Stone leaps for the hapless paparazzi.

The other paparazzi scatter, half filming, half running away in terror. Stone didn't get a superhero role simply by being pretty. He's muscled, fit, and has the endurance of a professional athlete. He uses those abilities to intimidate the paps to a distance, though they don't disappear.

Even Stone can't do that.

Breaths heavy, eyes concerned, he strips off his coat and covers me with it, hiding my face.

He takes my hand. "You're safe with me. Come on."

I let him lead me down the same path I had so effortlessly taken minutes ago. Where I'd felt safe and stayed comfortable under the advantage of privacy.

Now it's all shattered.

"How do they know me?" My ragged whisper comes through the flaps of Stone's jacket.

"I don't know," he mutters. "I've never mentioned your name. Not once. And you and I, we've done nothing in public."

"Other than go to a couple's cooking class together." My stomach plummets at the thought of having to give up those classes. "Were we followed?"

"I don't know."

"And they—he asked—they asked about my..." It's as if my body revolts, refusing to get the words out. "When I was pregnant."

Stone grinds to a halt. His eyes flash as they land on mine. "They what?"

"They know, Stone."

"No." He shakes his head. "Impossible."

"It's fully possible," I whisper. "If they have the right source."

Stone's eyes widen. "You think I had something to do with this? Noa, I received an alert on my phone as soon as you left this morning. I get one every time my name is in the press, and I had to read an article naming you as my high school sweetheart, who I'm rekindling with. There's a picture of you walking through town with me, totally unaware of the shit I've brought down on you. I came to find you as soon as I saw it. I don't know how they ... Someone in town must've talked. Maybe fucking Carly."

"Carly would never," I hiss. "I trust her like a sister. She's the only other person who knew about us, and I told her about it last night."

"Then how?" Stone throws his hands up.

He stares past me, noticing the reinvigorated paparazzi, and draws me forward again.

"Fuck this," he mutters. "This is just the start. We need to get inside. Now."

"What about your agent?" I retort. "Aaron. He loves putting you in the news. Keeping you relevant. Isn't that what you call it?"

Stone doesn't answer. He storms to the house with me firmly in his hand. This isn't like all those other times he grabbed me by the wrist. This is a command, tight and final, and if I don't do what he says, I'll be lost to the public eye.

Memories of the five months I had a baby inside me and

the agonizing five months after they removed her from me resurface, reddening my vision and making me stumble.

I lost my mother and my baby. It took me so long to live with that grief and now these strangers want to make it theirs.

Stone rights me, and when I buckle, when I sob harder, he picks me up and carries me into the house.

He sets me on the couch, keeping his arms around me as I cry into his neck. His tendons strain, but his hand rubs circles on my back. I don't want to see his face. I'm worried it'll be the same as mine—wounded with shock and horror.

"Noa, what's wrong?"

Mrs. Stalinski's soft voice comes from the corner.

I raise my head.

She's sitting in the sofa chair, comfortable under a heavy blanket and holding a steaming cup of tea. Stone must have carried her down.

"They know," Stone croaks over my head.

Mrs. Stalinski's expression falls. "Oh no." She looks past us out the window, probably watching the vultures circle. Her face hardens. "There's only one thing to do. Get out of here, Noa."

I sniffle, collecting myself. "I'm not leaving you."

"That's not your choice. It's mine and I'm telling you to get out of this house and go somewhere safe. Not home, but a hotel out of town. Somewhere you'll be out of view until we can get this under control."

"Ma, I don't know if Noa should be left alone right now."

Not, *I don't want to leave Noa*, I note.

"She damn well does." Mrs. Stalinski's voice rises to a level I haven't heard in over a year, full of conviction. "I love you, son, more than my own life, but you have brought nothing but pain to this girl. Involving yourself with her has made her endure it all over again. I was hoping it would be different. Seeing you two the way you were, even yesterday, was like a healing balm on my soul. If you two were happy, that's all I need to know before I let go. But this ..." She shakes her head as her eyes water. "I don't want this for you. I don't want people feasting on Noa's tragedy or my son's perceived coldness during that time. To have my two favorite people picked over—no. Just as it is Noa's job to care for me, it is your job to protect her, my boy."

"I get a decision in this," I protest, "and I'm not going anywhere without you."

"I accepted my boy's fame a long time ago," Mrs. Stalinski says levelly. "You did not, nor do you have to. And if you stay, it will be all people will talk about. They knew he was here for months yet only came at the mention of a high school sweetheart and a secret pregnancy. And they will stay for as long as they can get at that meat."

I can't argue with her. I drift away from Stone.

"Noa." Stone's plea comes out strangled. "I'm so sorry. But I don't want you to go. Call me selfish, but I do not want you to go out there. Stay with me. I'll protect you."

"Son," Mrs. Stalinski warns.

I give a solemn shake of my head in her direction, communicating that I agree with her. I say to Stone, "If they ask me more questions about my daughter, I won't be able to take it. Especially, *especially* if they call her unwanted." My voice cracks. It hurts to breathe.

"Noa ..." Stone reaches for me.

I rise, getting as far away from his embrace as I can.

"I can fix this." He stands with me. "I will track down who's responsible, and I'll raise hell."

"What's the point?" I ask. "It's out there now. My tragedy

is theirs. Your mother's right. I have to go. I can't be anywhere near you. The only way I'll be safe in Falcon Haven is when you leave."

Stone's expression warps into abject pain. He glances from his mother, then to me.

"I would never ask you to go," I whisper harshly. "You stay with your mother. I'll go. And I'll make sure the best nurse takes my place."

"I don't want another nurse," Stone shouts. "I want you, Noa. *You.* You're the best thing for this family. The reason this house isn't a skeletal, hollow version of what it could've turned into. You cared for my mom when I couldn't. Loved her when I wasn't here. And I'm—you've ... you can't leave. You just can't."

I swipe at the wetness on my cheeks. My lips are salty and damp. The tears just keep flowing.

And I say the one thing that will make him stop pushing. "Your mother doesn't deserve this."

Stone recoils like I've slapped him. Mrs. Stalinski's mouth turns grim, her eyes dimming, but she gives me a tight nod.

"She deserves peace," I continue, my words stilted. "Stability. Constant media at her doorstep would derail everything we've tried to build in this house."

"They won't leave just because you do," Stone says stubbornly.

"But they'll go a lot sooner," I reason. "When they get bored with your routine with your mother and I'm not here, living with you and going to couples things with you, and..." *loving you.*

A pained line forms between Stone's brows. He grimaces like his very muscles are atrophying under his skin. "You know

I can't argue with a statement like that. So fine. Go. But I'll go first."

He whirls, throwing the front door open.

"Where are you going?" Mrs. Stalinski asks.

I stare at him, my heart rusted like an anchor lost at sea.

"To break down Aaron's door and make him explain what the *fuck* just happened," he shouts.

The door slams shut behind him.

I sniff and wipe my nose on my sleeve, the only sound in a house plunged into silence.

"I'll stay until he comes back," I murmur to her.

"Dear, you're staying until you're okay to leave." She pats the spot beside her. I do as she says, curling into her as she wraps an arm around me.

Twenty-Eight

STONE

I STORM UP TO BIRDIE'S BREAD & BREAKFAST, THE gnarled hedges framing the walkway of the cheery yellow town-home resembling how my insides must look on this wintry, fuck-bluster day.

He's staying in a room on the third floor, the biggest they have because that's how he is as a bachelor living it up in my hometown.

I don't knock on the heavy mahogany door to his suite. I pound.

"Jesus, where's the fire?" I hear him call.

His footsteps pad closer, and he swings open the door.

Aaron's clad in a white towel wrapped around his torso, his water dripping down his hair and into his face. He blinks the water away and assesses me, heaving inside his doorway.

"Stone? What's up?"

"Did you do it?" I snarl.

Aaron's lips purse. His forehead wrinkles. If I weren't so

overflowing with rage, I might give him points for his honest surprise.

"Do what?" he asks.

"Don't give me that." I push past him and stalk inside. "You basically have trackers put into all your clients. You know exactly what I'm referring to."

The room appears untouched, the king-sized bed with thick down covers made up without a wrinkle, Aaron's open suitcase showcasing perfectly folded clothing, and his open wardrobe hanging a rack of suits. It's just like Aaron not to live in a room.

"Oh. That." Aaron shuts the door and turns to me.

"It's a lot more than *that*. I had to peel Noa off the pavement this morning after the paps mobbed her. The pictures they must've gotten, the way she had to find this out..." I scrape my fingers through my hair and wheel around. "I've never seen her like this. And it's all because of me. Or *you*."

Aaron holds a hand to his bare chest. "Me?"

"Goddammit, Aar," I seethe. "Did you leak her existence to the press?"

Aaron considers my question.

That silent hesitation turns into his greatest mistake.

I leap for him, teeth bared, and slam him into the wall. He lets me, his expression benign as I shove my face into his.

"How could you? You were more than my agent. More than a friend. You turned into my fucking brother, and you sell me out? For what? *What*?" I yell, spittle flying into his face.

My chest is tight. It's hard to breathe. My rib cage feels like it wants to crack open and rid itself of my swollen, infected heart.

Aaron doesn't flinch. He stares me right in the face. "If you think for one second I would sell you out like that, I'm not the agent for you. Nor am I the brother you always wanted."

My lips curl. Another snarl escapes my throat. I slam him back by the shoulders once more, then whirl away, scrubbing my face. My skin is so damned *hot*, my blood boiling. Noa's shattered expression imprints on the backs of my eyelids every time I blink.

I take a breath. My arms go slack. "Then who? Who could do this?"

"Who do you think?"

I peer at him over my shoulder. Aaron lifts off the wall, righting his towel as he strides toward me, his skin reddened where I grabbed him.

"Who has a serious vendetta against you, Stone? Your partying ways have made you a lot of enemies, but there are two I can think of that have you at the top of their lists at the moment."

I pinch my bottom lip as I stare at him. "Fuck. Ravynn and Bradley Mitchell."

"Yup." Aaron moves to the closet. "Mind if I change so I don't get beat up while in a towel?"

"I'm past wanting to punch you."

"That's a positive, at least. And yes, I saw the article the same time you did." Hangers scrape against metal as he flips through his suits. "I wanted to be certain of my hunch before talking to you, so I made some calls. It looks like Ravynn's exposé on you is more in depth than you and I thought."

"That makes no sense. I never spoke about Noa to Ravynn. Ever."

Ever since I left her, Noa was a wound I never thought would heal. When it did, she became pink scar tissue, the kind that puffs up and you always feel, the type that never goes away.

She stayed inside me, my secret scar, and I never spoke of her to my Hollywood crowd. Aaron hadn't even heard of her until recently, and that was mostly because he banished me to Falcon Haven while he sorted my shit out.

Shit that, I'm coming to realize, I should've handled myself.

Aaron chooses a navy blazer and slacks, pulling them out. "I'll call her people, see if we can come to some kind of arrangement."

"No."

Aaron pauses in laying his suit carefully on the bed. "Come again?"

"I can't have you fixing this all on your own. I have to do something."

"Stone, this is exactly why you hired me and the type of shit I deal with." Aaron folds his arms over his chest as he regards me. "Well, me and your attorney."

"Noa's having to relive the worst moments of her life because of me. My mother has to endure press at her door because of me. Falcon Haven will be swarmed by the exact types of people they hate—tourists who don't pay for anything —and I can't be responsible. I may have left this town because I felt like I was bigger than it, but I am not leaving my home to fight a monster." I nod the further I get into my argument. "I'll face it myself. Hold a press conference."

"*Whoa.*" Aaron holds out a hand. "Slow down. We are *not* talking to the press. What would you say? Is this pregnancy they're talking about real? Did she get an abortion? Did you pay for it? These are things I have to know before you pick up a microphone, buddy."

I ignore his questions. "I can't have somebody else speak for me anymore." I stride toward the door. "And I'm done running."

"Stone." Aaron's tone is sharp with warning. "Don't you turn that doorknob."

I fling the door open.

"*Stone!*"

Aaron's painstaking methods of getting clean and dressed work against him. He can't chase me down in a towel, and I rely on that as I take the stairs two at a time and burst out into the blustery air.

Twenty-Nine

NOA

I'M ABLE TO LEAVE MRS. STALINSKI'S HOUSE WHILE Stone is gone. Having him there to watch me pack would've been unbearable.

I make sure Mrs. Stalinski is comfortable on the couch with a blanket and a book before I head upstairs and collect my things. By the time I return to the living room with my suitcases, Moo has curled up between her legs and the couch cushion, purring loudly as she strokes him.

She looks up at my entrance, smiling gently. "Did you get everything, dear?"

"I think so." My voice is raw. "I'm so sorry I have to go."

"It's hardly your fault. Besides, seek pleasure because I'm now at the mercy of Berta."

Mrs. Stalinski pulls a smile from me. "I'll tell her to take it easy on you."

"I can face that dragon just fine. You make sure to get where you're going safe and sound, you hear?"

"I will." I turn my attention to my cat, that old curmudgeon looking so comfortable where he is. The empty cat carrier sits next to my bags, and Moo's lifted his head, eyeing it distrustfully. "Do you mind if Moo stays here? I hate moving him places. In his old age, he hates change."

Mrs. Stalinski barks with laughter. "I can empathize. Yes, of course he can stay, as long as you don't need him for comfort."

I walk over and brush my fingers over his fur. "He's given me so much. I feel I owe it to him to keep him where he's happy, and he loves it here."

"I'm fairly sure that's because Stone feeds him anchovies nightly."

The mention of Stone's name causes a pang in my heart. I flex my fingers, then withdraw them from Moo. Moo's also a reminder of *us* and those moments of stolen happiness we had with each other.

"I'll be back."

I'm not sure who I say it to, whether it's Moo or Mrs. Stalinski, or both.

Mrs. Stalinski catches my hand and laces her fingers with mine. "I'll hold the paparazzi off until you're ready to return."

She makes me smile again, but it quickly falls as I compare her strength to mine. "Do you think I'm weak for running away?"

Mrs. Stalinski's gaze narrows. "I don't think any such thing. I was with you when you miscarried, remember, and when your mother passed. And I was with you when you bounced back both times. You have an enormous amount of strength in you, and you draw upon it when you must. To walk around strong all the time, that eats at the soul. What makes life worth living is the difficulties, the moments of softness coupled with the broken and the boring. Take this time for yourself, dear. I don't think you've done that since my son hightailed it to Hollywood thinking he wasn't leaving anything behind."

"Why do I feel like I'm burying my head in the sand and hiding?"

"You're dealing with another beast entirely. It's a wonder to me that Stone has kept you out of the press this long. It convinces me that despite his mistakes, he truly is a good man. He wants to protect you. Let him."

Swallowing, I nod. "I'll keep in touch."

"You better."

Walking away from Mrs. Stalinski is a lot harder than I predicted. I battle back tears as I get to my car and dump all my things inside.

Berta, the new nurse, drives up just as I've turned the ignition to warm up the inside, and I walk over to her and give her last-minute instructions before leaving.

"She's the best patient you'll ever have," I assure Berta as she steps out of her pickup truck.

"I'll take good care of her, Noa," she assures.

"She has nightmares sometimes. I like to leave a glass of water next to her bed for when she wakes up parched. Oh, and sometimes she has trouble getting to the bathroom with her walker, so I bought a baby monitor just in case you can't hear her."

"Got it."

"And—"

"I don't mean this as an insult, sweetie, but I have twenty-five years experience, and nobody's died on my watch. She will be okay. Okay?"

I bite back more instructions and nod. "Okay."

Berta softens. "What's been written about you sucks. I hope it goes away soon."

"Me too."

I get in the car and refuse to look in the rearview mirror as Mrs. Stalinski's house shrinks into the distance.

I'm doing the right thing, refusing to be a sitting duck at Stone's house. Even as I leave her long drive and hit the road, the paparazzi swarms. They shout through my window and block my car. I have to inch forward, blasting the horn, and for the first time in my life, I contemplate running over another person.

My lurching and hard braking eventually gives me enough of a gap to gun through, and I leave all those men dressed in black with dangling cameras and equipment behind. To think Stone goes through this daily when he's in California boggles my mind. How he tolerates it is even more perplexing.

I drive for what seems like hours. No destination in mind —just away. Thoughts of Stone keep trying to surface, but I mentally bat them away or drown them out with music.

When it starts to get dark out, I choose a chain hotel off the highway. I figure once I've eaten, showered, and rested, I can come up with a better long-term plan.

Check in is easy, since I'm not exactly at a popular destination, and once I drop my bags on the floor of my hotel room and splay out on the bed, I check my phone.

There are a concerning number of missed calls from an LA-based number, coupled with voicemails. I listen to them, noting Aaron's nonplussed voice and his instruction for me to call him so we can put our heads together and come at this as a solid unit.

It's not a bad idea, but I need more time to process. I decide to call him later.

There are also multiple texts from Stone.

Call me. Please.

I just got home. You left so fast.

I can fix this.

Give me a chance to explain.

The last one gets me the most.

You don't have to relive this alone. Let me be with you.

My knuckles go white against the phone. I let it fall onto my chest as I stare at the ceiling, wondering if walking away from Stone was the best decision.

Yes, he hurt me deeply all those years ago, but this time with him has shown me he's changed. He's a man now, one with a public life and strangers who live off his scandals and feast on his mistakes. Everything he does is picked apart and discerned. If I stayed with him, I'd be flayed open. The little girl I never had will become public property.

And unlike him, I didn't choose this.

My phone vibrates against my chest. I think about ignoring it until I reason it could be Mrs. Stalinski, so I check the display.

It's the number of *C'est Trois*.

Confused, I rise on my elbows. If this is Stone's way of getting creative and tricking me into answering the phone ...

"Stop calling me," I say after I answer the call.

"Interesting, considering I've never contacted you before," Saint's voice drawls.

"Oh! Shit—I mean, oh, hi." I pop up, pressing the phone hard into my ear. "How can I help you?"

Saint's deep chuckle resonates through the phone. "That's a funny thing to ask, considering you're the one in the hot seat at the moment."

I slump forward. "So you've heard."

"I haven't been a small-town resident for long, but yeah, the grapevine here is faster than any winery I've been to."

"Yeah." I rub my eyes with my free hand. "It's likely the juiciest gossip Falcon Haven's had since, well, since Stone's fame."

"For what it's worth, I'm sorry this happened to you."

"Thanks." I chew on my lower lip. "Is that why you called? To check on me?"

"No, actually. I was wondering why you're not in class this evening."

"I would think that'd be obvious."

"Silly me, I took you for a woman of determination and focus, not one who scurries into a corner as soon as the shit hits the fan."

I straighten. "Ex*cuse* me?"

"Maybe it's the chef in me, but anyone who puts as much practice into the perfect plate as you have also has the gonads to continue her learning despite her personal life blowing up in her face."

"Has anyone told you that you do *not* have a way with words?"

"Why do you think I choose to spend most of my time with food? Get over here, Chef."

The way he says a title I don't deserve completely derails what I was about to say next. "I—I drove too far away."

"How far?"

"Uh..." I pull the phone away from my ear and check the maps. "Maybe an hour?"

"Class starts in forty-five. Be there."

"No—wait!" I say before he can hang up. "How can I get

through the paparazzi? They know Stone and I go to your restaurant every Tuesday."

"There's a back way. Park in the lot behind the restaurant, near the dumpster. Text me on my cell—I'll send you my number—and I'll meet you and sneak you in."

"Okay, but what about Stone? I cook with a couple. With another person, I mean. With Stone."

Ouch, it still scratches my throat to say his name.

"We'll work around it. I'll be your sous chef tonight."

"Huh? You? My couple cook?"

"Don't make me change my mind, Chef. Be here in forty-five."

Saint clicks off without saying goodbye, essentially denying me the chance to tell him where to shove it and that there's no way I'm returning to the lion's den, whose resident lion I narrowly escaped.

I stare at my phone, wondering what just happened.

Thirty

NOA

Saint meets me in the deserted parking lot as promised.

He appears from behind the dumpster as I get out of my car, his white chef coat reflecting as bright as the moonlight when he steps up to me.

"You're on time. Good," he says, gesturing with his chin for me to follow him.

I'm not sure how I got myself into this situation, but I follow him into the back of the restaurant, clinging to the words he said to me like *determination, focus, practice,* and *Chef.*

The potential he sees in me brought me here, and even during my darkest moments, I can't forget my dreams.

We enter the kitchen, where Dr. and Mr. Stanton are at their station, along with Rad and Danny. All four look up at the same time and applaud my entry.

"What? No, don't clap." I wave them off.

"Why not?" Dr. Stanton says. "You deserve it. We're glad you're here."

"Yes, don't let the scandal of a secret pregnancy with the hottest actor on the planet keep you away," Danny says.

There's no venom behind it, just a genuine grin, and I try to laugh at it in the way he must see it. It's a strange pull of my lips, to smile at what was once so painful, but I have to admit, it's different in a good way.

"Plus, I prefer to lose to my top competition through a fair fight, not because a bitchy diva kicked the spotlight away," Rad says.

To that, I laugh. "I'd prefer it, too."

"Enough chitchat," Saint says, clapping his hands together to get our attention. "Tonight's a tough one, and I'm not taking it easy on any of you. Noa, especially. As your de facto sous chef, I'll expect to see perfection in everything you do."

I nod, my chest lifting eagerly. This is exactly the distraction I need.

"Let's get started with coq au vin and pear galette. Two of my favorite meals, so don't fuck it up."

"He's so lovely," Danny mutters to Rad.

I jump to it, setting up my station and throwing myself into preparing the food.

Saint wasn't lying when he warned he'd become a sous chef nightmare. He critiqued everything I did, insulted my pastry methods, and all but tossed my first attempt in the trash beside our station.

If I wasn't so desperate to disappear into the bowl of macerating pears, I would've stormed out. If my storming out wasn't so parallel to how Stone behaved in this class, I would've thrown my apron at Saint and said none of this is worth it. A couples' cooking class isn't supposed to be so *mean*.

When, in fact, it completely distracted me from my real life.

I took each of his criticisms on the chin, redoing my cuts and re-chopping—essentially starting over every time he snapped, "Nope."

I had brief respites when he'd move on to the other stations, but he always returned, his footsteps soundless but his expression speaking volumes.

By the time I'm finished, I'm covered in flour and smelling like chicken fat and vanilla—not a great combo.

But my dishes look fantastic.

Even Rad gives an impressed downturn of his lips as he passes. His husband, Danny, hugs me tightly before leaving, as does Dr. Stanton. They clean up a lot faster than me since they didn't have to repeat the recipes three times, but I don't mind. Where do I have to be? I made it so I could disappear.

"You have talent," Saint says, standing in front of my station.

"Really? Because I was about to ask if you convinced me to return simply for your twisted entertainment."

Saint smirks. "I seek better forms of entertainment than watching an amateur slice chicken."

"Ah. So I'm back to an amateur cook." I scrape the remnants into the trash.

"An amateur with promise."

"I'll write that on my next plaque." I stack the dishes and wipe down my counter. "Or hey, in my online review of this restaurant."

"Touché." Saint chuckles. "I've said this before, but this was my father's idea. A way to endear ourselves to this town."

"Nice work."

"He didn't say *I* had to be nice. He's the man out front, greeting all our patrons by name. I'm the one getting the menu up to standard and offering lessons to people who consider cooking a hobby rather than a serious vocation."

"Is that what you think I'm doing? Treating this like I would a yoga class or knitting circle? Cooking is in my blood. Becoming a chef was my dream until—" I stop, shake my head. "I guess it's not a secret anymore. I still can't say it, though. It's like it gets stuck in my throat, swallows me whole."

"I know."

His acknowledgment stops me short.

When I lift my eyes to his, I'm surprised to find the tropical warmth I assumed he lacked.

"I have a daughter. I can only imagine the pain you felt."

"Thank you," I whisper.

"I can also see the reason behind your dream. You're very good, even after all these years with no practice. You have the skill, Noa. The patience and the drive. It's difficult, working your way up, but if you were willing, there's no age limit in pursuing a chef's career."

My answering laugh comes out uncomfortable. "I couldn't."

"Why not?"

His direct question makes me stumble. "Because—because I'm needed here."

"By whom?"

I don't think Saint means it as hurtful as it comes out. At least, I don't think he does.

"My patients," I explain slowly. "People I care about and take care of."

"And what about yourself? Have you ever heard of self-care?"

"Of course I have," I scoff. "I just don't have time for it."

"Make time," he snaps, and I jolt. "Most of those under me

would've burst into tears after what I put you through tonight. Many would've quit three weeks ago when we started. But you continued to show up, even when that man of yours told you that you deserved better. But that's the way of dreams, isn't it? You're willing to trudge through a lot of nightmares to reach them."

"I ... it's too late."

"It's never too late." Saint leans forward, palming my station and bringing us face-to-face. "What if I told you I had an opening for you?"

My eyes go wide. "Here? In this restaurant? I could never. And I don't know when I'll feel safe enough to walk through this town, never mind work at a popular restaurant."

"Not here." Saint keeps his stare level with mine. It's disconcerting how darkly handsome he is. How intimidating. "This is my father's restaurant. Mine is in Paris."

"Whaaaat?" The word comes out in a nervous melody.

"I'm here as a favor." His gaze shutters for a moment, telling me he's not being entirely truthful. "But my restaurants are still very much in business. I could get you in as a commis chef, nothing special, and you could work your way up while attending culinary school. Intakes at Le Cordon Bleu start in January."

"I'm aware." My heart rate spikes just hearing him speak of it.

"The only downside is that I'm a very impatient man, and I'd need you to fly over there right about now before I replace you with someone else."

"No way." I rear back, splaying my hands. "I'm not anyone's charity case, despite what the media tells you. This— what's going on with Stone and I—is a blip. I'm a better

295

woman than what you see in front of you. I'm not normally this messy. I'm not *broken* and in need of help."

"Who's discussing you as a woman?" Saint is openly thrown. "I'm talking about your culinary abilities. I'm sure as hell not a therapist who can listen to you unpack anything else. And I don't do charity. I see potential, and I want to capitalize on it. And I *will* make money off you if you take my advice, get out of Falcon Haven, and do something better for yourself."

I don't know how to answer him, so I just stare.

He sighs. "I'll let you finish up. Then I'll walk you to your car, and you can think about it."

Saint doesn't give me time to answer, walking away until he disappears around the corner.

Leaving me with the biggest, most life-changing decision of my life as his salute.

Thirty-One

NOA

Carly's waiting in front of my hotel when I pull in.

"What are you doing here?" I ask, shutting my car door. "And—*how*?"

Carly holds up her phone in answer. "Find My Friends, friend. I can locate you anywhere, especially in a crisis where you have to leave town in order to save face."

My head lolls back and I stare at the starry sky in exhaustion. Puffs of my exhale obscure the brilliant view. "The more I think about it, the more I wonder if running away fixes anything."

Carly makes a sympathetic sound as she slips her arm around my waist, and we walk inside. "It's probably one of those catch-22 situations. You can't win either way, just do what's best for you."

"You sound like Mrs. Stalinski," I say longingly. "I miss her."

"Not as much as I'm sure you miss a cold glass of chardonnay. As your bestie, it's my job to direct you to the nearest bar."

My body angles toward her, agreeing with that notion before my mind does. It's been an exhausting day compounded by a demanding night—and capped off with a heavy decision. It's on my lips to unload on Carly, tell her about this crazy Paris opportunity that I didn't see coming, but I stop myself, thinking it's better to do this after a few sips of wine before I hear everything my lovely, opinionated friend has to say.

She isn't here as my drinking buddy. Carly wants to dissect the breaking news today and Stone's role in it. That alone will require some prolonged sips.

I'm not one to deny the friend that stood by me anything she wants to know, so I break the ice once we sit down and the hotel bartender takes our order. The bar area has an old-fashioned vibe meant for the cigar-smoking men of old, with dark wood, brass finishings, and embellished mirrors behind rows of liquor.

"Did you read the article?" I ask.

"Did I read the article," she repeats, snorting. "Hell yeah, I did. About twenty times. Say my favorite word to me, and I'll get right on it."

I respond with a small smile.

"C'mon," she nudges. "Do it. Say it."

"It's not libel," I admit, leaning back as far as I can on the barstool.

"Dammit. I meant for you to say it *without* canceling it out."

"You were there. Everything this reporter wrote about is the truth."

"I'd hardly call her a reporter. More like a *Gossip Girl* reject who probably has a lizard as a pet and plays online bingo in her spare time."

The bartender sets our glasses down at the perfect time. I'm in the middle of quenching my stress when Carly bursts out with that line, and I nearly choke.

"Your loyalty is unmatched, even when it makes no sense," I say after collecting myself. "But sadly, there's nothing other than our mutual opinion of her to go on."

"You're annoyingly correct." Carly rests her chin in her hands and sighs. "I turned that article upside-down and sideways. She alluded to an abortion, but not enough to sue. The joy of the First Amendment." She lifts her wine. "Cheers to that."

"Your support means a lot. And coming here when it's completely out of your way."

"Are you kidding? I'm here for you, Noa. Always. We're there for each other, no matter what. So take another sip. Or gulp. Go on." She tilts my glass farther when it reaches my lips. "Up, up, up. There we go. Now you can tell me how fucking Stone has fucked this day up further."

I cough, pulling the glass away from my mouth. The bartender gives us the side-eye. Wiping the droplets with the back of my hand, I respond, "That's all it was. Fucking. Very astute of you to notice."

She makes *tsk* sound. "Sorry, babe. Overruled."

"You're not a judge. You're a lawyer."

"I'm whoever I damn well want to be when probing into your sex life. Tell me the truth. That's the only way we'll get through this together."

I chuckle, rubbing my eyes. I'm exhausted, famished, and uplifted by her presence. "I might've caught some feelings."

"Some? More like the seeds of him that remained grew into

a giant weed that's overgrown and impossible to eradicate now."

"Your analogies are wonderful."

"The jurors love 'em. And you love Stone."

I whip toward her, appalled. "Do *not*."

"Stop bullshitting me, Noa. You can pretend to the town that you've moved on and bury yourself in a life of servitude because you blame yourself for your daughter's death and not saving your mother, but I *know* the truth. I can hear your heart a mile away, and it wants him. Frankly, you never left him. Not really."

I sniff hard, refusing to let any more tears fall and hide my face behind my wine. "You don't get to do that—say those things so easily, like I can be summed up in a sentence."

"That's not at all what I'm trying to do." Carly leans forward, her hair flashing into fire under the recessed lights. Her eyes don't contain the same flame. They simmer with low warmth. "Maybe I'm quick to say it because I'm fully aware of how much it kills you to hear it. But I was beside you on the bathroom floor. I slept in the same bed as you for weeks. It was my pre-mixed, burned, more rectangular than circular cookie that you ate after refusing meals for days. Stone didn't see any of it. I'm not sure I'll ever forgive him for that."

I exhale, leaning away. "I've learned it's more complicated. When it happened, I emailed his assistant and left him a voice-mail. That's all I did. It never occurred to me what reading or hearing it might do to him. I was convinced he forgot me as soon as he passed the *Welcome to Falcon Haven* sign. My contacting him was more closure for me, hoping that once I did I could move on, which, of course, I didn't."

"He fucking deserved it."

"No. That's the time he started partying, getting into trouble. I didn't realize that until we spoke and I looked back on his history in the tabloids. He got into drugs, too, Carly. Married someone he barely knew. Got arrested for a DUI, surrounded himself with people who didn't care about William Stalinski and just wanted Stone William's luck and money. Does that sound like a man who didn't care he lost a child?"

"He didn't call you. Didn't talk to you about it." Carly crosses her arms while flicking her gaze at the bartender for another round. "That's the least he could've done. Not act like the spoiled prick he did."

I nod. "And I could've told him why I stayed. Why I wasn't going with him to LA. His whole life, people have left him, his dad being the first. He believed I didn't give a shit about him, that I felt he wasn't worth more than an angry voicemail when we lost her."

"What was he going to do if you gave birth to a healthy baby? I'm sorry, Noa, but I need to ask this if this is the direction you're going. Her loss was—"

"Convenient for him?" My voice cracks. "That's what I thought, too, until we spoke. I may not have wanted him in my life, but he wanted to be a part of hers. He wanted to prove himself worthy, especially after I rejected him."

Carly purses her lips in thought. The bartender comes over, refreshing our glasses until Carly says, "Just give us the damn bottle," and swipes it out of his hand.

Her phone pings. Carly finishes pouring, hands me an overflowing glass, then checks it.

She frowns.

"What is it?" I ask.

"It's ..." She peers closer. "Huh. Stone's put out a statement."

"He *what*?"

I resist swiping the phone out of her hands. Then I do.

"It's a video," I say, staring at the screen. Stone's face is frozen in a lopsided grin, his dimples prominent. His eyes aren't as endearing. They're shadowed, his sapphire irises blackened by the pixelated quality and lined with tension. The background behind him looks suspiciously like Mrs. Stalinski's living room.

"What are you waiting for? Play the man," Carly says.

I tap play, and Stone's velvet, baritone voice flows into the space between Carly and me.

"By now, you've been made aware of my high school sweetheart and the tragedy that struck between us. I won't name her because an article written without our permission or input has shattered her privacy enough.

"Ten years ago, I wasn't famous. I wasn't interesting. Hell, I wasn't Stone Williams. I was William Stalinski, a boy who grew up on a farm but wanted nothing to do with it. I had a father who felt the same and a mother who sold that farm, worked two jobs, and made it her life's work to raise a good and noble son. If you look at my documented history, you might assume she failed. She would argue otherwise."

Stone's gaze moves off-camera, the skin around his eyes relaxing, his entire face transforming into one of adoration. When he returns to the camera, that love shuts off.

"I've never admitted or felt bad about my mistakes. They started off small, so why should I apologize? Yes, I caught barn rats along with the cats and unleashed them on my school so I didn't have to go. Yes, I sent a Trojan virus to the school principal known to open all his spam emails and click on suspicious links, and got finals suspended. Yes, I snuck into fairgrounds after hours and fell in love with a goody-two-shoes, shy, smart-mouthed

girl who told me to save a kitten if I wanted to get into her good graces.

"And I did. I would do anything for that girl and the woman she's turned into. I sure as hell didn't stop getting into shit, but I wanted less of it when I was with her. We made something together, she and I, and that glow, that gorgeous shot of lightning, will never be forgotten."

"Uh-oh," Carly murmurs, frantically searching for bar napkins before she hands me a stack.

It's just in time to catch the overflow.

"The way the media's portrayed her is more than hurtful to me. It's deplorable. You don't know this woman, and I don't want you to. I've given you an all-access pass to my life as it is, and that's okay by me. I love my fans, but I adore her, and I can't let this go on as it is. We had a chance at a child. We lost it. That's all you need to know. I'm sitting here, in my hometown, in my home, with my mother behind the camera, asking you to leave her be. You have my permission to discuss me however you want—my club fight with Bradley Mitchell, for one, or my two-day marriage to Ravynn—seriously, I give you guys a ton of crazy to dissect.

"But this woman, she's the afterglow of that lightning. The permanent scorch mark on the Earth. And I will not have her belittled or taken apart. She is mine. My light." Stone pats his chest. *"And despite all I've done and what I've made her endure, she has stayed for my family.*

"Sweetheart, if you're listening to this..."

I straighten in my seat.

"I have spent my entire life thinking about myself, my accolades, reaching the next level and always coming first. I should've put you in the forefront. It should've been you. And I've regretted my decision to leave you for over a decade. I don't want you

watching this away from me. I'd like you here, beside me, so I can tell you in person that I've stopped hiding where I've come from. Because that's you. You're my home."

"Holy shit." Carly presses the side of her face against mine, both of us enraptured by Stone's speech.

"Consider this my public withdrawal from the upcoming filming of Cascade. *I can't in good faith complete this film if I want to stop running and start focusing on what's important. And that's my family. Thank you for listening. I love you all. Goodbye."*

The last image is Stone reaching for the camera and the screen going black.

Silence stretches between Carly and me. She's so frozen in shock, she doesn't even reach for the wine bottle for something to do.

I laugh, a weird and free one, my hands shaking, a light sheen of sweat on my skin, and my heart bursting with adrenaline. "What the hell did he just do?"

She says, "Well, I guess you'd better call him."

I toss her phone at her and reach for mine.

Thirty-Two

NOA

Stone didn't answer any of my calls. After leaving two voicemails and a few texts, I decide to give it a rest.

He's probably been inundated with calls, emails, and text messages about his surprise stream. Aaron's blowing a gasket somewhere, no doubt screening Stone's calls, but what disappoints me is that I'm not one of those people being let through.

I finish the bottle with Carly, and *because* we finished the bottle, take her up to my hotel room to share a bed and sleep it off together.

I'm deep in dreamland where scenes and people don't exactly make sense when a buzzing wakes me.

Rolling, I pick up my phone and squint through the dark. I rise onto my side when I see the string of notifications.

8 missed calls.

3 voicemails.

1 text.

Frowning, I come into a sit, my eyes adjusting to the brightness of the screen as I tap on the text message first.

Stone: It's Mom.

I RACE through the hospital doors, familiar enough with the layout that I reach the oncology floor in minutes.

The elevators open directly into the waiting room where I find Stone pacing, hands on his head.

"Stone!" I rush up to him.

Fear and love pour into my body, urging me to put my hands on his waist and pull him close. Tensed muscle and the soft fabric of his shirt brushes against my palms. I dig my fingers in, and it's like trying to carve into a rock.

"It was so fast." Stone's voice is hoarse. He won't look at me. I stare up at the underside of his chin, covered with day-old scruff.

"What happened?"

"She fell walking to the bathroom."

"Berta's supposed to help her when she needs help at night." My brows draw together. I scan the waiting room where there is one other couple talking quietly in their seats and another man with his head thrown back, snoozing. No Berta.

"Where is she?" There's an edge to my voice. "How could she have missed—"

"I let her go."

My head snaps back to Stone. "You what?"

"I thought I could do it. I *wanted* to do it." Stone's voice breaks. He tears out of my grasp, digging his fingers in his hair as he whirls, the cords of his arms drawing a haphazard map along his skin.

"She's my mother. I should be able to help her through her worst moments. And I did everything you told me—set up the monitor next to my bed to listen for her. But she didn't call out. Not until..."

Stone's unable to finish.

"It's all right," I soothe.

"They won't tell me anything other than she's fractured her hip."

"Oh no."

With the cancer eating at her bones, Mrs. Stalinski's become unnaturally fragile for her age.

"The doc told me to wait, but I'm about to bust through those doors, alarm or not. I have to know if she's okay. It's my fault she's lying in a hospital with broken bones." Stone's voice wrenches.

I grab his face and force him to steady. "Listen to me. There is nothing you could have done. She didn't call out. She didn't ask for help. She got out of bed, and as wonderful as she is, your mother is a stubborn mule. Even if Berta stayed, she wouldn't have heard either."

Stone moves his head, shaking out of my hold, his eyes hazy with pain and responsibility. "I should've protected her. Slept next to her. Prevented this. What's fucked up is I don't know what *this* is. Nobody will talk to me!"

His shout draws the attention of others in the waiting room.

"I'll sort this out." I draw my shoulders up. "My credentials will get me past that door. Is Dr. Silver here?"

Stone nods, his stare remaining vacant. Somewhere else. "She's talking to the orthopedic surgeon."

Surgeon. My stomach plummets.

"I'll track them down and get answers." I turn to the doors, but Stone's voice stops me.

"Thank you, Noa. I don't know what I'd do without you."

I give him my profile, lowering my chin in a half nod. "I'd do more if I could."

Stone doesn't answer. He falls back into a bucket seat, slumping over and covering his face with his hands.

No matter what I say, he'll blame himself.

It's what we all do.

DR. SILVER and the orthopedic surgeon, Dr. Patel, give me the answers I need, none of them good.

I return to Stone in the waiting room. He's wide awake despite the early hour, his chin resting on his hand as he stares off at nothing.

As soon as he spots me, he jerks upright. "What did you find out?"

"She'll need hip surgery." I communicate the bad news as best I can, and as fast as I can. "But you knew that since Dr. Silver consulted with a surgeon. The problem is your mom's ability to handle anesthesia. Her immune system's compromised. In this situation, it's good she hasn't restarted chemo yet, but with the way she is now, there's about a fifty-fifty chance she'll pull through."

Stone swallows. "And if we choose not to do the surgery? Or wait?"

I work my jaw back and forth. "It wouldn't be good. She'd be in a lot of pain. The doctors are talking to your mom shortly. You can go on back and see her."

"Have you seen her?"

I shake my head.

In answer, Stone holds out his hand. And he says the three words I dreamed he would say when I rewrote our past and had him stay ten years ago.

"I need you."

His fingers intertwine with mine when I take his hand, and we both walk to Mrs. Stalinski's room together.

She's sitting upright in her private hospital room (probably a demand of Stone's), her eyes closed with purple bruising underneath. A thin blanket covers her. If we hadn't been told she'd fractured her hip, I'd think she was comfortably resting after a doctor's checkup. There isn't much to wrap a hip in, other than to keep it as still as possible.

Stone walks up to one side of her bed. I go on the other, careful of the morphine drip hanging on an IV stand, the button close to Mrs. Stalinski's slack hand.

"They have her on a lot of drugs," Stone observes when his mother doesn't twitch as he takes her hand.

"The best pain meds available," I assure him. "She doesn't feel a thing."

Stone cups his mother's hand in both of his own. Then he drops his head and cries.

I go to him, rounding the bed and twisting him to face me, though he resists. Stone hates crying. He always has. To him, it's a weakness he will never give someone else to wield against him.

But it's me.

"Stone. Stone, Stone ..." I repeat his name in soft bursts, each a beckoning call, until he folds into me, his tears coating the side of my neck.

I reach up, hugging as much of his broad frame as I can and

holding on tight. My hands span his back, his bones and tendons rippling with agony as he moans into my skin.

"I'm sorry," I say. It's a nothing statement, but that's okay, because nothing helps in this situation. Nobody can make it better.

It's at that moment the two doctors come in, their faces grim.

Stone lifts his head, moving his hands to my shoulders and gripping tight.

"Give it to me straight," he says hoarsely.

And they do.

Thirty-Three

NOA

MRS. STALINSKI'S HIP SURGERY WOULD TAKE THREE hours. Dr. Patel was particularly convincing, as he had a father with cancer who had to undergo the same surgery to maintain a comfortable quality of life.

It wasn't about fixing Mrs. Stalinski, but about keeping her as pain-free with as little suffering as possible during her final days.

Stone's permission was perfunctory. Mrs. Stalinski had given her consent and was fully aware of the situation before they gave her a heavy dose of morphine.

And, in typical Mrs. Stalinski fashion, she told them to do the darned thing and make the screaming pain go away already.

What Stone and I did not expect was to see Dr. Patel during what should've been an hour into the surgery.

Stone goes rigid beside me. I put a hand on his forearm. "It could just be an update. In the condition she's in, they know to keep loved ones in the loop so we don't worry too much."

Although, they'd usually send a nurse. I don't voice my thoughts as Dr. Patel strides toward our seats.

Stone's arm relaxes under my hand.

We stand when Dr. Patel reaches us.

He pinches his full lips, and I notice the pale cast to his light brown complexion.

The rest of my heart, what remained of it when my mother left, shrivels and falls to the floor.

Stone doesn't require the doctor to elaborate either. He emits a low sound, a groan of denial before his expression twists and it takes every shred of his being to remain still.

"I'm sorry," Dr. Patel says. "She didn't make it. We did everything we could."

My hearing tunnels. I lose all my senses my vision bleeding in and out, focused solely on the movement of Dr. Patel's lips.

I vaguely register Stone's arm encircling my waist and holding me against him.

The tears don't come yet as I cling to Mrs. Stalinski as I knew her yesterday. Tired, weakened, but alive and hugging me to her, assuring me I'd get through this blip the same way I've fought through every other tragedy in my life.

She believed in me.

I believed in her.

And now she's gone.

I twist my face into Stone, his sweater turning my tears into dew that coats my cheeks and dampens my hair.

His fingers dig into my shoulder. I feel his chin fall onto the top of my head.

"You can go back and see her. Spend as much time with her as you like. Say your goodbyes," Dr. Patel says softly.

His footsteps fade. Neither of us moves.

Stone's other arm comes around my shoulders, and we rock back and forth for as long as it takes.

And it'll take forever.

Mrs. Stalinski's funeral is exactly how she would have wanted it.

The entire town came together, all of Falcon Haven closing down for the memorial. Mrs. Stalinski didn't want to be buried in the cemetery. She asked that her ashes be spread on the nearby shores of the Atlantic Ocean. Stone planned on pouring her ashes privately and spending his last moments with her. Until then, Mrs. Stalinski asked for a memorial brimming with food and an open bar for the residents of Falcon Haven, courtesy of the Tipsy Falcon.

The one thing she couldn't plan for was the season she'd die. Although, with the seasonal flowers she chose and her pick of a gathering in the warmth of the Merc as opposed to the park she used to love daily walks in makes me believe she had a good idea as time ticked down.

Maisy had her baker prepare over one hundred Falcon's Talons, Mrs. Stalinski's favorite sweet treat, and she handed them out on the house as everyone trickled in that morning, no black clothing allowed.

I'm sipping on a coffee in the corner, dressed in Mrs. Stalinski's favorite color, red, my hair down and in waves and with heavy makeup. My eyes required extra attention since they're so swollen from crying. My cheeks, too, since they've lost all color.

The parallels between my mother and Stone's are almost too much to bear. My mom also opted for a memorial, but since she died in the summer, they held hers at the gazebo in the middle of Haven Park, with tulips and chocolate truffles as her favors to the crowd. I don't like to ponder that time—I'm adept at shutting that part of my brain off—but as I watch Mrs. Stalinski's neighbors and friends trickle into the Merc, faces somber with bright dresses and suits, my throat thickens, and I'm convinced I'll break down crying. Again.

In a fit of desperation, I scan the crowd for Stone's tall presence. I didn't have him when my mom passed, and to have him now, to be both a pillar of grief and support, causes mixed emotions in me I don't yet know how to interpret.

After Mrs. Stalinski's passing, he and I are both left without family. Adrift. Needing each other.

I'm not ashamed to admit I'm drawn to him like a magnet.

We've spoken little since the hospital. We haven't touched on the media leak or the source behind revealing the loss of my baby, but the very paparazzi that enjoyed making my life hell wait outside the Merc, eager to use their expensive cameras up against the windows and catch Stone's last moments with his mother.

Maisy, bless her, predicted their evil plans and has covered her windows in all the bed sheets she could get her hands on. Maroon, hunter green, and navy blue king-sized sheets block every window, a strange but loving ode to her friend, and in keeping with Christmas.

A tinkling sound runs through the crowd, people hitting their spoons against their coffee cups and drink glasses.

Heads turn, and at last, I catch Stone, using the small podium Maisy constructed in the middle of the cafe and a microphone stand on loan from the Tipsy Falcon.

Stone clears his throat. Even in grief, he's the handsomest

in the room, his pale skin contrasting with his dark, thick hair and piercing, though red-rimmed, eyes.

He is perfection, and my heart tugs at the sight of him. If I'm honest, my heart hasn't stopped being pulled toward him since the day we first met in high school.

"Thank you all for coming," he says. "It would mean a lot to my mother to see you all here, gathered in her honor and eating your weight in falcon's feet and booze."

Chuckles and laughter follow.

He smiles sadly. "Judy Stalinski grew up here. She had her son here, grew her roots here, and never wanted to move, despite her son's bribery of a mansion in Malibu to get her to leave."

More laughter. Even I grin at the thought of Mrs. Stalinski making herself at home in Malibu.

"But that was her. She didn't care what her son did, as long as he was happy—and stopped stealing the flowers from the box planters in front of Feather's Flowers." Stone gives his trademark grin. "Hey, they weren't part of the inventory and free, right?"

The owner of Feather's Flowers shakes her head and waggles her finger at him, but with a doting expression. I dip my chin in decades-old embarrassment since most often, he tossed those flowers he swiped into a haphazard bouquet for me, Stone's way of begging my forgiveness for whatever current shit he'd gotten himself into.

"Jokes aside," Stone continues as the lighthearted laughter dies down. "My mother is a woman who will never be replaced. I loved her so much. It's giving me an ungodly amount of pain to stand in front of you right now and acknowledge that she's not here anymore. I will see her every time I look in the mirror, but I won't have her life behind my eyes, or her wise smile, or her unwavering patience. She was a force, and though I am but a reflection of her, her spirit lives on in this town. Her one wish was to have me return to Falcon Haven, a place where her heart will always remain, and I know, every time I *do* return here, I will see her in the eyes of all of you. In the architecture she loved, the local businesses she made it her priority to support, and the friends she made and loved. I—" Stone abruptly stops, putting a fist to his mouth.

I start forward at the moment Maisy steps onto the podium and gently takes the microphone from him.

"We all love listening to Judy's pride and joy," she says, "but if you'll give me a few moments of your time, I'd love to say a few words about my dear friend."

Stone rubs Maisy's shoulder in thanks, departing from the podium with his head down.

He takes a direct line out of the cafe and into the grocery section. I part the crowd with quiet "excuse me" and "pardon me" to get to him, but he's moving too fast.

Concerned, I set my half-finished coffee down on the nearest flat surface and pick up my pace, leaving the crowd behind.

I pass Carly, who squeezes my arm in support, and Rome, who nods his respect, and even Aaron, leaning against the wall with his arms crossed as he subtly scrolls through his phone.

I have to believe he's working on important tasks relating to Stone. Otherwise, I'm sure Stone would've decked him on his way past.

It also serves as a stark reminder that I'll never understand Stone's life outside of Falcon Haven, one requiring constant management by other people because he's watched by the world at all times.

Maisy's borrowed bed sheets can only protect him for so long.

I follow Stone's steps into the back storage room, and though I've lost sight of him, a sudden arc of light in the darkened warehouse tells me he's leaving.

"Stone!" I call, hoping to stall him before he gets into his car.

Racing outside, I hold a hand to my eyes, the sun bright and blinding in a clear, cold sky.

In seconds, my body takes priority, demanding I wrap my arms around myself to protect my exposed skin from the cold.

Snow has yet to fall, but that doesn't mean the temperature is snowflake worthy.

"Stone!" My teeth chatter.

I don't see him in the back alley where a thin, one-way road allows for trucks and cars to park. I figured I'd see his sleek black vehicle as soon as my eyes adjusted, but all I face is frosted-over curbs and black tarmac.

I haven't heard the expensive purr of his engine, which gives me hope. My heels hit the pavement hard with my quick strides as I head to the corner.

Dread collects in my belly, ice chips trickling through my inner warmth. I don't know why, but I feel like if I don't catch him right now, I'll never see him again.

An instinct, the unavoidable nudge of history repeating itself, collects inside me. He'll say goodbye to his mother and leave for Hollywood again.

As much as we've been through together, I don't know if I'm enough for him to come back to.

It's a hopeless thought, dark, depressing, and perfectly encompassing my sadness over Mrs. Stalinski's death.

All I know is I need to see him. One more time. His speech

to the public plays like a reel inside my head, providing me with the strength to find him, but not enough to ask him to stay. Not if he doesn't want to.

"Hey! Noa!"

I whirl at the sound of my name, surprised to see Saint running toward me with my coat on his arm.

Shivering, I halt in the middle of the sidewalk.

"I saw you run out of there," he says, his breaths clouding the air between us. "Thought you might need this."

"T-Thank you." I turn, allowing him to settle the coat on my shoulders.

In time to see Stone round the corner and watch Saint smooth my jacket by my shoulders.

His expression hardens, his black woolen coat doing nothing to hide the bunching of his muscles underneath. He prowls closer.

"The fuck are you doing touching her?" he snaps at Saint.

Saint stays behind me, but I don't have to turn to predict his casual enjoyment as he watches Stone approach.

"Getting the lady her coat," Saint responds, "since it seems she was left to chase you down without one."

Stone's lip curls.

I raise my hand to Stone, quelling any insult or, let's be honest, fighting words. If it were any other day, I'd push at Stone and tell him to choke on his jealous streak because it is so damned unnecessary when he's the only man I see.

But today ... I just don't have the strength.

"It doesn't mean anything," I say to Stone. "I was looking for you. Worried about you."

Stone looks between me and Saint, suspicion lining his grief-stricken features.

"And, I assume, saying goodbye," Saint says.

I wheel around to pin him with a look. "Thanks for the coat. You can go now."

Saint rocks back on his heels, his hands tucked into his coat pockets. He's a typical, arrogant, fearless chef, but even he has his limits and can resist baiting a man who just lost his mother.

I brace myself for the opposite.

"I'm sorry for your loss," Saint says to Stone.

"Thanks," Stone mutters.

My shoulders relax.

"I didn't come here to start anything," Saint continues, "I was looking for Noa since you aren't returning any of my calls. Understandable, of course," he adds when I open my mouth to argue, and Stone puts a possessive hand on my arm. "I didn't know your mother, though she sounds like an outstanding woman, so I'll respectfully take my leave."

Stone relaxes his stance beside me. I finally allow myself to exhale.

"I just wanted to confirm you'll be coming with me to Paris," Saint says. "Our flight leaves in twenty-four hours."

Oh shit.

Stone's grip tightens like a vise. "What's he talking about?"

"Oh. Whoops." Saint widens his eyes theatrically. "I'll let you two figure it out."

I could kill him. I really could if too much death didn't already surround me. I settle for glaring daggers into his back as he walks away, mentally cataloging all the ways I'll threaten him later.

"Noa." Stone redirects my attention. "What the hell is he talking about?"

I sigh and face him; the wind picking up speed and billowing my hair behind me. It's ice-driven and freezing, enough to overtake the blush I thought I needed. "It's nothing like how he insinuated, and honestly, if it wasn't such an opportunity, I wouldn't go anywhere with that jerk."

"Go *where*?" Stone's eyes are as bright as the sky behind him. Bright, yearning, and concerned.

It hurts to look at him. "To work in his restaurant. And go to culinary school enrolling in January. In—"

"Paris," he finishes, his voice chilled.

I swallow and nod. "This was before your mom—"

Stone holds up a gloved hand to stop me. "You should go. She would want you to."

My chest turns to ice. "What? Really?"

"It's an amazing opportunity, like you said."

"It is," I agree, "but you're important to me, too. I'm not going anywhere until I know you're okay."

Stone's expression shutters, colder than the air surrounding us and as unmoving as his new name. "You won't say no to the chef because of me, right? I'm getting out of this town as soon as I can. Aaron booked me a flight to LA this evening."

"And you're going?" I hate how unsure my question sounds. Clingy and full of tremors, just like a decade ago. "But your speech just now..."

"Falcon Haven was important to my mother, yes. But she's not here anymore. And my home is in LA. I'm sorry, Noa. We got each other through a horrible time, and I can't thank you enough for being there for me and showing so much support, but I think it's time we move on. My mother wouldn't want us to stay here because we felt some sort of debt to each other."

My mouth falls open, and I balk at him. "Debt? That's what I am to you?"

He responds with a lopsided smile, the one that makes women melt because of how handsome, innocent, and beguiling it is.

I'm sickened under its scope.

"We needed each other to heal our wounds from when we were kids," he says. "It's time for us to grow up. What I said online, about staying here and giving up *Cascade*, I wasn't thinking right. I was angry, emotional, and not being smart about your future. You were never meant to be a nurse. You should pursue your passion the same way I pursued mine. I don't want to keep you from that."

"I..." I fold my arms over my middle, as if that can keep me from tearing apart. "I was going to say yes to Saint. Maybe"— and this part hurts the most— "you're right. Mrs. Stalinski would want me to go. And *I* want to go."

"So you should go," Stone repeats.

He jumps in place, retaining warmth as his cheeks and nose redden.

"Who were we going to spend Christmas with, anyway?" he asks.

You.

But if I say it out loud, I might break.

I can't believe he weakened me again. That I let him break through my carefully placed walls, that I could allow him to worm his way into a heart full of holes.

"Both our moms are gone. Any invitations would be pity," Stone reasons. "So go to Paris. Christmas in Paris is a sight to behold, and you deserve it."

My face freezes into one of disbelief. I can't look at him anymore, and my feet started retreating from the moment he snapped the remaining heartstring between us.

That's why I don't register the cold leather of his glove on my cheek or the way he yanks my face to his so abruptly and with such finality that I don't have time to gasp when his lips capture mine.

The fiery heat of his mouth thaws my lips. They part for him, his silken tongue sending fireworks into my mouth as he strokes. Our heads angle, our teeth cut into sensitive flesh. We press so hard together, we're icicles forming to a deadly point.

I moan into his mouth. It comes out as more of a lament, a *please don't go* kind of sound, and it brings tears to my eyes.

Stone rips away, leaving both of us gasping opaque white clouds.

He gives me one last stare, his blue irises broken shards of beauty. "I wish you the best of luck, Noa. I really do."

And with that, he turns, walking away for the final time.

I blink the tears back. My hands form fists at my sides.

And I remind myself that getting on that plane tomorrow is my damned decision and a chance to become the person I was always meant to be.

Thirty-Four

STONE

Letting Noa go was the worst and best decision I've ever made.

It's difficult to put her image at the backs of my eyes and focus on the present. Those wide eyes of hers, her stern look when I piss her off, the way she admonishes me, then strokes me with her tongue. How she looks at me like I'm still worthwhile, despite all I've done. And the moment she opened her arms to me, and I walked away.

That's the worst one—the hurt in her eyes, the kind I keep causing.

I couldn't hold her back a second time. That is exactly what I read in her eyes, that she'd sacrifice her dreams—again —for me.

It's the kind of girl she is, but I'm a different man now. It split me in two to push her away—fuck, did it ever. But if my mother has taught me anything, it's being selfless even when you are bearing the most pain you've ever endured before.

I'd be better off with Noa by my side. She would pick up where my mother left off, keeping me to high standards and giving herself to me wholly whenever I needed it.

I'm evolving, but I'm not so cocky as to believe I've transformed into a man as greedy as that. To separate Noa from her passion would be unforgivably selfish, and I meant what I said to her and go over every word every time I'm forced to be without her—she's my home. I can turn my back on that solace in favor of her happiness because I'm not so sure I'm hers.

And so, after spreading my mom's ashes on a borrowed boat and even seeing a humpback whale after I did it—*hi, Mom*, I'd thought through a frozen body and blurred vision—I board a private plane with Aaron and go back to the place I've called my home for over a decade.

There's no human component to my return. I dodge the press at the airport and hole up in my coastal mansion, reading scripts and catching up on the latest *Cascade* schedule.

I meant what I said when I'd walk away from the role. But then my mom died, and Noa received the chance of a lifetime (from a douchebag, but he's a talented douchebag with more connections than I could ever give her in the chef world), and Aaron reminded me of the fall-out if I broke my contract with the studio. I didn't need an excuse to immerse myself in the role and fly to Madrid to film.

I'm ever the professional, being such a good boy that both the domestic and international paparazzi became bored with me, and my history with Noa becomes old news.

Ravynn attempted a tell-all article about me and all but confirmed she leaked Noa's past, unearthed through a private investigator. The woman could not seem to let go of our brief mistake of an encounter, but the little I knew of her gave me enough to understand that ignoring her cries for attention would be the ultimate insult.

My talent for method acting came in handy—I became Matthew Chaise, a father wrongfully arrested for the death of his daughter while she studied abroad. The dark storyline is addictive as it is tragic, perfectly setting me up to forget my own life's plot.

I'm in craft services, breaking from a wrenching scene when Matthew discovers his daughter is alive and willfully framed her father with the help of her boyfriend (played by the illustrious Bradley Mitchell, if you were wondering), when Aaron approaches me by clapping me on the back.

Dust puffs out of my dirtied linen shirt when he does.

"Merry Christmas Eve, buddy," he says, helping himself to fries when he cuts in front of me.

I freeze with my plate in midair. "It's Christmas Eve?"

He answers after swallowing a mouthful. "Sure is. You wouldn't know it with this hot-as-balls weather, huh? Santa decorations or not, Christmas deserves snowfall."

I shrug. "I don't mind the heat."

"Well, good, because I booked us a nice restaurant to celebrate tonight."

His incessant chatter motivates me to keep moving and pile my plate. "What makes you think I have plans to celebrate Christmas Eve with you?"

Aaron barks with laughter. "Because like me, you have no one. I figured the two of us bachelors could close the best restaurant in Madrid with the most expensive bottle they have."

I slow down as we reach the desserts. "That's ... utterly sad."

"It is what it is, my friend." Aaron makes his way to an empty table and I follow suit. "Hey, we have each other."

I'm not sure how to respond. Aaron's good-natured about it, but isn't it entirely fucked up that we don't have anyone to be cozy with on the happiest of holidays? It makes me miss my mother something fierce. I could always rely on her to call me regardless of where I was. She'd bring home to me just by hearing her voice.

I sit across from Aaron with a heavy sigh, my gaze unfocused for the first time since putting on Matthew Chaise's skin.

"Don't look so depressed about my company. You might just wound me permanently," Aaron jokes before digging in.

I lift my fork to join him until we're interrupted by a, "Excuse me, Mr. Williams?"

A security guard has approached our table holding a paper-wrapped package.

I wipe my mouth with a napkin. "That's me."

"A delivery boy brought this to the gate. We checked it out. It looks harmless, but I don't recommend you eat it."

"I'm sorry. Did you just ask a movie star to *eat* a package?" Aaron clarifies.

I send Aaron a warning look. He loves messing with anyone stupid enough to engage with him.

"Thank you." I take the box from the confused security guard, though I'm equally perplexed.

"Did somebody send you food? Oh, wait." Aaron's expression clears. He leans forward, shadowing the table. "What's the return address?"

I slide it from under his busybody gaze. "Get back to your carbs."

"I'll be paying for this later," he mutters. "But dammit, it's the holidays."

Aaron resumes his seat, munching on his lunch but keeping his attention on me.

"Open it," he says.

"What if I want to do it in private?"

Aaron scoffs. "I'm your firewall. Do it."

He's not wrong. I unwrap the package and have to put aside some ice packs before getting to the small white carton in the middle.

"Hmm, the suspense continues," Aaron says.

A simple white card is nestled underneath it. Eagerness crawls into my throat until I stanch it.

It can't be from her, but it has to be from her. Who else would send me perishable goods?

Aaron solves that problem for me. "I had your assistants intercept a dozen cupcakes the other day. And cookies the day before that. All from fans hoping to make you fall in love with them through your stomach."

"Right." Despite my best efforts, my voice clogs with disappointment.

I made it clear to Noa that we were going our separate ways, and I can convince myself up and down that I did the right thing ... yet that damned eternal flame won't snuff out.

"You'd be surprised how many women send you edible delights," Aaron continues. I send him a wry *you've made your point* look, which he ignores. "One time, a woman sent you THC candies. I took those. For your protection, obviously."

"Obviously."

Aaron closes his mouth, studying me. "What's with the long face? We've done this at least six times, you and me, getting through the holidays like it's any other day."

"I don't know." I sit back and shove my plate aside. "I'm just thinking of ..."

His expression turns sympathetic. "Your mom?"

"Yeah."

I should finish there. Any person in my corner would be satisfied with that answer. But my mind has other ideas. I'm wondering how Maisy's doing without her good friend beside her on cribbage Fridays. Or if Rome is getting by without the free labor he loved to work into the ground and I enjoyed, too. Grunt work, yes, done by the real me, without cameras or recognition. I'm crossing my fingers that Devon's stayed out of trouble and away from drugs, wondering if I should've lectured him with a stern frown instead of just a whack upside the head.

I'm thinking about Noa and her celebrations tonight. If she misses me like I miss her. How she looked in the Stalinski house and how the house looked with her in it. Her laughter coaxing Ma out of misery, the delicious smells drawing us all into the kitchen for family meals. Her sweet smile. Her judgment-free touch. The way she regarded me as a regular man, her man, no spotlight, no expectations, other than to be a good one.

My stomach lurches. I've lost my appetite.

"If I didn't know any better," Aaron muses, "I'd say you're homesick."

I grunt an acknowledgment.

"No way that's the case since your whole pitch to me when you wanted me to represent you was that you wanted to shed your down-home image and be the next Tom Cruise."

"I did not say that."

"Eh." Aaron makes a seesaw motion with his head. "Came pretty close."

"I'm fine."

I'm wondering what Noa's doing right now.

I bring my plate back to the center, pressing my elbows on either side of it.

Is Rome prepared for the coming freeze? The weather app on my phone is still tailored to Falcon Haven. I should change it but haven't gotten around to it.

"I'm told Falcon Haven sure looks pretty on Christmas," Aaron says.

"Fuck," I mumble, internally lecturing myself to snap out of it and get back to work.

I pull out the card, opening it and reading.

To THE WORST sous chef I've ever had the displeasure of teaching,

Your girl is doing wonderfully. I'm overnighting you this delicious Financier pastry she made without her knowledge. Not because I'm thinking of you, more because I feel sorry for both of you.

I've never met a more frustrating pair, other than myself.

Noa excels at her position in my restaurant and was accepted into Le Cordon Bleu. She's doing fabulous, as you'd expect, but she is not the same.

If you would get over your own ego—as I have defeated mine by writing you this asinine note—you will come to her.

Today is my last day in Paris. I'll be re-joining my father and daughter in Falcon Haven. The last place I want to be is in a small town in the middle of nowhere, but it currently houses the people I hold the most dear.

Your lady is all alone and unhappy in Paris.

Think about that.

~ S.

"WELL? WHO'S IT FROM?" Aaron asks.

"My Ghost of Christmas Past, Present, and Future," I mutter while pushing to my feet. "The arrogant fuck."

Aaron asks, without being prompted, "What should I tell the director?"

"I'll do it."

As if summoned, Bradley's head pops up from another table. "What are you doing, old man? We have to be back on set in five."

"I won't make it."

"Huh?" Bradley rises, his handsome, surgically re-aligned face genuinely confused.

"I shouldn't have to say it again, but why not. Get fucked, Bradley. Take my role. Win the Oscar. I have a better goal in mind."

I've never been more honest with myself in my fucking life. I really don't care if he gets the Oscar and I never touch one for the rest of my life.

My golden girl is waiting for me when she shouldn't. I should've been there from the beginning.

I promised her I was back. That I wouldn't leave her again. For a brief, insane moment, I entertained the idea of living without her.

As my mother would say, *get your head to stop wobbling and make her yours. She's already a Stalinski, you dolt.*

"You're right, Ma," I say under my breath.

I leave craft services behind. Aaron leans back in his seat. To my shock, he doesn't yell at me to snap out of it and go earn him his commission. He watches me depart with a strange, satisfied grin on his face.

The same type of smile pulls on my lips when I realize what I have to do.

What I should've done then, now, and will do in Paris.

Thirty-Five

NOA

CHRISTMAS CAROLS PLAY ON AN INCESSANT LOOP AT Saint's restaurant.

At first, I loved the nostalgia the music brought as well as the new enjoyment hearing them all in French gave me. But on the fourteenth run of the playlist and when closing up the restaurant, I was done with it all.

I'm one of three people willing to stay late on Christmas Eve, now the last. Marcel bids me adieu on his way out, eager to get home to his family. Saint is remarkably fair to his staff, paying us overtime for keeping his business open on Christmas Eve while he's returned to his family. His salty nature isn't in keeping with a gesture so kind, but I'm not about to look a gift horse in the mouth while he works me to the ground and makes sure I understand every aspect of the kitchen before releasing me into culinary school.

Once Marcel leaves, I dart to the stereo and turn the music off. The resulting silence is a balm on my ears, the soft traffic seeping through the chilled window-front as I turn down lights and turn the last of the chairs over.

Saint's benevolence doesn't end with a commis chef position in his kitchen. His apartment is also available because of his mysterious move to Falcon Haven, and he offered it to me, so long as I house-sit his plants appropriately. The large, vacant interior would be incredibly lonely had I not brought Moo along with me. He'll be waiting with his tail puffed in aggravation and a prissy look on his face when I return to him tonight. Moo hasn't gotten over the indecency of a long flight where not only did we have to fly in economy but he also had to stay in his carrier for the entire six hours.

With Moo in mind, I pocket the remaining sardines that lay fresh and unclaimed in the freezer. I do a last once-over of the kitchen, and, satisfied, I head to the entrance, the key ring jingling in my hand.

My steps stall, then come to a complete stop when I notice a large, bulky figure on the other side of the door.

One with startlingly blue eyes, even at night.

It takes time for my brain to come to terms with who it is. Time enough for the man to press his palm to the window, the heat of his hand condensing into a temporary handprint as he mouths, "*I'm sorry.*"

My breaths were falling naturally until my mind shouted his name. Then they stuttered, gasped, and I choked on wordless anguish until my body knew enough to burst forward and unlock the door.

Stone pushes at the same time I pull, bringing the cold night in with him. A black beanie rests tight against his ears and forehead, and he's pulled his coat's collar to protect him from the Parisian winter. His cheeks are flushed red, his eyes blazing, as he shadows my form in a single step.

"Noa," he rasps.

Tears brim as I look up at him.

"William," I whisper.

We stare at each other, each unmoving within a thrumming city, the door softly shutting behind him.

Stone is the first to break the quiet. "I made a mistake. No, scratch that," he says before I can respond. "I've made so many fuckups with you. I didn't appreciate you. Didn't worship you. Didn't love you the way I should've the instant I realized you loved me back."

"Which time?" I ask, both shocked and pleased that my voice comes out level. "Because I've fallen in love with you twice now."

His mouth goes slack with breath as my words hit him. "I didn't need a reason other than thinking of you here, all alone, but after saying something like that..."

I pray I can stay strong with him standing in front of me, all but making my dreams come true. *He's here.*

"We said our goodbyes," I say. "You made sure they were absolute. You even sealed it with a kiss. I moved to Paris, and you went to Madrid. We were willing to start over again without each other."

Stone takes a moment to think, but his eyes don't stray from mine. They burn so much that I'm turning into flames just by keeping us connected.

He says, "It took a letter from a dick for me to realize what my mother was also trying to say by putting you and me in the same house again. Putting distance between us didn't make a difference, either. I'm pulled to you, wherever I am."

He feels the draw, too. Elation floats me sky-high until I lecture it down again.

I retreat. I have to. "Physically, maybe. But mentally,

emotionally, I can't handle more of this, Stone. I've *missed* you. I woke up with you on my mind every morning but seeing you now, it's pure agony. I can't play these games anymore. I can't choose between a life of passion with you or my dream."

"I know that." Stone moves forward, clasping my hands in his. Despite his hot, searing gaze, his hands are ice cold. "Hell, I know too well how much I've hurt you. I'm not here to make you choose, sweetheart. I never want to do that to you again. I want..."

I raise my head, desperate to hear more, but so, so afraid. "Yes?"

"I want you. Always. I've spent years wondering what it is I was running from when I was meant to be with you from the beginning. Was it fear? Did I think I could find something better? Hell no. You were perfection then, and you are now. It took my mother dying, losing everything that mattered, to realize my dream was never to move away from you." Stone dips his head until his nose brushes against mine.

I'm disheveled, exhausted, and smell like garlic and sardines, but I've never felt more beautiful under his scope.

"I want to believe you," I say.

He nods, my skin tingling where he touches mine. "I've gone over and over in my head why I didn't choose you, then and now. And all I can come up with is I didn't know how. My pops left me, and Ma worked so hard to fill that gap—so much that I felt ashamed she had to work so hard on account of me. I've been a burden on everyone I met, and the last thing I wanted was to be a burden on you, a woman who makes everyone in her life a priority. I wasn't worthy of your love. Not then. But now? Now I want to prove to both you and myself that we deserve each other. I deserve you."

My hand rasps against his cheek. I resist digging the pads of my fingers into his skin, clinging to him, clinging to *hope*. "I don't love people who don't deserve it."

Stone chuckles darkly and moves to kiss my palm. As if I might stray, he reaches up and holds it there by my wrist.

"This is how I'm gonna prove our worth," he says into my palm. "I won't force you to choose between me and your dream. I want you to have both. I want to taste all your meals, be your guinea pig for any recipe inspirations, curl up beside you while I sleep off your high-calorie creations and be there for you when you open your own restaurant."

My arm goes slack in his hold. "You were supposed to win an Oscar next year."

"Oscar will be just fine without me. Me, though, I'd rather hold you. I want to spend the rest of my life with you. No accolade in the world would match the feeling you give me every time you walk into the same room I'm in."

My eyes water. My mascara clumps together, and my nose burns with the warning of an incoming sob.

Stone tips my chin, his gaze diving into mine, into *me*, until that string I tried to cut, or tangle, or drift away from, grows tighter, until nothing but hesitant inches separate us.

"Do you forgive me?" he asks, drawing me into him, encircling me with all he has to give.

"I forgive you," I respond, softly but with certainty.

Stone's expression falls as if the weight of bearing the reality of my pain leaves his shoulders.

"Thank you," he whispers hoarsely.

He's in the midst of collecting himself when I add, "I love you."

He stares down at me, and in that gaze, the rest of our burdens drift away. "I love you, too. My God, do I love you."

And then he kisses me.

Our lips match each other in fervor and warmth. A familiar sigh escapes my lips, and he laps at it hungrily. He sheds his coat without breaking off our kiss and unbuttons my chef's jacket before he pulls me against him. We fit together in perfect, rekindled harmony.

It's the kiss I've always wanted. My dream within a dream. I don't know if I'll ever come to terms with the fact that I'm achieving everything I've ever wanted. I picture Mrs. Stalinski, Mom, and our unborn daughter looking down at us with pride.

"It's snowing in Falcon Haven," he murmurs into my mouth.

I smile, keeping my lips on his. "It is?"

"Sure is, sweetheart." He tightens his arms around me. "Let's go home and see it."

I nod, half laughing, half sobbing, as he lifts me and spins me while we kiss.

No matter where I end up, I find Stone Williams. William Stalinski. The boy and the man.

We've returned to each other. Come home.

And this time? It's for always.

Epilogue

ONE YEAR LATER

"I'm nervous," I say.

No one's listening. Or maybe they can't hear me due to the last-minute hammering and scraping of heavy wooden tables and chairs as the contractors drag them into place.

Well, the contractors and Stone.

His broad back faces me as he twists the last high-top into alignment with the others beside the front-facing windows overlooking Main Street.

A deep V of sweat runs between the middle of his shoulder blades, the thin navy cotton damp and melting into the grooves of his muscles as he works.

I swallow at the sight, ignoring the untimely tingles my vagina gives off at the sight of Stone with his dirty jeans and wood-dusted skin carrying a sheen of salt. As far as I'm concerned, America can have him as their perfect poster boy and sexiest man alive, because I'm more than happy to call this version my man.

To my surprise, Stone answers without turning around. "I know you're nervous, sweetheart. But you have nothing to worry about. The layout is perfect. Your food is fantastic. You are, in fact..." He turns to me. I'm already in the midst of preening under his grit-laced voice, the overworked tone something I usually receive after a marathon night of sex with him.

"...Incredible," he finishes with a side-cocked, seductive smile.

The responsive flutters in my belly are both from his bedroom eyes and the reminder that my new restaurant, my sole focus since graduating culinary school, my *baby*, opens tonight.

"I don't know." I force my leg muscles to relax their anxious vibrations and move toward him. "Maybe it's too soon. I should've waited. Or opened in LA instead of Falcon Haven. Or researched more states to know which has the best successful restaurant opening rate—"

Stone steals my second-guesses by pressing his lips to mine. My tongue flicks out. I taste wood, salt, and his unique sweetness.

He pulls away as soon as I melt into his body, holding me steady by squeezing my upper arms. Stone's magnetic blues, softened by a love that hasn't faded—will never fade—with time, he says, "This is the perfect spot. You're next door to Maisy, one of your favorite people and unrepentant cheerleader. You're far enough away from Saint's spot that he won't consider you competition and set fire to your restaurant. You have the whole town chattering about your modern American take on food. And believe me, getting this town to talk about anything other than ranching, where to get the best grits, and who's hooking up with who, ain't easy." Stone gives a wry smile. "I should know."

I stare past his shoulder, scanning the exposed wooden beams in the ceiling, the blonde wood tables, and the walls containing posters, tin signs, and street art of all the places I dreamed of visiting after catching the travel bug in Paris. After witnessing the transformation, Stone vowed to take me to every city, island, or mountain I wanted, so long as I set roots with him and named a permanent piece of land our home.

I agreed, even though I've learned that anywhere I go with Stone *is* my home, because he's with me.

Stone grinned when I said we should keep his mother's house, a place she so carefully tended and that was full of love, and make it our glowing lighthouse within the globe of our world. His eyes misted and he had to clear his throat multiple times when, after poring over budgets, business plans, and profit analyses, I wanted to name my restaurant Judy Lynn's, after our mothers.

I'm overwhelmed with the responsibility of representing our mothers, our relationship, and showcasing it all to Falcon Haven, a town that knows me all too well and can judge me just as easily. My breath grows tight. My lips part slightly to let a squeak of air through.

Stone notices, a line forming between his brows as he stares deep into my eyes, then pivots me by the shoulders.

"See that?" he says behind me.

He's spun me to look at the central piece of art in the restaurant, on the wall immediate to the front entrance. It's a large mural Stone commissioned to copy his favorite photo of me that he took in Paris. I'm wearing a traditional chef hat and white apron, my profile grinning as I stare down at the dough I'm kneading in the culinary school's kitchen.

At first, I didn't want it. I thought a photo of the two of us would be better, since he helped finance this dream of mine and has become my other half.

Stone refused, saying this was for me. My dream, my restaurant, my executive chef role.

"You are at the forefront," he says now, into my ear. "I can't think of a better time for me to step back and allow my girlfriend and all-time badass chef to have the spotlight for as long as she wants."

"You've never shared the spotlight," I joke, one side of my lips tilting up.

Stone twists me back to him so we're facing each other again. "That's because I'm not sharing. I'm giving it to you. Happily." He pulls me in for another kiss, murmuring against my lips, "You *are* my spotlight, Noa. Always."

I smile against his lips until he catches them with his teeth and sucks them into his mouth.

A groan escapes my throat. His erection presses into my stomach and I lean into it, subtly rubbing against his cock and wishing I wasn't wearing jeans and could lift my leg and let him enter—

"Oi! Some of us are working here!"

At our lead contractor's booming voice, drawing the attention of the others, Stone and I laugh against each other's mouths and reluctantly part.

Stone takes my hand as I use my other one to rub the blush out of my cheeks. "How about I buy you a milkshake at the Merc before the big reveal?"

I huff out a laugh and nod. "Sure. Dairy on a nervous stomach sounds great."

We walk hand-in-hand out into the bright, searingly blue day. Before we turn right and into the Merc, I swing a stare over my shoulder, taking one last look at the black-and-white sign, written in a combination of Judy and my mother's cursive, each writing their own name.

Judy Lynn's.

I squeeze Stone's hand a little tighter. He squeezes back.

That tiny gesture is all I need to be certain that despite all my pain, all our troubles and the loss that came before, I did it.

I found my happily ever after.

more books from ketley

all in kindle unlimited

If you like your grump to be a single dad (or a dad-to-be), read:

Trust

Rock

Play

If you like your men to fall in love in a small town, read:

Lover

If you like your playboys with a dash of suspense, read:

Dare

If you like your tattooed bad boys and morally gray heroes, read:

Rebel

Crave

If you like thriller with your romance, read:

To Have and to Hold

From This Day Forward

If you want enemies to lovers with a side of secret societies and gothic academies, read:

Briarcliff Academy Series

Rival

Virtue

Fiend

Reign

Thorne of Winthorpe Series

Thorne

Crush

Liar

If you like dark romance and mafia men, read

Titan Falls Standalone

Cruel Promise

Corrupt Empire Duet

Underground Prince

Jaded Princess

About the Author

Ketley Allison has always been a romantic at heart and loves writing over-the-top, plot-twisty romance and characters. Ketley was born in Canada, moved to Australia, then to California, and finally to New York City to attend law school, but most of that time was spent in coffee shops thinking about her next book.

Her other passions include her two daughters, wine, coffee, Big Macs, her cat, and her husband, possibly in that order.

Visit Ketley's Website:

f facebook.com/ketleyallison
♪ tiktok.com/ketleyallison
○ instagram.com/ketleyallison

Lightning Source UK Ltd.
Milton Keynes UK
UKHW022111281222
414549UK00019B/202